Kirk Munroe, Victor Semon Pérard

Fighting for the Lone Star Flag

A Tale of Texas

Kirk Munroe, Victor Semon Pérard

Fighting for the Lone Star Flag
A Tale of Texas

ISBN/EAN: 9783743367227

Manufactured in Europe, USA, Canada, Australia, Japa

Cover: Foto ©Andreas Hilbeck / pixelio.de

Manufactured and distributed by brebook publishing software (www.brebook.com)

Kirk Munroe, Victor Semon Pérard

Fighting for the Lone Star Flag

WITH CROCKETT AND BOWIE

OR

FIGHTING FOR THE LONE-STAR FLAG

A TALE OF TEXAS

BY

KIRK MUNROE

AUTHOR OF "THE WHITE CONQUERORS," "AT WAR WITH PONTIAC," "THROUGH SWAMP AND GLADE," ETC.

ILLUSTRATED BY V. PERARD

NEW YORK
CHARLES SCRIBNER'S SONS
1898

Norwood Press
J. S. Cushing & Co. — Berwick & Smith
Norwood, Mass. U.S.A.

TO MY READERS

The following story of the struggle by which
Texas gained her independence from Mexico is his-
torically true so far as I may rely upon Yoakum's
History of Texas, and the memory of one who took
an active part in the conflict, the late John C. Duval
of Austin. For the benefit of many who have lost
sight of the fact, I would state that after Rex,
Tawny, and their associates had achieved the freedom of Texas, she remained an independent republic
for nine years, or until 1845. Then, of her own
free will, she became the twenty-eighth and greatest
state of the great American Union.

The 21st of April, or San Jacinto day, is annu-
ally celebrated throughout the state with great rejoicings, and the church of the Alamo, still standing
in San Antonio, is the monument most reverenced
by the sons and daughters of Texas.

THE AUTHOR.

BISCAYNE BAY, FLORIDA.

TABLE OF CONTENTS

CONTENTS

LIST OF ILLUSTRATIONS

WITH CROCKETT AND BOWIE

CHAPTER I

A HOME IN THE WILDERNESS

A BOY and a horse, both breathing hard and trembling from recent exertions, stood gazing at each other dubiously, and each was wondering whether the struggle in which they had been engaged for the past two hours was to be resumed or not. The boy, who was a slender lad with a very determined expression on his sun-tanned face, was so covered with dirt and perspiration that it would have been hard to decide whether he was good looking or not. His close-cropped head was bare, for he had long since parted company with his broad-brimmed sombrero, his flannel shirt was soiled and torn, and even the stout trousers of homespun, tucked into the legs of heavy cowhide boots, bore sad traces of the recent fray. One side of his face was bruised and so swollen that the eye was nearly closed. Thus taken altogether, Rex

Harden, only son of "Squire" Ellis Harden of the great Herrera Ranch, was at that moment a very disreputable looking young man.

The horse at which he was gazing with a comical expression of mingled doubt and admiration was in no better plight than himself. In fact, he seemed a little worse off than the boy. He was a splendid chestnut stallion, four or five years old, clean limbed, full chested, with flowing mane and tail of hair so dark as to be nearly black, and without blemish or spot on his body, save only a clearly outlined white star on his forehead. His beauty was, however, sadly dimmed just then; for he was covered with lather and dirt, a bloody froth dropped from his mouth, his breath came in choking sobs, his dripping flanks heaved like a bellows, and his slender limbs trembled so that he could hardly stand.

Not far away was a small band of mares and foals pawing the earth impatiently, tossing their heads, ready to take flight at a sign of danger, and yet rooted to the spot by an eager curiosity to learn what their splendid and hitherto untamed leader could be doing.

On all sides of these two groups was spread a vast extent of brown, rolling prairie, broken in the northeast by a range of blue hills, and on the west by a dark line of timber marking the course of a river. The soft wind that rustled the dry grasses and fanned the heated brow of the only human being to be seen in all the landscape swept up from the warm waters of the Mexican Gulf, for this was a Texas prairie, and Rex Harden was a native of the Lone Star State.

As we catch our first glimpse of him, it is evident that both he and the fine animal beside him have just regained their feet after an ugly fall and are still doubtful as to whether their bones are whole or not. The boy's head was in a whirl as he picked himself up, and many stars shot athwart the glance cast at his companion in adversity. He drew a hand swiftly across his still serviceable eye to clear its vision, and then, stepping to the horse, threw an arm impulsively across the beautiful creature's neck, saying as he did so:

"Tawny, old fellow, let's make up and be friends. I don't believe you want any more of this racket, and I'm sure I do not, for another cropper like that one would lay us both out. So I'll give in if you will."

As if in answer the horse rested his head on the boy's shoulder, and with their cheeks touching, the latter had not the slightest doubt but that Tawny had understood every word said to him. He at any rate readily comprehended the animal's movement, and knew that their battle was ended. He also knew, or at least fully believed, that in that moment he had gained a friend that would be faithful even unto death, for Rex Harden dearly loved horses, and knew that the affection of a thoroughbred once gained would never be withdrawn.

At the conclusion of this treaty of peace and friendship the boy tore out a sleeve of his tattered shirt, and with it wiped the dirt and foam from Tawny's nostrils. He loosened the cruel cord that, fastened tightly about the animal's lower jaw, had served instead of a bridle, and threw off the folded blanket that, cinched with a leather surcingle, had taken the place of a saddle. Then he rubbed the horse vigorously until every trace of lather and dirt was removed, giving him a dry polish with the remaining sleeve of his useful flannel shirt, which he also tore out without hesitation.

Although this was the very first grooming that Tawny had ever received in all his wild free life, he did not move during the operation. He even allowed the blanket saddle to be replaced without opposition, and the hated cord to be again slipped over his lower jaw. Only when the lad climbed stiffly to his back and intimated that it was time to be moving did he give a convulsive start and then stand quivering.

The boy spoke a few soothing words, patted the arching neck, and at the same moment pressed his heels against the animal's flanks. This time he was obeyed, and Tawny, king of the prairie, hitherto wildest of the wild and freest of the free, a horse that many men had declared would never be caught nor tamed unless first "creased" with a rifle bullet, stepped forth the willing bearer of a burden.

At this moment the ragged, bruised, and astonishingly dirty but triumphant lad on his back was so thrilled with the glorious victory just achieved that it was all he could do to repress a yell of delight. He did repress it, however, and devoted his entire attention to a further soothing of the splendid horse that had just become his by right of conquest. At the same time he turned him gently in the direction of the distant river, towards which they started on an easy lope, with the little band of mares and foals following them curiously a short distance behind.

The disreputable looking but happy lad riding thus proudly across the brown prairie was a son of one of the earliest American pioneers to settle in what was then the Mexican state of Texas. His father, a Kentuckian, had in the first flush of manhood gone to the wars with General Andrew Jackson, and had lost a leg in his first and only battle. Recovering health and strength after a weary illness, he had promptly offered to release the Kentucky sweetheart who had nursed him, from her engagement to a "fractional man." She had as promptly refused to be released, and so they were married.

Directly afterwards Ellis Harden took the modest portion of this world's goods allotted to him, and with dauntless energy sought to make a home for his wife and himself in the little known Mexican state of Texas. They settled at Nacogdoches, a busy frontier town close to the boundary line between Mexico and the United States, and here the young Kentuckian prospered beyond his hopes. Here were born his two children, Rector or "Rex," as he was always called, and Mabel. Here, too, during the revolution by which Mexico threw off the galling yoke of Spain, Ellis Harden was enabled to render important aid to Don Manuel Herrera, Mexican Commissioner to the United States. A few years later on account of this service he was granted a noble property on the Cibolo River in Southwestern Texas, some twenty-five miles from the town of San Antonio de Bexar (Behar).

In 1821, the Mexicans under Augustin Iturbide established their independence, and three years later they adopted a liberal constitution modelled after that of the United States. At the same time they offered tempting inducements to emigrants to settle in Texas. Under these circumstances Ellis Harden decided to take possession of his property on the beautiful Cibolo, and there established himself as a ranchman. In honor of the friend through whom he had received his grant he named the new home Rancho Herrera. Here with the opening of this story he and his had dwelt for ten years in comparative peace and ever-increasing prosperity.

The stalwart but crippled American was a man of

such fearless integrity that the scattered settlers of that section formed a habit of referring all their disputes to him for adjustment rather than entrust them to the Mexican Alcaldes of either San Antonio or Gonzales, and for this reason he became known far and wide as "Squire" Harden.

Having a certain amount of capital to start with and being possessed of unbounded energy, Squire Harden, in spite of being a "fractional" man, had developed his property until the Rancho Herrera was one of the finest in the state. It boasted thousands of cattle, great fields of corn, cane, and cotton, and hundreds of horses bred from imported Kentucky stock, the fame of which had spread even to the Mexican capital, where they were always in demand for service in the army. As the vast estate bordered on the highway between San Antonio and Gonzales, and lay midway between the two towns, it was a favorite halting-place for travellers, to whom its generous hospitality was never denied. If they were Americans, they were entertained at the great house, while natives were equally well cared for in the quarters of the peons, a large number of whom were employed on the ranch as herdsmen or cultivators of the soil.

Among other things, not then common in that country, the Rancho Herrera supported its own grist-mill, cotton gin, and smithy, while deft-handed Mexican women wove both wool and cotton, raised on the place, into blankets and such stuffs as were needed by its people.

Here, then, Rector Harden had grown from childhood to sturdy youth, and this was the home he loved. Here was the noble father whom he regarded as the best and wisest of men, the devoted mother who had so bravely ventured into this far land for the sake of her loved ones, and the brown-haired sister only a year younger than himself, known to her mother as Mabel, but called "Daughter" by her father, "Dulce" (Sweet) by Rex, and "Honey" by Aunty Day, her old negro mammy.

Rex was proud of being a Texan, and his only present ambition was to aid his father in making the Rancho Herrera the finest property of its kind in the country. He already knew a great deal about cattle and crops, was a fearless horseman, a good shot, and could throw a riata or lasso with the best vaquero on the ranch. Nor had his education in other subjects been neglected; for, besides being carefully taught at home, he had been sent for three years to a military school in New Orleans, from which he returned to the ranch for the long vacations.

As there were no railroads nor even stages in Texas in those days, he had always made the journey to and from New Orleans in one of the trading schooners plying between there and Matagorda, the seaport nearest to his home. Of course he talked

Spanish as well as did the Mexicans among whom he lived, and in New Orleans he had gained a fair knowledge of French. Thus our lad had been given advantages far beyond those enjoyed by most boys of his age in that new country. Best of all, he had been taught from his earliest childhood to be a gentleman.

Having thus introduced him, we will precede him to his home, and stand ready to receive him as he rides proudly past the great house, on the porch of which his father holds conversation with a newly arrived stranger, and leads his little drove of horses to one of the corrals in its rear.

CHAPTER II

REX AND TAWNY

TAWNY had long been a source of pride and perplexity to the whole ranch. On all its broad prairies there was no horse to compare with him in beauty or speed. In some way he had escaped the branding-iron when a colt, nor had he ever since been captured, though many attempts against his liberty had been made by the Herrera vaqueros. No one had enjoyed these efforts, with their exciting races over the broad plains, more than Tawny himself, and he had always entered into them with a joyful readiness.

On such occasions he would stand with proudly uplifted head and distended nostrils until his would-be captors were just ready to throw their entangling ropes ; when, with a snort of defiance and a toss of his silken mane, he would dash away at a speed that none of his pursuers could hope to equal. Still they always followed him, and each time with fresh hope. He invariably ran in a great circle that caused the race to finish near its place of starting, and during its continuance he would slacken his pace at intervals until his pursuers were close at hand, only to dart away again with increased speed just when they thought they had him.

So aggravating were these tactics, and he showed such a knowledge of the steps it was proposed to take for his capture, that the superstitious Mexicans came to regard him as possessed of uncanny powers, and named him "El Diablo." But for strict orders issued by the master of the ranch that not a hair of his glossy coat was to be harmed, more than one of his baffled pursuers would have tried to overcome him by the dangerous and doubtful method of "creasing," which is stunning by means of a rifle ball so carefully aimed as to cut a crease on the upper side of the animal's neck, without otherwise injuring him.

Rex, who had loved the horse from the first and longed to possess him, called him "Tawny," by which name he came to be generally known. Although the lad had joined in many a chase of the superb animal, he had never really wished them success in their efforts for his overthrow. He rejoiced that this descendant from Kentucky thoroughbreds should outwit the craftiest of Mexican vaqueros, and took as much pleasure in witnessing their defeats as in the mad racing. Another cause for rejoicing at their failures was a promise from his father, that if he should ever, alone and unaided, succeed in capturing Tawny, the horse should be his from that moment. Many a fruitless race unseen by the others had our lad given the wild horse after receiving this promise, and each failure to capture the beautiful creature only made him seem the more desirable.

Tawny fully realized that the ranch was his home, and never strayed very far from it. Next to racing with would-be captors he enjoyed lording it over the other semi-wild horses of the estate, and was always accompanied by a band of admiring followers, most of whom were young mares with sleek skins and velvety noses, belonging to the best equine families.

During his study of Tawny and his companions, Rex discovered that one of their favorite midday resorts was the shade of a great live-oak that stood by itself on the edge of the prairie a hundred yards removed from any other timber. Here they would remain for hours, lazily switching their long tails, lying down, standing, with slim heads caressingly extended over each other's necks, playfully biting, squealing, or kicking at one another, or staring intently motionless at the antics of a squirrel or at something else that attracted their curiosity. After breaking up these pleasant parties several times by sudden outrushes from the neighboring timber, Rex conceived the plan of concealing himself amid the lower branches of their favorite tree during a time of their absence from it, awaiting their coming, and then attempting to throw a noose over Tawny's neck from that point of vantage.

For the carrying out of this purpose he stored a blanket, a surcingle, and several stout ropes in the tree, and established himself on one of its lower limbs for several days in succession, spending three or four hours there each time, before he had the pleasure of seeing the unsuspecting horses led by Tawny the superb trot jauntily into its wide shadow.

The lad was thrilled at finding the animal he so coveted almost within reach of his hand, and his heart beat high with hope. At the same time he almost stopped breathing and hardly dared move, for he knew that the slightest sound would send the keen-witted creatures off like the wind. He had previously fastened one end of a noosed rope to the limb on which he sat, and now he held the noose ready for dropping, the moment an opportunity offered.

Several minutes passed before Tawny came to that side of the tree, and Rex had about decided that he could not bear the pain of his constrained position a moment longer, when all at once the stallion appeared immediately beneath him. In an instant the darting rope had settled over the proud neck, and, as the startled animal sprang away, it tautened with a cruel, choking jerk, that flung him heavily to the ground. At the same moment, and before the terrified horse could regain his feet, Rex dropped from his hiding-place. Within two minutes he had Tawny's legs so secured that he could not rise. Then he loosened the choking neck-rope and spent a quarter of an hour in soothing and stroking his captive.

The next move was to allow the horse to regain his feet, hobble him so that he could not move without falling, and strap a folded blanket to his back. Five times did Tawny throw himself in striving to avoid this indignity before the blanket was securely fastened in place. The securing of a noosed cord about his lower jaw was attended with still greater difficulty, but even that was finally accomplished. Then the entangling leg-ropes were cast loose, and Rex vaulted into his blanket saddle. The horse made several convulsive movements, each of which was checked by the rope still encircling his neck and choking him with every pull upon it. Then he stood still while the boy, retaining his seat, soothed and talked to him.

At length Rex severed the taut rope with a single stroke of his hunting-knife, dropped the weapon, twined his fingers in the thick mane, gripped the animal's body with his knees, and found himself speeding through space as though he were astride a runaway locomotive.

As the stallion reached the place to which his terrified comrades had retreated at the first alarm, he began to make furious efforts to rid himself of his burden. He reared until it seemed as though he must topple over backwards, pitched, bucked, leaped sideways, and even rolled on the ground. When-

HE REARED, PITCHED, BUCKED, LEAPED, AND EVEN ROLLED

ever he attempted this last manœuvre the boy flung himself to one side, but sprang again to the animal's back the instant the latter began to regain his feet. At the same time he never once relaxed a steady pull on the slender cord about Tawny's lower jaw. Once he was flung to the ground, and was dragged by it for a short distance, but the strain on the horse was so painful that he was forced to come to a stop, and in a moment Rex was again seated on his back.

Then the animal bolted and ran, or rather flew, at a speed that filled the boy with a delirium of excitement, up hill and down, across broad levels, mile after mile and league after league. At first the young rider gave him his head and allowed him to take his own direction. Then he gradually resumed his pull on the cruel cord and, little by little, changed the course of his flying steed until at length they were headed almost in the direction from which they had come.

After a while the fearful pace began to tell, and the sobbing animal began to falter in his stride, but now Rex urged him on with shout and blow until finally Tawny plunged heavily forward and fell, flinging his rider far over his head. That neither of them gained broken bones was a miracle, but both of them were young, and so neither of them did. When they picked themselves up they gazed at each other with that feeling of mutual respect that, between worthy opponents, often leads to sincerest friendship.

When our proudly happy lad had ridden his prize home and into a stout corral, he did not leave him until he had removed the blanket saddle and cord bridle that formed Tawny's badges of servitude, and had given him another thorough rubbing down, during which he talked incessantly to the horse, often calling him by name. Then he brought the thirsty creature a bucket of water, and fed him with a small measure of salted oats, a luxury of civilization that Tawny had never before tasted.

Through all this the horse was so quiet and docile that Rex began to wonder if he had not given him too severe a lesson, and broken his spirit so completely that he would never regain it.

After having thus extended the hospitalities of the ranch to his newly acquired friend, and leaving orders with a peon to have all the animals cared for, the young horse-tamer, recalled to his own aches, bruises, and general dilapidation, made his way to the house.

This ranch house was a large, comfortable affair of squared logs, having a great central hall running through it from front to rear and open at both ends. On either side of this were two large rooms. In the hall a rude stairway, hewn from the trunk of an oak tree, led to an upper story which was at once store-room and bed-chamber for an indefinite number of guests. From this upper room a ladder gave access to the roof, on which was a platform enclosed within a breastwork of logs; for this house was intended as a fortress as well as a dwelling, and was admirably planned for defence against those Indians who then roamed over the whole of Texas.

A detached kitchen stood behind the house, while in front, commanding a fine view of both the road and river, was a broad porch overrun with roses.

Rex entered the lower hall from its rear end, hoping for a chance to render himself more presentable before meeting any of the family or the stranger whom he had seen talking with his father. But Squire Harden caught sight of him and called him.

"What horse was that you were riding, son?" he asked, as Rex appeared on the porch.

"It was Tawny, sir."

"Tawny, the wild stallion! You don't mean it."

"Yes, I do," laughed the boy. "We had a big fight and then made friends with each other afterwards."

"Prettiest fight 'tween man and hoss that ever I seen," remarked the stranger to whom Squire Harden had been talking, and who was a spare, smooth-faced man, clad in buckskin.

"Did you see us, sir?" asked the lad, in a tone of surprise. "I didn't know there was a soul within miles of us."

"I expect thar's many a man seen by Deaf Smith, who never sees him," laughed the Squire. "Son, I want to present you to my old and valued friend, Mr. Erastus Smith, better known as 'Deaf Smith,' the scout, whom I think you must have known long ago by reputation."

CHAPTER III

A HORSE WITH LIKES AND DISLIKES

DEAF SMITH, most famous of Texan scouts, was a New Yorker by birth, brought up amid the wild scenes of Mississippi Territory and an early pioneer to Texas, where he helped found the American town of Gonzales on the Guadalupe River some fifty miles east of the Mexican city of San Antonio. He had not been content to settle down there or elsewhere; but had spent years in wandering alone over the vast southwestern wilderness, hunting buffalo, capturing wild horses, and leading the life of the Indians, who either as friends or foes were for months at a time the only human beings with whom he held intercourse. On one occasion while Rex was away at school he had appeared at the Rancho Herrera, bleeding from an arrow wound, with the warning of a contemplated attack from a war-party of Comanches. With this timely notice, and aided by the brave scout, Squire Harden was enabled to prepare a complete surprise for the savages and drive them off with such heavy loss that they had not cared to molest him since.

At that time a strong liking for each other had

sprung up between the two men, and Deaf Smith·
had ever afterwards been a welcome guest at the
ranch, though he rarely visited it more than once
a year. Thus it happened that until now he and
Rex had never met, though of course the boy had
learned many thrilling tales concerning the famous
scout, that he afterwards related with fine effect to
his school-fellows at New Orleans.

Smith had also heard much about his friend's son;
but, fearing that he would be unfitted for Texas life
by his schooling and residence in a great city, had
purposely avoided meeting him. Now that such a
meeting was forced upon him, he gazed at the lad
curiously as he took his extended hand and held it
in a firm grasp.

While our hero's present appearance might not
have produced a favorable impression in New Orleans
society, it seemed exactly to suit the scout's idea of
what was fitting and proper; for, after a moment of
such searching gaze as seemed to read the lad's soul,
he said:

"Young man, I am proud to make your acquaintance, for your own sake as well as your dad's, but
I'm free to confess that if I hadn't seen you awhile
ago wrastling with that hoss, and met you bearing
signs of a tussle, I wouldn't have believed you had
the grit you've just showed. It does look, though,
like your schooling hadn't done you no great harm
after all."

"You are very kind to say so," replied Rex, flushing at what he felt was a great compliment, coming as it did from Deaf Smith, "and I am awfully glad to meet you, for I've heard more about you than about any other man in Texas. I would like to know, though, where you were when you saw Tawny and me getting acquainted."

"On my way here from Gonzales," was the reply.

"But I was not anywhere near the Gonzales road."

"No more was I. To my mind a road is a mighty dangersome place, and I never set foot on one when I can travel by a grass trail. When I fust seed you cavortin' over the perarer, I mistook you for a Comanch, and laid low. Even when I found you was white, I still laid low to watch the fight between you and the critter. Same time I never mistrusted who you war, though I knowed the hoss. When you went streaking off, like you never meant to stop this side the Sabine, I came on here and told the Squire thar was two devils fighting over yonder, one human and one hoss. He 'lowed that the human devil would get the wust of it, seeing as how El Diablo hadn't never yet met his master. Same time, seein' what I seen, I was willin' to bet on the human comin' out ahead. Of cose I hadn't no idee who he war till you rid past awhile back, and the Squire 'lowed that you bore some faint likeness to his son. Even then, he was dubersome about the hoss, and reckoned it couldn't be El Diablo."

"And it wasn't," laughed Rex, joyously, "for his name is Tawny, and he is the dearest and gentlest and most splendid horse ever raised in Texas. He is my very own too, isn't he, father?"

"I expect he is, son," replied Squire Harden; "for you seem to have won him in fair fight, though I must confess that I would rather you had set your affections on any other horse in the whole cavallado. This one has such a devilish temper, that—"

"Oh, father!" interrupted Rex, reproachfully, "you wouldn't say that if you only knew how gentle and loving he really is. Why—"

Just here the lad was, in turn, startlingly interrupted by such a confusion of shouts, screams, and general uproar, coming from the direction of the corrals, that the three occupants of the porch sprang to their feet and hastened to the scene of disturbance.

The corral in which Rex had left his little band of horses was a stout post-and-rail enclosure divided into two parts. Between these was a gateway of two posts some seven feet in height connected at the top by a bar of timber. According to young Harden's instructions this gate had been opened, that the horses might have access to a water trough in the further division of the corral.

The capture of the famous stallion had created great excitement in all quarters of the ranch, but especially among the vaqueros who had so often failed to accomplish it themselves. These were consumed with jealousy that the hero of the hour should be a mere boy, for so they regarded Rex. And one of their number, a surly fellow named Domingo, who was only retained on the estate because of his horsemanship, was particularly bitter in his comments upon the *muchacho* who, he declared, could never have captured El Diablo unaided. While a number of his fellows were gathered about the corral, gazing at the horses, this man, armed with a raw-hide quirt, entered it and began with vicious blows to vent his spite upon the captive animals, under pretence of driving them into the further enclosure.

At first he expended his efforts on the mares and foals, which, blind with terror, rushed frantically from one enclosure to the other and back again. Tawny, evidently bewildered and uncertain how to act, followed them. As he returned through the gateway, the scowling Mexican, who stood close beside the barrier, struck him a stinging blow. With a shrill scream of rage and pain the animal wheeled and charged furiously at his cowardly assailant.

With a single leap the terrified man gained the topmost rail of the dividing fence and started to swing himself up on the bar connecting the two posts. As he did so, the horse seized one leg of his flapping cotton trousers and strove to pull him down. The man yelled with fright, but clung so stoutly to the post that the cloth tore away and in another moment he was perched on the narrow bar, in comparative safety.

He was still so nearly within reach of his enraged enemy that he dared not let either hand or foot hang a single inch below the timber beneath which the horse was dashing furiously, back and forth, seeking for some way to get at him. He even reared and struck at the posts with his fore feet, shaking them so violently as to very nearly dislodge the man from his uncertain refuge. The latter screamed for help, the spectators shouted wildly, and some of them made fruitless efforts to lasso the horse, while, as Rex reached the scene, one man was in the act of levelling a rifle at the superb creature.

The lad was just in time to disconcert this fellow with a shout and to snatch the gun from his hands before a shot could be fired. Then without a moment's hesitation he vaulted over the fence into the corral and ran toward the gateway in which the maddened stallion was still striving to reach his enemy.

"Tawny! Tawny! You, sir! Behave yourself!" shouted the lad as he drew near, and the effect was so magical that the spectators stared in amazed silence. At the sound of the voice that he had already learned was that of his master the horse instantly desisted from his furious efforts and stood motionless, gazing inquiringly at the approaching figure. Walking directly up to him, Rex threw an arm over the proud neck and petted him for a few moments, all the while talking in soothing tones. Then he led him into the further enclosure, where the other horses were grouped in one corner, and closed the gate.

" Now, coward, you can come down," he shouted, at the same time stooping to pick up a raw hide quirt that he discovered lying on the ground. As he raised his eyes, he saw that the Mexican had already taken advantage of this diversion in his favor to make good his retreat toward the outer fence, from which his comrades were greeting his forlorn appearance with shouts of laughter. At the same moment Rex caught sight of the long welt across Tawny's back raised by Domingo's spiteful blow, and instantly realized what had happened.

Filled with a sudden rage, he tightened his grasp on the quirt and sprang after the cowardly Mexican. If he had overtaken him, it is not likely that even Domingo's bulk would have saved him from a thrashing, but the man had already cleared the barrier, and by the time Rex reached it had disappeared to be seen no more at the Rancho Herrera. So Tawny's young master was forced to content himself with giving the swarthy peons a fierce warning of what would happen to any one of them who should ever dare lift a hand against his horse. While he was delivering this harangue, that was listened to in sullen silence, a gentle touch on his shoulder caused him to look around.

A young girl, simply clad, but glowing with health, and the beauty that health alone can give, stood by his side, while close at hand were the squire on his crutches and the scout.

" Why, Dulce ! " exclaimed the lad, " what brings you out here ? "

" I came to see your beautiful horse. But, Rex, whatever have you been doing ? You look as though you had gone through the wars."

" Well, I haven't," laughed her brother. " I would go through a kind of war, though, if I could lay hands on that scoundrel Domingo. To think of his daring to thrash Tawny ! It makes my blood boil, and if ever I catch him — Well, no matter. Isn't he a beauty though ? "

" Who ? Domingo ? "

" Of course not. I mean Tawny — that chestnut stallion. And, Dulce, he is my very own. Come, and I will introduce you."

A few minutes later the superb creature had been enticed to the bars and, assured by Rex that it was perfectly safe to do so, was daintily nibbling sugar from Mabel's hand.

From that hour Tawny readily admitted to his friendship those who were properly introduced and vouched for by his young master, always provided they wore white skins ; but for any whose skins were dark he held a bitter hatred to the day of his death.

CHAPTER IV

THAT same evening after supper Deaf Smith took his departure, and to the surprise of Rex, Squire Harden had not urged him to remain with them over night. This was so contrary to the usual hospitable custom in the Rancho Herrera that, after our lad had courteously walked with the guest to where his horse awaited him, and returned to the porch on which the family were assembled, he could not forbear commenting on the occurrence.

" I wish Mr. Smith could have passed the night with us," he remarked, " for I wanted so much to hear of some of his adventures from his own lips. Why was he in such a hurry, father? "

" He is charged with a duty that may not be delayed," replied the squire, who appeared to be in a mood at once thoughtful and troubled. " The fact is," he continued, " there is a rumor that President Santa Anna has sent an army in this direction to proclaim martial law in Texas, deprive us of our civil liberty, and force us to acknowledge his dictatorship, as he has already done with every other Mexican state. It is reported that this army, commanded by the President's brother-in-law, General Martin Perfecto Cos, is to come by sea, land on our coast, and overrun the country. So Deaf Smith has been sent out by the Committee of Safety to watch for his arrival and notify them of his approach.

"It is further stated that General Cos has orders to disarm all American settlers, drive from the state those who have entered it since 1830, and to arrest on the charge of treason a number of persons, among whom is your friend Travis."

"Will Travis, father!" exclaimed Rex. "Why should they arrest him? What has he done?"

"He headed the first armed opposition to Santa Anna in Texas, by leading the party that drove his military tax-collectors from Anahuac on Galveston Bay a few months ago. Since then he has publicly declared that Texas must either become an independent republic or else be annexed to the United States."

"How I wish I had been with him!" cried Rex, his imagination already on fire. "And wouldn't it be fine if Texas could only become a republic all by herself? That would be worth fighting for."

"It certainly would," replied Squire Harden, with a smile at his son's enthusiasm. "But I think it would be better if, after winning our independence, we could join the glorious American union of States. Texas rightfully belongs to the United States anyhow."

"How so, father? I thought Texas had always belonged to Mexico."

"So do a good many other persons think so, and that is what the Mexicans claim; but, nevertheless, it is a false notion. Texas was discovered and settled by the French under La Salle, who, in 1685, planted a colony on Matagorda Bay. As he had already discovered the mouth of the Mississippi, and taken possession of Louisiana on behalf of the King of France, so he now took possession of Texas and declared it to be a part of the same territory. At that time the nearest Spanish settlement in Mexico was so far away that the Rio Grande flowed midway between it and La Salle's colony on Matagorda Bay. Thus, according to the law of nations regulating the discovery and acquisition of new countries, the French territory of Louisiana extended to the Rio Grande."

"Then," demanded Rex, "when France sold Louisiana to the United States, why didn't we claim the Rio Grande as its western boundary?"

"We did," replied his father; "but in the meantime La Salle's colony having been destroyed, and no more Frenchmen having come to reëstablish it, the Spaniards overran the country and occupied it after a fashion for more than one hundred years. During that time they pushed as far east as the Red River, which they declared was the western boundary of French territory. When, in 1803, France sold

Louisiana to the United States for fifteen millions of dollars, the question of a boundary between it and Mexico was instantly raised. Spain now claimed the Mississippi as the dividing line, and we claimed the Rio Grande. Finally the Sabine River, about midway between the two, was agreed upon, and since then it has been generally admitted that Texas is legally a Mexican state.

"When, in 1821, Mexico threw off the hated yoke of Spain, she found no firmer friends, nor braver fighters in the cause of her freedom than the Americans of Texas. Upon the adoption of a liberal constitution in 1824 all Texans rejoiced and swore to support it. Relying upon its promises, thousands of settlers flocked to Texas and made new homes within her borders. Finally, their members so aroused the jealousy of the Mexicans that in 1830 President Bustamente issued a decree forbidding any further immigration from the United States and revoking many of the privileges granted to those of us already settled here. At the same time troops were sent to enforce these measures, and it was ordered that the money for their maintenance should be raised in Texas. Thus we were not only required to submit to our oppressors, but to support them.

"In 1832, when Santa Anna raised the standard of revolt against Bustamente and declared for the Constitution of 1824, the Texans hailed him as a liberator and took up arms in his cause. They were

everywhere successful and showed such a capacity
for self-defence that when Santa Anna assumed the
title of Dictator, he became more intensely jealous of
the growing American power in Texas than any of
his predecessors. So in January of this year (1835)
the Mexican Congress, composed almost wholly of
members selected by Santa Anna, overthrew the
Constitution of 1824, meeting with opposition only
from the representatives of our own state and those
from Zacatecas. Then Congress passed two acts, the
first of which declared Zacatecas to be in a state of
rebellion. The second reduced the militia to one
soldier for every five hundred inhabitants, and
ordered all other citizens to be disarmed."

"Does that mean," asked Rex, indignantly, "that
they are going to take away all our rifles, and leave
us without the means of defence against Indians, or
for hunting?"

"It means that they are going to attempt something of that sort," replied Squire Harden, significantly.

"Well, they can't do it! that's all, and I would
just like to see them try," cried the lad, hotly.
"It is the most outrageous proposition I ever heard
of."

"I am afraid your desire will be granted," rejoined
the squire; "for it looks very much as though Santa
Anna was going to try and enforce his unjust decrees
without further delay. He began by leading an army

against Zacatecas and gave the alleged rebels a most terrible punishment. In one battle he killed two thousand of them and made prisoners of twenty-seven hundred more. Then he marched into the capital of the state, which was one of the wealthiest cities in Mexico, and for two days allowed his soldiers unrestrained license to kill and plunder the unfortunate inhabitants. In consequence of this crushing blow the state has submitted to his will, and now he proposes to turn his attention to us.

" At Monclovia our legislature has already been dispersed, and our governor has been made a prisoner by Santa Anna's troops. There is, as you know, a strong garrison at San Antonio. General Cos is reported to be on his way to reënforce it, and the Dictator has declared that if we make any show of resistance to his authority, he himself will take the field with an army powerful enough to sweep every American from Texas."

" Oh, if he only does come ! " cried Rex, " what a lesson we will teach him ! "

"Don't brag, son, and don't be too confident," admonished his father. " Remember that over-confidence is as fatal to success as indecision. Consider, too, the fearful odds that will be arrayed against us. The Texans are poor, few in number, without any form of military organization, dwelling in a country filled with enemies, and, worst of all, they are divided into factions that are working against each other with might and main. We are, moreover, without a leader; and, in case of an uprising, must be regarded by the world as rebels against legally constituted authority."

"I don't care a snap!" exclaimed Rex. "If we are few in numbers, one Texan is worth ten Mexicans any day, when it comes to fighting. If we are poor, then we have so much the less to lose and more to gain. If we have no military organization, then we will fight without one, as the Comanches do, and the Mexicans have never yet been able to whip them. An invasion will consolidate factions, and a leader will be found when we really need him. As for being rebels, I for one should be more proud of being called a rebel in such a cause than anything else I can think of."

"And here is another rebel!" cried impulsive Mabel, moving to her brother's side and throwing an arm about him.

"I am afraid, Ellis, that I too shall have to join the rebels," laughed Mrs. Harden. "I didn't know that I was one until this evening; but you have explained the situation so clearly that I can't be a Texan without being a rebel, and so I mean to be both."

"A pretty state of affairs, upon my word!" cried the squire. "But if you think I am going to be left out of this rebellion that already claims those whom I love best and whatever I hold most dear, you are mightily mistaken. No indeed! and I hereby declare myself to be the arch-rebel of all this rebellious company, since the case I have just presented was exactly calculated to bring about this happy result. It will be a sad day for Santa Anna and a glorious one for Texas when every family in the state becomes as united in rebellion against the despotism of Mexico as mine is at this moment. Then will we win independence for our beloved country."

"We will win it anyhow, father; I know we will," declared Rex.

"Yes, son, I believe we will, though it is going to be a hard fight, and one in which victory will only be gained after many bitter reverses. Mexico is populous and wealthy. Her people are united under a leader skilled in war, who is as cruel and unscrupulous as he is ambitious. He has already denounced all Americans who may take up arms in the cause of Texas as pirates, and declares that he shall deal with them as such. He is supported by a regular army of veteran soldiers, and can bring the resources of a nation to the crushing of a single state. He has everything, while we have nothing."

"But, father, have I not heard you say that an Englishman never knows when he is whipped, and the greater the odds are against him, the better he fights? If that is true of the English, is it not equally so of their American descendants? and consequently ought not the odds against us to be counted as just so many points in our favor?"

"That is good logic, son, and does credit to your schooling," admitted the squire. "I only pray God that it may be sustained by results."

CHAPTER V

JAMES BOWIE, FIGHTER

FOR a week after the exciting day that witnessed Rex Harden's capture of the horse he had so long coveted, the lad devoted every spare moment to winning Tawny's affections and to training him for future usefulness. He alone fed, groomed, and cared for the animal, the only exception to this rule being that Mabel was allowed to win a share of his regard through occasional treats of sugar. Every day Rex and he took long splendid runs across the brown prairies, and from each one they returned better acquainted with each other than before.

The most important lesson learned by Tawny during this schooling was that of repressing any sign of nervousness at the sound of firearms. At first he was made familiar with the report of a pistol fired from the saddle, but ere the week was ended a rifle might be discharged between his ears without causing him to flinch. Rex also practised a certain shrill whistle that he always sounded at feeding time until Tawny learned to recognize it and come at its call.

Absorbed as he thus was in educating the superb creature that acknowledged him as master, Rex by no means forgot the conversation with his father that had in a few minutes transformed him from a loyal Mexican subject into a bitter young Texan rebel. His long rides afforded him ample time for thought, and the more he reflected upon the wretched condition of his native state under Mexican rule, and dreamed of her glorious future, if only she could achieve independence, the more ardently did he long for the time to come when even he might strike a blow in the cause of freedom. He had not yet dared express his hopes and longings to his parents, but with Mabel he had talked freely concerning them. Into Tawny's sensitive ears he also whispered of the daring things he meant to do if war should be declared, and of how brave they both must be if ever they found themselves in a battle.

Towards the end of the week it was noticed at the ranch that while travellers were still occasionally seen on their way westward or in the direction of San Antonio, none had come from that place in several days. The last to do so had been a messenger from the Mexican Commandant of the district to the people of Gonzales. He bore a demand for the return of a brass field-piece borrowed by them some years before for defence against Indians. They promptly refused to give up the gun, declaring that they still needed it for defence, and with this answer the messenger returned to San Antonio. Since then the inmates of the Rancho Herrera had heard nothing concerning the affair, and were growing decidedly anxious as to how it might result.

One afternoon while they were in this frame of mind a horseman coming from the east reined up before the great house, and was cordially greeted by Squire Harden. He was tall and handsome, fair-haired and blue-eyed, carried himself with a military air, and had the look of one who would be either a loyal friend or a bitter enemy. He was both; for he was James Bowie, the most noted duellist in the southwest at that moment, and the best-known man in Texas. As a son-in-law of ex-Governor Vera-mendi of San Antonio, whose eldest daughter he had married some years before, he possessed influence among Mexicans as well as with Americans, though by the former he was more feared than liked.

"Well, James, what news do you bring?" asked Squire Harden, after he had seen his guest provided with refreshments and comfortably established on the porch.

"The best and the worst, squire," replied the new-comer. "I bring the news that Texans everywhere are declaring for independence, and also that war can no longer be averted, since Cos has landed at Matagorda with dire threats against all Americans."

"That Cos has landed is indeed news," said the squire, thoughtfully. "How did you learn it?"

"Deaf Smith brought the report to Gonzales yesterday, and has gone on to notify Austin at San Felipe as well as Houston at Nacogdoches. I am on my way to San Antonio to discover the state of public feeling there, to remove my wife and her sister to a place of greater safety, and last but not least, to notify you as chief of the Committee of Safety for this district, that you are urged to repair without delay to San Felipe and assist in establishing a permanent State Council."

"I suppose that is all that a cripple is fit for," replied the squire, bitterly, "but I would willingly give ten years of my life to shoulder a rifle, and march on two sound legs against those who propose to enslave us. To remain idle at a safe distance and allow others to fight for him is indeed a hard fate for one whose chief desire in life is for his country's freedom."

"I know how you feel, squire," answered Bowie, gently, "and I honor your sentiments. At the same time there is another side to the question. While it is certain that Texas can never gain her freedom without fighting for it, it is equally certain that she cannot fight without an army, and that an army cannot be raised without authority. It must also be equipped, maintained, and directed by the authority that calls it into existence. And this is only a small portion of the labor that will devolve upon that same authority. So, squire, you won't have a chance to be idle in San Felipe, nor will you be even safe. Santa Anna will set a price on the head of every member of that Council, and unless we can successfully resist him you will be the especial objects of his vengeance. Texas has plenty of men to fight for her, but very few fitted by nature or education to do her thinking. You are one of those few, and even if you had the legs of a centipede combined with the strength of a Goliath, we could not spare you from our Council."

"There is much truth in what you say, James, and of course, since I am useless as a fighter, I will go to San Felipe as a talker."

"And as a worker, a writer, and a planner, squire, — one who will cheer on the brave, encourage the faltering, and shame the cowardly. I tell you, my dear friend, it will be a fine thing for the fighters to feel that they are backed up in their government by such thinkers as you."

"That may all be, James, and I will do what I can in any way that offers. At the same time it is very certain that you will find many more men in Texas ready to talk than to fight for her. However, of one thing I am assured : those who do fight will fight to the bitter end."

"You are right, squire. They surely will," answered Bowie, with a flash in his blue eyes that told how he would fight.

"I wish," continued the other, meditatively, "that I knew the exact state of affairs in San Antonio, for I cannot join the Council without first providing for the safety of my family."

"Let me ride to town with Colonel Bowie, and find out what is going on," suggested Rex, who had been an eager though silent listener to the foregoing conversation.

"You, son!" exclaimed Squire Harden, gazing at the speaker doubtfully, as though surprised that one so young should even think of undertaking such a mission. "No, of course I can't let you go. San Antonio is altogether too dangerous a place for young Texas rebels just now. And yet I don't know," he added, with a sudden realizing sense that the sturdy, well-knit figure standing before him was no longer a child, but as gallant a youth as could be found in a day's ride. "You are as tall as I am. You have two sound legs, you whipped Tawny in fair fight, and it may be that on this errand you will find a chance to render Texas a service. Yes, boy, you may go. At the same time, do not delay your return; for we shall not only be anxious concerning you during every minute of your absence, but your report will determine our plans."

"Don't you fret, squire. I'll see that the lad comes to no harm," said Bowie, as Rex hurried away to prepare Tawny for the ride that was to be undertaken at once.

"Thank you, James; I know that he could not begin his career in safer hands than yours."

A few minutes later Bowie and his young companion, whose superb mount excited the other's enthusiastic admiration, had taken their departure, and in less than three hours they were within sight of the ancient Spanish town of San Antonio de Bexar.

Old as this principal city of Western Texas was even at that time, and populous as it has become since the Americans made it their own, in the year 1835 it contained less than two thousand souls and was of but small commercial importance. Located on the west bank of the San Antonio River, some five miles south of where that limpid stream springs in full volume from the Guadalupe foot-hills, the town as Bowie and Rex saw it consisted of a few hundred low stone or adobe houses lining narrow streets and thickly clustered about a cathedral that faced an open plaza. Not more than a dozen of the better houses rose above a single story, but most of them were flat roofed, and all had stout walls covered on the outside with a white plaster. Beyond these clustered houses was a ragged fringe of jacals or hovels built of sticks, cornstalks, mud, or anything else that came to hand, and occupied by the peons or servants of the town.

Through several of the unpaved streets, which were quagmires in wet weather and beds of dust in dry, ran accquias or ditches of clear water, from which the domestic supply was drawn.

The eastern portion of the town was enclosed within a great ⊃ shaped bend of the river, which might be crossed at a shallow ford or by means of a single bridge. On a slight elevation northeast of this bridge, and a quarter of a mile from it, or a half a mile from the Plaza, stood the mission of the Alamo, long since diverted from its original use and become a barracks for the garrison of San Antonio.

Besides the Alamo and the mission of San Fernando, to which the cathedral belonged, there were four other missions located on alternate sides of the river south of the city at distances of from two to nine miles from it. Thus San Antonio was essentially a Spanish mission city in which, up to the outbreak of the revolution, very few Americans had made their homes, and now most of these had left, to escape the threatened storm of war.

As our travellers drew near to this ancient city, it was bathed in a glow from the setting sun and presented a picture of perfect peace. Peons were home returning from the irrigated fields, flocks and herds were being driven to their safe corrals, the evening bells of San Fernando were answering the distant chime of the mission San José, and from the grim Alamo the mellow notes of a cavalry trumpet rang out clear and sweet on the still air.

The two horsemen passed the garita or lookout, a

stout block-house crowning a gentle slope a mile east of the town, without observing any signs of human presence. If, however, they had glanced back after passing it, they would have seen a quick waving of signal flags from its roof. But they did not turn their heads, and so had no suspicion that their coming was already noted and reported to the troops in the distant Alamo.

CHAPTER VI

IN THE STREETS OF SAN ANTONIO

ALTHOUGH neither Rex nor Bowie looked back after passing the garita, they realized that a certain amount of danger might await them in a city filled with troops intended for the subjugation of their country. Therefore as they descended into the river bottom and entered the shadow of its bordering belt of timber, Bowie asked his companion if he knew of any place on that side where he could leave his horse in safety.

"If you do," he continued, "I think it would be well to conceal him and enter the city on foot, for it is possible that so fine an animal might be seized for use in the army if the soldiers caught sight of him. At the same time an emergency might arise in which you would have urgent need of his services."

"Yes," replied Rex, after a moment's thought, "I think I know of such a place; though as Tawny will allow no one but me to care for him, I cannot leave him there very long."

"I don't think you will need to leave him for more than an hour or two," rejoined the other; "but I am convinced that it will be best for us to separate before appearing in town, and for you to enter it on foot. They won't dare interfere with my movements, at least not for a while, and so I shall ride directly to the Veramendi house. There I can quickly obtain all necessary information, and shall look for you to rejoin me as soon as it becomes fairly dark. You are sure that your proposed hiding-place is a safe one ? "

" Oh, yes," replied Rex, " for it is the house of Manuel Peralta, who is under obligations to my father that he is anxious to repay."

" Humph! " ejaculated Bowie, sceptically. " I know the place, and if you don't turn up within an hour, I shall visit it in search of you. But here is the road to it now. So adios, for a little."

Thus they parted, Bowie taking the road to the bridge, and Rex that leading to the ford near which stood Manuel Peralta's little adobe house. At the bridge the former was halted by a guard, the officer of which demanded to know what had become of his companion.

" I have no companion," replied Bowie.

" But you had one when you passed the garita.",

" That may be."

" What has become of him ? "

" Quien sabe ! " (who knows).

" That you do not answer, Señor Americano, makes it plain that you are a character of suspicion. As such I am compelled to lead you to the Commandante.

who will no doubt derive great pleasure from your conversation."

"Thanks.   But I have no desire to meet the general to-night, and in fact am too busy.   Therefore I regret that I cannot accompany you, Señor Teniente."

"But you must!" cried the officer, angrily. "Soldados, seize him!"

"Stand back, soldades!   Don't you dare lay a hand on James Bowie," thundered the American, at the same time clapping spurs to his horse.

The animal sprang forward with such violence that one of the guard was hurled to the ground, while the others instinctively drew back, awed as much by the name they had just heard, as by the man's bold move.

"Buenas noches, señores!" shouted back Bowie, mockingly, as he flew down the street leading to the heart of the town and disappeared in the gathering dusk.

"Carrajo!" hissed the baffled officer between his teeth. "Señor James Bowie shall answer with blood for this insult.   He has entered the city, but like a rat, easily entering a trap, he will find the difficulty in getting out again.   Now will I look for the other rat, who has doubtless gone by the ford.   It is then fortunate that I stationed a guard also at that place."

Manuel Peralta had been a herder on the Rancho Herrera until an accident so crippled him as to compel the use of crutches.   Feeling a deep sympathy for the man on account of the similarity in their misfortunes, Squire Harden had loaned him sufficient money to purchase a small house near San Antonio and establish himself as a zapatero, or shoemaker. Not one peso of this money had yet been repaid, although the man seemed to have a fairly good business, and was always ready to promise that he would pay something on account within a few days.

He had one son, a bright little chap of perhaps ten years old, named Murillo. This child was a great favorite with Rex, who rarely failed to bring him some present when he visited the city, and who was regarded by the little one with an ardent admiration.

It was at this place, then, on the outskirts of the town, and close to the ford, that Rex proposed to leave Tawny while he crossed the river and visited his friends of the Veramendi household. He might have hesitated before doing so had he known that, since the coming of troops to San Antonio, Peralta had found the selling of liquor to the soldiers so much more profitable than the making of shoes that he had turned his establishment into a pulqueria, or place for drinking.

Ignorant of this fact, Rex, after parting from Bowie, turned his horse towards the ford and a few minutes later reached the little adobe house, which stood in the shadow of a wide-spreading umbrella tree. Behind it was a tiny stable for the accommodation of the donkey on which Manuel Peralta rode into town whenever business called him that far from home.

As Rex drew near, he heard the sound of so many voices coming from the front of the house that he cautiously turned to one side, determined to secure Tawny in the stable before making his presence known. Riding up to this and dismounting, he discovered his little friend Murillo seated on the ground just outside, and feeding with bits of meat a superb fighting cock which he recognized as one he had presented to the child when it was still a chicken nearly a year before.

The boy was so intent upon his occupation that he did not observe his friend's approach until the latter stood beside him, saying:

"Hello, 'Rillo! What are you doing?"

At this the child scrambled to his feet in affright. In another instant his face beamed with joy, and without wasting any time in the formalities of greeting he at once began to talk of his wonderful chicken, which, as Rex now saw, was tethered by one leg to a small stake.

"Oh, Señor Rex, you are come just in time for the battle royal, the greatest cock fight ever seen in San Antonio. It will be on Sunday, which is to-morrow, and no chicken in the city will stand up for more than one minute before El Bravo. All the soldados say the same, and Domingo, who knows the most of any, is to handle him, and will divide with me the pesos that he will win. He is to wear spurs of steel that will tear like the thorns of the mesquite and cut like knives. Also, Señor — "

"I have no doubt it will all be very fine," interrupted Rex, "and I hope El Bravo will win the battle, of course; but before I hear any more about it I want you to help me put my horse in the stable of the donkey, and fetch him some water, as well as some corn, if you know where to find any."

Eager to do anything to oblige his dear friend, the child promptly routed the indignant donkey from his comfortable quarters, of which Tawny was quickly placed in possession, showed Rex where to find corn, and ran to the river for a bucket of water.

When the new-comer had seen his horse thus cared for, though he did not deem it best to remove either saddle or bridle, he asked 'Rillo why so many persons were gathered before the house, and who they were.

"They are the soldados who guard the ford, that none may cross after the Angelus, and they are come for a glass of pulque," was the unexpected answer. "Of course," continued the child, "they will permit you to cross if you wish, for they are my friends, and I will tell them that you, also, are my best friend of all. Come quick that you may know them, for already they are leaving and will go back to the other side."

"Hold on!" cried Rex, in a low tone, at the same time drawing the boy inside the stable, that they might not be seen by the departing soldiers. When they were thus hidden from view, he said:

"'Rillo, if I am your best friend, you will do something for me, will you not?"

"I will do anything that the señor shall demand," answered the child, loyally; "even if he desired El Bravo, he should have him."

"Oh no! I shall not ask anything so great as that. I only want you to promise not to let your friends, the soldiers, know of my coming to this place."

"Of course I promise. That is easy."

"And tell me, is there not a boat of some kind on the river below the ford, in which I can cross to the other side? I would not keep it long, for I shall soon come back."

"There is the canoa of Pedro, but he gets money from those who use it, and without money he will not let them cross."

"I will give you money for him, and as much more for yourself, as well, if you will lead me to that canoe," said Rex. "See, here is a silver peso, that shall be for you and him to divide."

'Rillo being thus satisfied that he was about to make a fine bargain for both Pedro and himself, willingly consented to disclose the hiding-place of the canoe. Thus within a few minutes Rex had gained it unobserved, thanks to the darkness that had now fallen, and found himself poling Pedro's sluggish craft across the swift current. Although he was carried some distance down stream, he succeeded in gaining the opposite bank, and in making a landing not far from the Plaza.

Moving swiftly but cautiously along the dirty streets, and keeping in the deepest shadows, he had very nearly gained the house in which he hoped to find James Bowie, when a door close at hand was flung open, allowing a flood of light to shine full upon him.

At the moment he was thus discovered a stern voice from across the street ordered him to halt. The command was accompanied by the ominous rattle of weapons, and for an instant Rex faltered. Then he sprang forward, determined to risk everything rather than surrender, and ran plump into a patrol of soldiers who were just turning in from a side street.

CHAPTER VII

BENEATH THE VERAMENDI GARDENS

So unexpected and impetuous was our lad's dash among the members of that astonished patrol, that, although several of them clutched at him as he shot past, he had cleared them and was flying up the street before they fairly realized what had happened. Then with angry cries they started in hot pursuit, and even sent a couple of musket balls whistling in the direction he had taken.

In an instant the quiet street was filled with an uproar. Doors and windows were flung open. Shouting men and screaming women poured from the houses, and harmless shots were fired into the air from ancient bell-mouthed blunderbusses, whose owners had been aching for a safe opportunity to test their noise-producing power. Every one believed that the city either had been or was about to be attacked, and cries of Los Americanos! Los Tejanos! (the Texans) were heard on all sides.

Suddenly these cries were silenced by a blare of trumpets, and the populace shrank back to make room for a dark mass of cavalry, that, coming from their encampment in the Plaza, were making their way to the ford of the river, and completely filled the narrow street from house to house in their passage. Forty files, of four troopers each, swept past, and after them rumbled half a dozen heavy wagons drawn by four mules, showing that some expedition more serious than a mere reconnoissance was on foot.

Some of the spectators said this was the advance guard of General Cos's army, and others that the brave cavalrymen were hastening to repel an attack about to be made on the city at the ford. But all was speculation, for the secret of the movement was so well kept that it was not known to a dozen persons in the city.

James Bowie knew it, though; for Nelita, his dark-eyed little sister-in-law, had told him even amid her joyous greetings, and for many minutes he stood in the open doorway of the Veramendi house, awaiting anxiously the appearance of his young friend.

He started at the sudden uproar of shouts and firing, and in the intentness of his listening was barely conscious of two pair of soft hands that grasped his arms as though seeking his protection. So indeed they were; for, with parents dead, and their only brother Florio a soldier on duty at the Mexican capital, Ysobel Bowie and Nelita Veramendi, her younger sister, knew not where to turn for protection during these stormy times, save to the stalwart American who had given one of them his name.

As they clung to him, trembling with apprehension, and he peered anxiously forth into the darkness, there came a sound of flying feet, and in another moment Rex Harden stood breathlessly beside them.

"Hide me quick!" he panted. "The soldiers are after me!"

For answer James Bowie deliberately closed the stout doors, dropped a heavy wooden bar into iron sockets behind them, and said:

"Now, lad, you are safely hidden, for the time being, and can have a full five minutes in which to regain your breath. Tell us what has happened, and hear our news. That will do, Queridita. Don't choke the boy."

This last was addressed to his wife, who had impulsively thrown her arms about the lad's neck and kissed him; while Nelita shyly allowed him to clasp her extended hand. It will thus be seen that our Rex was on intimate terms with the Veramendi family, the younger members of which had been his playmates in childhood, while their father and his had been the best of friends.

Within two minutes the young fugitive had recovered his breath and related his recent thrilling experiences. As he concluded Bowie said:

"Fetch something to eat and drink, Ysobel, quick as you can, for Rex must be off again at once. You see there are so many others who want him that we must not keep him long."

Even as he spoke there came a furious pounding against the outer doors, and loud demands that they be opened ; but without heeding these, Bowie continued :

" The ball is to be opened this very night, Rex, and probably this very hour, by Castonado, who is ordered to march on Gonzales with two companies of cavalry to capture the disputed field-piece. He is also commissioned to disarm such Americans as he may find, and last but not least, to arrest your father and bring him to San Antonio for trial as a conspirator against the Government. So, lad, your work is pretty plainly cut out for you, and there is a ride before you that if successful will become as famous as that of Paul Revere. Not only must you warn the settlers, including your own father, of Castonado's advance, which, with only cavalry in his command, will be a rapid one, but you must manage to give the people of Gonzales several hours' notice of his coming before he appears."

" But how am I to get away from here ? " demanded Rex, whose nerves were tingling with the exciting news he had just heard, as well as with the responsibility so suddenly thrust upon him.

It is no wonder that he was dismayed by the apparent hopelessness of his position, for such a storm of blows was now falling on the outer door as announced a determination to break it in if it were not speedily opened, and already a sound of angry voices from behind the house proclaimed it to be surrounded.

"Nelita will show you a way out," answered Bowie, calmly. "So drink this chocolate, stuff these cakes into your pockets, and be off while I commune with the idiots who are raising such an infernal racket outside. Now, 'Lita, he is ready. Adios, lad, until we meet again."

Intimate as Rex had been with the Veramendi family, and well as he thought he knew the low, rambling house in which they dwelt, he had never even heard of the underground passage to which he was now conducted by the girl, whose strong friendship for Americans combined with her sense of justice to make her an ardent champion of their cause. It led from a dark cellar where its opening was so ingeniously concealed that days might have been spent in fruitless search for it, even after its existence was known, and it extended under the gardens to the river, a hundred yards away.

Nelita only accompanied him to its entrance, for she had been bidden to return with all haste, in order that she might not be missed from the household when Bowie should admit the soldiers. Rex would gladly have talked longer with her, but he too had urgent cause for haste. So after a few words of instruction concerning the passage, and a warm handclasp between the two, he entered the absolute blackness of the narrow tunnel, and Nelita closed its door behind him.

The place in which our lad now found himself was so low that he could not stand upright, but was, at the same time, so free from obstructions that even in a stooping posture he advanced rapidly until brought to a sudden stand by an angry snarl from close at hand. Instantly the boy was bathed in perspiration, and found himself trembling violently, but in a moment his courage returned. He knew that he could not retreat, and so must advance in spite of whatever danger opposed him. Thus thinking, he drew his hunting-knife and, holding it well to the front, sprang forward, at the same time uttering a shout. A scamper of soft footfalls proclaimed a retreat of the beast that had protested against his presence, and in another minute he had emerged from the stifling passage into a dense thicket beneath a slightly overhanging bank of the river.

The darkness of the outer world seemed almost daylight compared with that from which he had just come, and he experienced little difficulty in making his way along the stream to where it turned sharply eastward. Here he knew that in order to save precious time he must cut across the great bend, and pass through that part of the town lying in its mouth. He dreaded to attempt this, but only hesitated long enough to raise himself cautiously above the bank and make a careful survey of his surroundings. As he could neither see nor hear anything to alarm him, he started down a narrow lane and nearly reached the opposite arm of the bend without meeting a soul.

Then he ran plump into a soldier, and for a moment believed that he must either submit to arrest or fight for his liberty; but fortunately for him the soldier was so full of pulque as to be maudlin. He apologized profusely for having collided with his dear friend, and insisted that Rex should take a drink with him in token of forgiveness. The lad attempted to shake him off; but the fellow clung to him so persistently and claimed his friendship so loudly that in desperation Rex knocked him down with a well-placed blow, and dashed away, leaving the soldier to alarm the neighborhood with his cries.

By the time the young fugitive reached his canoe many persons were running hither and thither with excited inquiries as to what had happened, but none of them discovered him, and he was allowed to shove off without molestation. By the time he gained the opposite bank he was half a mile below the house of Peralta, and careless of what became of the canoe, he hastened towards it with all speed.

As he drew near to the pulqueria, he became aware of a great splashing in the water of the ford, and the sound of many voices mingled with the rattle of arms and a tramp of horses. With a sinking heart he realized that Castonado's troops were already crossing the river, and that many of them were now gathered at the very place where he had left his horse.

Creeping as close to them as he dared, he crouched behind a tree and anxiously awaited developments. It was evident that Peralta was doing a rushing business with the troopers, who waited to see their wagons safely across the river before resuming their march. Many horses were fastened to trees and fences while their owners made merry in the pulqueria. Bitterly as Rex would regret the leaving of Tawny behind, he wondered if he could not secure one of these animals, and dash away without running any risk save that of a few scattering shots! Upon him depended the safety of the dear ones at home, and every minute was of the utmost value. Yes, he must secure a horse at any cost, though to recover Tawny seemed out of the question.

Thus thinking, Rex slipped from his hiding-place and had started towards the nearest group of tethered animals, when his steps were abruptly arrested by a great outcry from a score of voices and the sounds of a fierce struggle in the vicinity of Peralta's little stable. Amid the general uproar he heard shouts of "El Diablo! El Diablo!" Then came shrill screams followed by the rushing gallop of a horse, and Rex instinctively knew that his Tawny had fought with the enemies of Texas and won the first battle for liberty.

CHAPTER VIII

As the sound of galloping hoofs died away in the distance, sharp words of command were issued by the Mexican officers, the men sprang to their tethered horses, and with a heavy heart, Rex knew that his chance for securing one of these had vanished. For a moment he stood irresolute, and then, moved by a sudden impulse he slipped softly away. Reaching a safe distance he began to run at the top of his speed in the direction taken by Tawny, which fortunately was also the direction of the Gonzales road.

He did not of course expect to run the whole twenty miles to his home, nor even, while on foot, to outstrip the horsemen who would follow closely after him, but he did hope to find a horse somewhere. He felt keenly the loss of Tawny, and wondered if he should ever see him again. To be sure, it was possible that the horse might make his way back to the ranch ; but Rex feared he would not do so until after it had been abandoned. Then he would fall into possession of the enemy, and the mere thought of such a fate for his beautiful horse made the lad hot with anger. He hoped the soldiers had not known whose horse they had found in Manuel Peralta's stable, and that by leaving him there he had not brought trouble upon the crippled zapatero. If he had been aware of the real facts in the case, he would not have been thus worried.

Little 'Rillo had not betrayed his friend's secret, but it was discovered by Domingo, late vaquero on the Rancho Herrera, now a soldier in the troop of Castonado. This man, who was a noted cock-fighter, had been delighted to discover at Peralta's pulqueria a chicken of the famous Herrera breed, and had consented to handle it during the forthcoming battle. Of course, when he was ordered out with his troop, the cock fight must be postponed. When Castonado halted his men at the ford, Domingo paid a visit to El Bravo in company with Peralta, to examine into his condition and decide upon a change of diet.

As these two entered the little stable, they were amazed to find it occupied and nearly filled by a horse in place of the donkey for which it had been built. Hastily procuring a light with which to view this unexpected tenant, Domingo recognized him at once as the redoubtable Herrera stallion that had so often defied him, and had finally driven him from the ranch.

"Peste!" he exclaimed. "The young gringo who claims to have captured this beast, and to be a better rider than any vaquero in Texas, must have come to this place. Doubtless he is sent to spy out and give warning of the very expedition on which we are engaged. Perchance thou hast him hid, friend Peralta, and so are in a fair way to be shot for sheltering this spawn of rebels."

"I have not! Indeed I have not!" protested the other, trembling with fright at this suggestion. "I know nothing of him! And how this brute of a horse came into my stable I have no knowledge."

"The youth has then had the assurance to place his vile horse here without thy permission, and so to endanger thy life, relying for thy forbearance upon thy great love for his father?"

"But of that I have none. His father, the tyrant Harden, pesters me continually for a few wretched pesos that he owed me for long service, but which he claims to have advanced as a loan. Bah! I hate him and spit upon him!"

"If he owes thee money, let us take this horse and sell him. In any case, as the property of a rebel, he is our lawful spoil, and may we not do as we please with our own? El Capitan Castonado will gladly buy him, for he is very wealthy, and every month he kills a horse. So I have heard him boast, and also do I know that he is not pleased with his present mount. If it is hinted that one must needs be a perfect horseman to ride this diablo, then will El Capitan be eager to purchase him, for he boasts that he can unaided break the heart of any horse that lives. Within one month then will this brute be dead, for the noble Castonado finds the same pleasure in killing horses that a more soft-hearted person does in the death of bulls."

As Peralta readily agreed to this scheme, Domingo informed the sergeant of his troop that the pulquero had in his stable the finest horse in all Texas, one of the famous Herrera breed. It had been given him in payment for services; but as the animal was much too spirited for him to ride, he would sell it for a very small sum. Did not his excellency, the sergeant, think that El Capitan Castonado would be pleased to hear of such a bargain in horseflesh?"

His excellency the sergeant did think so, and accordingly reported what he had heard to a lieutenant. He, in turn, ventured to tell the captain of the wonderful horse just discovered that no one could ride, and which might in consequence be bought for a song.

Upon this, the noble Castonado, declaring that he had yet to meet the horse he could not ride, started towards the little stable in which Tawny was chafing at his unusual confinement. He was followed by the lieutenant, the sergeant, Domingo, Peralta, and a score of eager soldiers, several of whom bore torches.

"Bring him forth," commanded El Capitan, and Domingo with half a dozen others sprang to obey the order.

The horse showed such docility in allowing them

to back him from the stable, that the spectators declared him to be of coward blood and an animal of no spirit. As if understanding and resenting this imputation, Tawny was no sooner clear of the doorway than he turned upon them with all the concentrated fury of his wild nature. Within two seconds his gleaming teeth and flying heels had cleared a wide circle about him, and Domingo, clinging doggedly to his bridle, had been seized in the powerful jaws, shaken, and flung aside as a terrier flings a rat.

Then, with a rush that knocked down the great Castonado himself, besides the lieutenant and sergeant and several others of minor importance, the mighty horse sprang into the darkness and disappeared. As the discomfited captain stiffly regained his feet, he swore with fierce oaths that he believed this to be a plot of the devilish Texans to kill him, and that all who had been implicated in it should be sweetly punished upon his return from chastising the rebels. Then ordering that his command instantly take the road, he sulkily mounted a horse that would allow himself to be abused or even killed at the will of his cruel master.

In the meantime, Rex Harden, running along the eastern road, reached a point two-thirds of the way to the garita without incident. Then he was startled by seeing what he believed to be a horseman looming above a slight rise of ground before him. Halting, and ready for a dash to one side in case his liberty should be threatened, he watched closely to see whether the suspicious figure were coming or going. After a moment he decided that it was not doing either, but was standing with its head to the ground. A great hope sprang into the boy's breast. Could it be Tawny cropping the wayside grass?

Softly he breathed the whistle signal, the meaning of which was understood by his beloved horse alone. At its sound the animal lifted his head and listened. A repetition of the signal was answered by a whinny of recognition. One minute later Rex, his heart overflowing with gratitude, was seated on Tawny's back, and the reunited friends were speeding joyously eastward.

As our young rider knew nothing of the guard stationed at the garita, he was unprepared for the stern challenge of " Quien va ! " that greeted him as he approached it. Instantly appreciating the situation, however, he lay flat on Tawny's neck, urged him to increased speed, and dashed like a thunderbolt past the block-house. The angry roar of a musket greeted this defiance of authority, and a bullet whizzed spitefully after him. It did no harm, and Rex was rapidly becoming so used to being under fire, that he only laughed at this fruitless attempt to stop a pair of Texas rebels who had made up their minds to go ahead.

At the same moment a greater anxiety than that attending a mere musket shot was caused by the clear notes of a trumpet borne faintly to him on the heavy night air from the direction of the ford. At sound of this ominous warning the lad bent low and whispered to his flying steed that for many miles their headlong speed must not be slackened.

Twice during the next hour did the young rider make slight detours from his road to warn American settlers of Castonado's coming with orders for their forcible disarming. At these places, while his foam-flecked horse was rubbed down by willing hands and given a mouthful of water, Rex was surrounded by groups of resolute men, pale-faced women, and excited children, who heard his news with breathless interest. By these it was certain to be spread, and in each case he left the little communities making hasty preparations for a flight to the eastward.

It was midnight when Tawny's flying hoof-beats, his rider's shouts, and a joyous barking of dogs roused the inmates of the Rancho Herrera, and brought them to door and window. As Rex flung himself to the porch, a figure appeared in the hall-way, and Squire Harden's voice demanded :

" Who's there ? "

" It is I, father, and a Mexican army is on its way to arrest you."

" Thank Heaven, son, that you are safe ! " cried the squire. " I feared worse news. But why need they send an army to arrest a single man ? "

"It is also sent to capture the field-piece at Gonzales and to disarm all Americans whom they can find."

"It will take an army to do those things," replied the squire, grimly, and, Mrs. Harden now appearing with a light, Rex saw that his father, supported by his crutches, held a pistol in each hand.

"How far behind you are they?"

"An hour, at least,—probably more; for Tawny has brought me like the wind."

"You have done well, son, and gained for us plenty of time."

"I am also charged to warn Gonzales, and all between here and there."

"It is a noble errand, and we will go with you; but to accomplish it, both you and Tawny must have rest and refreshment."

Turning to the two American overseers of the ranch, who slept in the great house and had appeared in the lower hall, fully armed, at the first alarm, the squire added:

"Tom, take the fleetest horse in the corral and scout along the San Antonio road until you sight this Mexican advance. Then fly back with all speed. If we have left, follow us to Gonzales. Richards, harness four mules to the light wagon, saddle the two best horses you can find, and have all in readiness at this door within half an hour. You, Rex, must first care for Tawny, and then come to the house for refreshment. Wife, do you and Mabel collect such things as are necessary to your comfort on a long journey, but not to exceed a single trunkful. In less than an hour from now we must be off ; and remember, all of you, not one word of this news to a single Mexican on the place."

CHAPTER IX

MIDNIGHT FLIGHT OF THE SETTLERS

WITH each person performing an allotted task the preparations for flight proceeded so rapidly that within the appointed time all was in readiness for an abandonment of the ranch. The covered wagon, with four fleet-footed mules attached, was drawn up before the porch. In it were stored two mattresses, together with blankets and pillows, a trunk, provisions, everything in the way of arms and ammunition that the house afforded, and Aunty Day.

On the front seat were Mabel and her mother, both of whom were expert handlers of reins, and who were to take turns at driving. Squire Harden and his man Richards, armed with rifles and pistols, were to ride beside it. Rex, also armed and mounted on Tawny, was to ride ahead with all speed, carrying the alarm to settlers on the west bank of the Guadalupe and into Gonzales. Already had two parties of fugitives passed the ranch, but they had not halted, for the squire had shouted that he would shortly overtake them.

As the Hardens were bidding a sad farewell to the home they loved so dearly, and which they feared they might never see again, there came a clatter of hoofs, and the scout who had been sent back along the road dashed up to the wagon. He brought the startling intelligence that the Mexican advance was pressing forward so rapidly as to be already within a mile of that place, and liable to appear at any moment.

" Let them come ! " cried the squire, with assumed cheerfulness ; " they will find the nest deserted and the birds flown."

In another minute the light wagon was spinning along the Gonzales road with its nimble-footed mules on a run, while Rex and Tawny were speeding eastward like the wind nearly a mile in advance.

Despite the precautions taken to keep the news of the night from the Mexican peons, it had spread to all quarters of the ranch, and, as the Hardens began their flight, a dark group of blanketed figures, gathered close to the walls of the house, sullenly watched their departure. Then they rushed into it, with the hope of plunder, and began to batter down the heavy doors of the several rooms.

While they were thus engaged, but before they had effected an entrance, a squad of a dozen cavalrymen, swarthy as themselves, appeared on the scene and drove them from their work. It was the Mexican advance led by Castonado himself, and he was furious at the discovery that his expected prisoner had made good his escape. How a warning had been conveyed to him, the Mexican captain could not imagine ; for, so far as he knew, only a riderless horse had left San Antonio in advance of him and passed the garita that night.

When he learned from the peons that Rex Harden, mounted on that same horse, had reached the ranch an hour before, he was more puzzled than ever, but he did not waste time in seeking to solve the mystery. As the fugitives had only a few minutes' start of him, and were encumbered by a wagon, they might still be within his reach. So, leaving a couple of soldiers to guard the house, which, with its broad estate, he had long coveted, and which he now believed might soon become his own, El Capitan Castonado again set forth on his pursuit of the hated Americans.

An hour later the Harden party had just over-taken another wagon-load of fugitives guarded by two horsemen, when the squire, who with senses keenly alert brought up the rear, detected the beat of galloping hoofs on the road behind him. The pursuit had been hotter than he anticipated, and he realized that the time for desperate measures had arrived. Spurring to the front, he urged on the mules to greater speed, and, as the wagons bounded forward, he hastily explained his plan to the four men who guarded them. His own team could easily have outstripped the other, but the thought of allowing such a thing never entered the mind

of the brave Kentuckian. To him the fate of one must be the fate of all, and the speed of both wagons must be regulated by that of the slowest mule in the two teams. When the squire saw that every animal was doing its utmost, he dropped behind the rear wagon, and the other men followed him.

Ranging themselves in a line across the road, they cocked their rifles and waited. They were barely in position before they heard the sound of galloping horses, and a minute later they could distinguish through the darkness a still darker mass rushing towards them.

"Aim low, men," ordered Squire Harden. "Ready! Fire!"

The five rifles spoke as one. Five jets of flame leaped forth, and two of the oncoming horses plunged heavily forward, flinging their riders to the ground far beyond them. Others were wounded, and the whole Mexican squad was thrown into such dire confusion by the unexpectedness of the attack, that half of them turned and fled without waiting to discover their enemies' strength. Being thus deserted, Castonado, with the three or four who remained firm, deemed it wiser to retire from the field rather than risk a further encounter with an unknown force.

Thus was danger averted from the fugitives for a time; and when the defenders of the wagons again overtook them, they were confident that present pursuit was given over. In this belief a halt was called, and the jaded mules, which had been driven for fifteen miles at their utmost speed, were given an hour's rest by the roadside.

Although it is doubtful if the exhausted animals could have continued their flight much longer without this breathing-spell, it came very near to resulting in disaster. About daybreak, shortly after they were once more on the road, a picket who had been left behind came in with tidings that the Mexicans were again on their trail.

This was only too true; for Castonado, reënforced by a number of his troopers whose inferior mounts had caused them to drop behind, and having obtained fresh horses from a deserted ranch, had determined to make one more effort to capture the fugitives.

So the mules were once more lashed into a run, and the fierce race for liberty was resumed. With increasing daylight the occupants of the wagons could look back and see their pursuers topping some distant rise of the road or disappearing in a hollow. Each time as they came into view, they were plainly nearer than before, and after a time their exulting shouts could be clearly heard. Now, too, the speed of the mules began visibly to slacken; they no longer sprang forward at the sting of the lash, and it was evident that they had come to the end of their strength.   In a few minutes more the race must end.

But it must not end with the tame surrender of cowards ; and although the Mexicans outnumbered the defenders of the wagons by three to one, the latter determined to make one more attempt at driving them off.   So with a brave show of confidence that he did not feel Squire Harden urged his horse to the side of the flying wagon, and shouted, " Hold out a a little longer, wife, while we drop back again and teach those fellows another lesson.   Good-by ! "

" Wait, father !   Wait a moment ! " screamed Mabel.   " Look there ! "

The excited girl was standing up clinging with one hand to the swaying wagon top and pointing with the other in the direction they were going.

In the glory of the rising sun a cloud of dust rose on the keen morning air.   In it were moving figures that momentarily grew more distinct.

" Hurrah ! " shouted Squire Harden.   " Anda, mula ! Anda ! One more effort, boys, and we are saved.   Only friends can come from that direction."

And so it proved ; for out of the golden dust cloud came a dozen hard-riding Texans, waving their rifles, yelling like wild Indians, and led by a slender lad on a magnificent chestnut horse, who set the headlong pace as easily as though he were fresh from a night of rest.

Rex had ridden to the Guadalupe, carried his warning to the settlers on the bank, sent a message across to Gonzales, and then turned back to meet the fugitives from the Cibolo, accompanied by a squad of eager volunteers, whose numbers were increased as they advanced.

The new-comers opened their ranks with a ringing cheer to allow the wagons passage, and then reënforced by five more men, closed again for a charge upon those who had maintained their relentless pursuit through the night. But the Mexicans did not await their onset. Warned by the Texan shouts, they had already drawn rein, and as the wild riders swept into view from beyond the wagons, Castonado with his troopers turned and fled like leaves before an autumn gale.

For a mile the Texans followed them, firing an occasional rifle shot to accelerate their speed. Then they clattered happily back to where the women had halted their wagons by the roadside, and were already preparing a breakfast for the heroes of this glorious though bloodless victory.

How light-hearted every one was, now that the terrible strain of the night was relaxed, and what a joyous meal they made of that rude camp breakfast! How they all talked and laughed at the same time! How the women were complimented on their pluck, and the men for their bravery! Squire Harden tried in vain to express his gratitude to the new-comers for the promptness of their aid ; but they interrupted him with shouts of :

"That's all right, squire. We'd been worse than greasers if we hadn't come, seeing that you had weakened your own fighting force by sending your son to warn us of danger."

"All the same, men," insisted the squire, "I do thank you from the bottom of my heart. And, Rex, I am more than proud of you for this night's work."

"It was Tawny's work, father, more than mine ; for I don't believe there is another horse in Texas that could have done what he has since leaving San Antonio last evening."

"No, son," admitted the squire ; "I don't believe there is." And to this opinion every man present agreed.

Before noon of that day every American settler on the west bank of the Guadalupe had been ferried safely across to Gonzales, and every boat had been removed to that side of the river. Already were messengers, mounted on fleet horses, speeding eastward with the news of Castonado's advance, and bearing appeals for aid in repelling it.

With the departure of these, less than a score of fighting men were left in the village. But this handful calmly awaited the Mexican approach, confident that their rifles could hold the crossing against Castonado's swarthy troopers until the aid for which they had sent could arrive.

CHAPTER X

ORGANIZING THE FIRST TEXAS ARMY

ACCORDING to Castonado's orders, the main body of his little army had halted at the Rancho Herrera. To that place, therefore, after failing to disarm a single American, or to capture the man who was regarded as the most pernicious rebel of that district, the Mexican leader retired to await further instructions from the Commandant at San Antonio. Thus were our fugitives given a day and a half of rest in Gonzales before any further move was made against them.

Squire Harden had intended to push on to San Felipe on the Brazos, a hundred miles farther to the eastward; but now he could not leave a point at which every Texas rifle was of such infinite value, and so he determined to remain at Gonzales until the present crisis should be past. Having thus decided, he pitched a tent on the river bank, and it at once became a headquarters to which persons of all conditions flocked for advice or assistance.

Rex with half a dozen of the younger men constituted themselves a picket guard to watch the ford half a mile down the river; and, as his comrades jokingly called our lad "Corporal of the Guard," he was soon known on all sides as "Corporal Rex." Feeling that in this exalted position he ought to wear some distinguishing badge of office, he asked Mabel if she could not suggest and make him one. Gladly accepting this task, the quick-witted girl promised to comply with his request; and, while he slept in the wagon after a night of watching, she smuggled his hat into the tent and busied herself with it for several hours.

When Rex awoke, the hat lay beside him and was the first object to catch his eye. He gazed at it for a moment in perplexity, and then, seizing it, he sprang from the wagon with a shout. On its front was embroidered a tiny blue flag in which was centred a white five-pointed star.

"The star on Tawny's forehead suggested it," said Mabel, who was watching to note how he liked it.

"It's the very thing," cried Rex, "and you are a perfect trump to have thought of it. Hurrah, for the lone-star flag of Texas!"

Then, giving his sister a kiss and a hug, the young corporal set forth to display through the village his newly acquired insignia of rank. But he was not long allowed to be the sole bearer of the lone-star flag; for the device caught like wild-fire, and every one who saw it instantly desired to wear this first distinctive emblem of Texas. Already was Mabel busily at work on one for her father, and within half an hour every needlewoman in Gonzales was either embroidering little lone-star flags or making them from bits of blue silk.

Texas had not yet achieved her independence nor even declared it. In fact, her people still regarded themselves as loyal citizens of Mexico, and were only intent upon defending the rights guaranteed them by the constitution of 1824, against the despotism of an usurper. At the same time the destinies of nations hang by such slight threads, that every Texan who accepted and wore one of the badges made that day impressed upon his heart a symbol that he would never relinquish and one that he would maintain through suffering and disaster even unto death. Texas has long since cast her fortunes with the great sisterhood of the stars and stripes, but she still cherishes the lone-star banner as her state flag, and no other line ever penned can so inspire her sons as does

"Hurrah for the Bonnie Blue Flag that bears the single star!"

While the refugees gathered at Gonzales guarded its approaches, devised emblems distinctive of their beloved state, and waited for the volunteers who they were certain must be hastening to their aid, Castonado had resumed his line of march towards them. About noon on Tuesday, the 29th of Septem-

ber, a scout dashed into the village with tidings that
the enemy was close at hand. Shortly afterwards
anxious watchers on the river bank caught sight of
the pennons, plumes, and glittering trappings of the
Mexican cavalry as it advanced through the open
timber on the opposite side of the stream and halted
at the water's edge.

"Send over a boat that I may cross and deliver
my message to the inhabitants of Gonzales," shouted
Castonado, angrily.

"We will not put you to the inconvenience of
crossing," replied Squire Harden, politely. "If you
will speak your message from where you stand, we
shall hear it the more quickly."

"I do not choose to hold converse with rebels, but
demand speech with the alcalde," retorted Castonado.

"Unfortunately he is absent, and may not return
until night."

"Then in the name of His Excellency, General
Santa Anna, President of the Republic of Mexico,
whom the people of the state of Texas are sworn to
obey, I demand that the men of Gonzales relinquish
to me the brass field-piece loaned them by the military governor of San Antonio de Bexar, but now
needed on the fortifications of that place. If it
be not delivered at once, I have authority to take
it by force, and shall do so regardless of consequences."

The men of Gonzales would have replied to this arrogant speech with a shout of defiance, but Squire Harden reminded them that while they were but eighteen against one hundred and sixty, discretion was, for the moment, the better part of valor. Then he politely informed the Mexican commander that his demand should be considered upon the return to town of its alcalde ; but that, without his sanction, the citizens of Gonzales were powerless to take action in so important a matter.

With this, Castonado, who had not yet discovered the weakness of the Americans, was forced to be content, and, after allowing his hearers until the morrow for a consideration of his demands, he retired his troops to the open prairie and went into camp.

That night volunteers began to reach the scene of action, from Bastrop on the Colorado, and even from the distant Brazos, until by morning the Texan force was nearly one hundred strong.

On the following day, Castonado, attired in gorgeous uniform, and escorted by twenty troopers, again made his demand for the cannon, from across the river. This time those on the opposite bank replied with shouts of scornful laughter, and bade him come and get the gun, if he really wanted it.

At this the face of the Mexican became black with rage, and he at once despatched a company of his cavalry to the ford. They were ordered to take such a circuit as should conceal their movements, until they were close to the river bank, and then make a dash for the opposite shore. In the meantime he kept up a pretence of parleying, and caused his escort to spread out among the trees, so as to convey the impression that nearly, if not quite his whole force was at his back.

In doing this he labored under the belief that no American would have dared cross to his side of the river, and that no knowledge of his plan could reach Gonzales. It was a sad mistake on his part, for Rex Harden, and Deaf Smith who had arrived during the night, had crossed the ford before daylight, leaving their horses on its opposite bank, and had scouted about the Mexican camp until they had mastered its every detail, including the number of its troops.

They were still on hand when the movement towards the ford was ordered; and the moment they were convinced that those troops were about to attempt the surprise of that point, Rex ran to it with the speed of a deer, waded breast deep through its cold waters, notified the guard what to expect, sprang on Tawny's back, and was off like the wind towards the village, while Deaf Smith remained to watch Castonado.

Fortunately, the young scout found most of the volunteers in their camp, where they were gathered, for an election of officers. On receipt of his news, this business was indefinitely postponed, and fifty men, snatching their rifles, sprang to their horses, and, without waiting to saddle, set off, at a break-neck pace, for the ford. Here they concealed themselves in the underbrush bordering the trail that led to the water's edge.

Two minutes later the Mexican cavalry appeared on the opposite bank, and seeing nothing to hinder them, dashed into the shallow water. As they did so, they were startled, and frightened almost out of their senses, by the sudden appearance, only thirty yards away, of a double line of resolute Texans, each pointing a deadly rifle at them.

"Don't fire unless they advance," Rex had pleaded a moment before. "War has not yet been declared, you know, and we shall have a better cause if we let them begin it."

As this advice, which Rex had learned from his father, was acknowledged to be good, it was adopted, and the stalwart Texans only levelled their guns at the badly rattled troops. It was enough; for within one minute they had wheeled sharply and were riding for dear life up the bank they had just left. As they disappeared they were followed by shout after shout of derisive laughter from the riflemen, who, without firing a shot, had thus gained so signal a victory.

When the last of Castonado's cavalrymen had thus scampered out of sight, the Texans returned leisurely to their camp and resumed their interrupted election. Rex took an active interest in this business until, after a colonel and a captain had been chosen, he was covered with confusion at hearing himself nominated for the position of lieutenant.

"Rector Harden," declared the speaker, "is not only a descendant of soldiers, but has himself received a military training; moreover, he has already, as we all know, proved himself to be a brave and devoted son of Texas.   Therefore I nominate him for the vacant lieutenancy of this company."

"Second the nomination!" shouted a dozen voices.

"You have heard the nomination, gentlemen. All in favor will signify it in the usual manner."

"Aye!" shouted every man present.

"Contrary minded?"

A dead silence.

"Lieutenant Harden," said the smiling chairman of the meeting, "I congratulate you on the unanimity of your election, and at the same time congratulate the assembled company upon their choice of a junior officer."

"They couldn't have made a better," called out a deep voice from the outer edge of the assembly, "nor one who will fight more loyally for the flag that I see he has already raised.   Let me in, boys, that I may shake hands with him."

With this a big man forced his way through the crowd, and in another moment Rex, proudly happy, though covered with confusion at the honor just thrust upon him, was shaking hands with his friend James Bowie.

The latter had just arrived from San Antonio by way of Bastrop, and when he had congratulated the young lieutenant he again raised his voice to say :

" Now, boys, let's carry our gun across the river and give those chaps a chance to take it from us if they can."

CHAPTER XI

THE ABSURD BATTLE OF GONZALES

WHILE the bold proposition of James Bowie was hailed with acclamation, and a majority of the volunteers were in favor of crossing the river at once, the cooler counsels of Squire Harden and others, who realized how much depended upon the success of the movement, restrained them until the following day. By that time late arrivals had so strengthened their force that their numbers were equal to those of the Mexicans, and there was no longer a doubt that the latter could be beaten in fair fight.

The Texans waited until darkness should conceal their movements, and then, all being in readiness, the crossing of the river was ordered to begin. The mounted men, fifty in all, were the first to leave camp, their destination being the ford, which they were to hold. They were also bidden to make a demonstration from that direction to attract attention from the main body of volunteers, who, taking the famous brass field-piece with them, were to cross in boats half a mile higher up stream.

Rex Harden went with the former body, and to

him was accorded the proud distinction of leading the advance,—a picked squad of twelve splendidly mounted horsemen, every one of whom was eager to strike the first blow for Texas. As these dashed through the ford and mounted its farther bank, the young leader was in a fever of excitement and found himself trembling violently, but he only leaned over his horse's neck to whisper :

"We are going into battle, Tawny, you and I; but we must keep cool—"

At that moment came a sharp challenge from the timber, the roar of an escopetta, and a ball whizzed spitefully close above the lad's head.

The first shot had been fired, and it had come from the other side. Half a dozen others instantly followed it.

"Steady, men!" cried the young lieutenant, sitting erect in his saddle, with every trace of nervousness gone. "It's only a picket that needs to be driven in. Forward! *Charge!*"

The squad responded with a yell whose volume would have done credit to a full company, clapped spurs to their horses, and rushed like a cyclone through the narrow belt of timber, beyond which the Mexican picket was already in full flight.

Close up to the enemy's camp did the Texans hold their headlong course without drawing rein. Into it they poured a volley of rifle shots, receiving a scattering and harmless fire in return, and having thus very thoroughly attracted attention to themselves they wheeled and dashed away in the direction from which they had come.

"It was like prodding a hornets' nest," remarked Tom Gallup to Rex as they listened to the blaring trumpets, the angry drums, and the fierce shouts of the aroused camp behind them.

"Yes, and wasn't it fine?"

"You bet it was. Beats buffalo-hunting and roping wild horses all hollow. I only hope they won't run away before we've had another chance at them."

In spite of this hope it seemed, a few hours later, as though the Mexicans had run away. The volunteers were so delayed in their crossing of the river by a dense fog that settled down while Rex and his little command were driving in the picket, that it was after midnight before they were ready for an advance. Then the scouts sent to locate the enemy's camp brought back word that it was abandoned.

With this Rex was ordered out with three men to discover, if possible, what had become of Castonado and his force. Moving as quietly as possible, these scouted for several miles along the San Antonio road until satisfied that the retreat had not taken that direction. Then dividing into two parties, they made long detours on either side as they returned.

"It's awfully puzzling," remarked the young lieutenant to Tom Gallup, who was his only companion.

"It is so, and I'm afraid in some way they've

given us the slip, after all. We could run 'em down, though, if only this confounded fog would lift so as to give us a chance at the trail. Hist! What's that?"

Both lads reined their horses to a standstill and listened. A sound as of digging came to their ears, and with it a low murmur of voices.

At this moment Tawny lifted his head and sounded a shrill neigh of challenge. It was promptly answered from close at hand. At the same moment jet after jet of flame pierced the fog on the scouts' left, and a volley of shots rattled in their direction. One of the bullets grazed Rex on an arm, though he did not realize at the time that he had been hit.

Wheeling sharply, without firing a shot in return, the two lads spurred back toward the road, with a troop of Mexican cavalry in hot pursuit.

A few minutes later the young scouts, shouting that they were friends, dashed into the Texan bivouac, while a discharge of the brass field-piece that, as was afterwards discovered, killed a man and a horse, caused the Mexicans to wheel in turn and hurry away through the fog.

"We found them, sir," reported Rex to Colonel Moore.

"I see you did," replied the officer, grimly, "and apparently they came near finding you. Where are they?"

"About half a mile to the right of their old

camp, and I should say entrenching themselves on that little mound just beyond Carter's cornfield."

"Can you lead us to the spot?"

"I think so, sir, now that daylight has come."

"But, lad, you are wounded!" exclaimed the colonel, as he noted that blood was dripping from the young lieutenant's left hand. As he talked, Rex had been unconsciously wiping this away with his other hand.

"Oh, I guess not, sir," he replied, hastily wiping away another trickle of blood as he spoke.

"You are, though. Here, let me look."

With this the speaker caught Rex by the arm, ripped open his sleeve at a place where a tiny hole betrayed the course of a bullet, and laid bare the wound. It was only a slight furrow on the inside of the arm, but the ball had gone within an inch of the boy's heart, and for a moment a sense of his narrow escape from death turned him faint.

"Bring water and rags, quick," ordered the officer.

Both were speedily forthcoming, and a few minutes later the wound had been bound up with rude skill.

"There, that will do until you can get across the river," said the colonel, "and I am very grateful not to have lost one of my most valued officers on his first day of service."

"Thank you, sir," murmured Rex. "But surely, colonel, you are not going to send me to the rear for a scratch like that. Just as you are about to engage the enemy too. Really, I don't feel it at all, and am as strong as ever I was. Besides, I know just where to find them, and — "

" That will do," laughed the other. " I give in, and you may come along if you like. Now, men, fall in."

Two minutes later the little Texan army was pressing eagerly forward with Rex Harden, as proud of his wound as he was of the blue emblem on his hat, riding beside the colonel to point out the way.

After a mile of rapid marching he said : " There is the cornfield, sir, and they are just beyond it."

At this Colonel Moore halted his men and formed them in line of battle, with their single piece of artillery in the centre. This was hardly done when the fog, which had been thinning away since day-break, lifted entirely and disclosed the opposing forces to each other not more than two hundred yards apart. The Mexicans had indeed thrown up a line of low earthworks on rising ground, behind which they awaited the Texan advance.

Before this could be ordered a man bearing a white flag was seen to leave the enemy's line. As he came near, he was recognized to be an American whom Castonado had taken prisoner. He brought word that the Mexican commander desired an interview with Colonel Moore.

Upon this the Texan leader rode forward and, halting midway between the two forces, was there met by Castonado.

"I trust, señor," began the latter, suavely, "that there is to be no trouble between us, and that you have come to surrender the cannon, which I see you have brought with you."

"Then your trust is wholly misplaced, sir," replied Colonel Moore, "for I have brought that gun for use against the enemies of Texas, as you will find to your sorrow, unless you prove yourself her friend by joining in our struggle for liberty or surrender your command as prisoners of war."

The Mexican's face blazed with anger. "You insult me, sir!" he cried, "and I will die at the head of my brave troops before even considering either of your propositions."

Upon this, and without exchanging another word, the leaders parted and returned to their respective commands.

"Don't be worried, boys," said the ranchman, who had remained with his friends, and had already found a place in the ranks. "Them fellows over there are pretty nigh scared to death now, and one roar from this little 'barker' will about use 'em up. They sent off their wagons more than an hour ago."

The impatient Texans did not need this encouragement. Their only worry just then was lest the enemy should run away without waiting to fight, and the result proved their fears to be well grounded.

As Colonel Moore rejoined his men, he gave orders to fire one volley and then charge without waiting to reload. A moment later the roar of the six-pounder was drowned in a crash of rifles. Then, with a wild yell, the Texans dashed across the intervening space and up the gentle slope. The Mexicans fired but a single answering volley, every shot of which flew above the heads of the oncoming volunteers. Then they leaped on their horses and fled, pell-mell, down the opposite side of the rise, a panic-stricken mob of fugitives, in spite of Castonado's furious efforts to check them.

Thus, when the Texans gained the breastworks, all that they found were a few dead and wounded men and horses, while the remainder of Castonado's valiant force was rapidly vanishing in a flight that was only ended at San Antonio.

"Looks like the King of France and his forty thousand men," remarked Tom Gallup to his friend, Rex Harden, as he gazed comically at the dust cloud hiding their recent foes.

It was all so absurd that, while some of the Texans swore and others stared in open-mouthed amazement, the majority laughed until they ached, over the farce that had just been enacted. For all that, they had won a victory, the effects of which were to be felt far beyond the borders of their beloved state.

CHAPTER XII

WHY THE MEXICAN TROOPS FOUGHT BADLY

BY the affair of Gonzales the spirit of revolution in Texas was fanned into so fierce a flame that it could never again be quenched save by the gaining of an absolute independence. When the victorious volunteers, after chasing Castonado out of sight, recrossed the river, proudly carrying with them the field-piece they had sworn never to give up, they were received with the wildest demonstrations of joy. Congratulations, speeches, and feasting filled the day, and at night the jubilant Texans gathered about huge bonfires to discuss over and over every detail of their first stand against the tyranny of Santa Anna.

Couriers had been despatched east, north, and south, with the glorious news, and it was everywhere received with wildest enthusiasm. From all quarters came the cry:

"Drive the Mexicans beyond the Rio Grande!"

In Eastern Texas company after company of volunteers was raised and hurried to the front. General Sam Houston, Ex-United States Senator, Ex-Governor of Tennessee, and recently arrived in

Texas to discover its present condition and prospects, was unanimously chosen commander-in-chief. Two companies were raised in New Orleans, and a battalion in Georgia. The citizens of Cincinnati subscribed for two cannon to be immediately cast and sent as a present to the Texans.

James Bowie hurried with all speed to his plantation on the Mississippi. He had already issued invitations for the grandest barbecue ever seen in the Southwest, to be held there in the interest of an American Texas. At it he was to report to the thousands who would be gathered the result of his observations on the scene of action. David Crockett of Tennessee, renowned as a rifle shot, a backwoods politician, a fighter, and for his homely wit, was one of the principal speakers at this great meeting. He aroused such enthusiasm, that when he left it for Nacogdoches he was accompanied by hundreds of sturdy frontiersmen armed with rifles and bowie knives, pledged to fight in the cause of Texas.

Gonzales was the appointed place of rendezvous, and Stephen Austin, just escaped from a Mexican prison, and one of the most popular men in the state, was elected to command the forces there collected. At the same time one member from each of the committees of safety, which were well scattered all over Texas, proceeded to San Felipe, where they organized a provisional government for carrying on the war.

As a result of all this energy a force of five hundred well-armed volunteers was gathered on the east bank of the Guadalupe, ready for a march to San Antonio within ten days after the absurd but important battle of Gonzales.

On the other hand, the news of the Texas uprising was received in Mexico with angry amazement and a determination to suppress it before it could assume formidable proportions.

Castonado's flying troops reached San Antonio on the fourth of October, and their appearance so aroused the fury of the Commandant at that place, that on the very next day he set out for Gonzales with five hundred troops and three pieces of artillery. He threatened the direst vengeance against the heretic Americanos who had insulted him and dared resist his authority. No one of them should be left alive, and their town should be burned to the ground. In spite of his brave words and the confidence with which he set forth, the reports brought in by his scouts of the rapidly increasing strength of the Texans so cooled his ardor that his marches became slower and his halts longer, until finally he dared advance no further.

The Texan army was at length equal in force to his own, and when he heard that it crossed the river to meet him, he in turn fled back to San Antonio almost as precipitately as had Castonado only a week before.

In regard to the cowardice thus manifested by the Mexican troops it should be said that while most of their officers were men of undoubted bravery, the soldiers with whom they were expected to subdue Texas had all been pressed into service, and fifty per cent. of them were convicts or jail-birds, compelled to serve out their terms in the army. These troops could only be induced to fight when their overwhelming numbers gave them an assurance of success, or when fear of their own officers was greater than their dread of the enemy.

Such men were absolutely without shame in running away from inferior forces, were sustained by no sentiment of patriotism, and were mercilessly cruel wherever they found themselves in a position to be so. Of such as these were the permanent Mexican garrisons in Texas composed; and when General Cos was sent to reënforce them, several hundred of his one thousand men wore manacles on their arms and legs until they reached San Antonio.

Even when Santa Anna advanced into Texas, some months later, two thousand of his six thousand troops were poor Yucatan Indians, ruthlessly dragged from their homes to fight a people with whom they had no quarrel, and of whom most of them had never heard.

With such soldiers at his back it is not then surprising that the Commandant who had set out to punish the rebels at Gonzales should have deemed it the part of wisdom to retreat before an equal force of

Texans, who were not only aching for a fight, and had everything to fight for, but were among the most expert riflemen of the world.

Before leaving Gonzales, General Stephen Austin despatched a force of one hundred mounted men to the southward against the Mexican garrisons of Victoria on the Guadalupe, and Goliad on the west bank of the San Antonio. If these could be captured or forced to retreat, and at the same time Bexar could be taken, Texas would be free from the presence of Mexican troops.

After the absurd battle of Gonzales, Rex Harden, as the only one wounded on the Texan side, had been the hero of the hour. He was made so much of that he finally grew ashamed of the scratch that his admirers insisted upon dignifying as a wound, and to tire of being questioned concerning it. Therefore, when it was decided to send a mounted force to the southward, he applied for, and received, permission to accompany it.

Not only was Rex impatient for further action, but he was decidedly lonely since his father had felt obliged to push on toward San Felipe on the very day that Castonado was put to flight. Of course Mrs. Harden and Mabel had gone with him, as had the latter's dearest friend, Nelita Veramendi, whom the Bowies had left in Squire Harden's care when they hastened eastward to the great barbecue.

So the young lieutenant gladly rode away with

one hundred of the best mounted among the Texas volunteers; and among all their fine horses there was none to compare with his Tawny.

At the very first bivouac he was approached by the leader of the expedition, who said:

"I am told, Harden, that you can talk Mexican like a native. Is that so?"

"I believe it is, sir."

"And that you have the best mount of the entire troop?"

"My horse is certainly a good one."

"You have also done some very creditable scouting during the past two weeks."

"Thank you, sir."

"Are you willing to undertake another job of the same kind?"

"Certainly, if you wish me to."

"Well, I do. We are, as you know, bound first for Victoria, which place I expect to reach to-morrow evening. As the Mexican garrison is small, it is not likely that we shall be detained there very long. At any rate we shall hasten on to Goliad as quickly as possible. Now I know nothing of the latter place, nor of its strength, but am very desirous of gaining all possible information before reaching there, in order to plan an immediate attack. Therefore, I want a scout to cut across country from here to Goliad, gain what knowledge he can concerning the strength of the place to-morrow night, and meet me somewhere on the Victoria road the day following. Can I count on you for this duty?"

"I think you may, sir. At any rate, I am willing to undertake it, and will do the best I can."

"How many men will you want?"

"I would rather go alone."

"But the country between here and there may be infested by Cos's troops."

"So much the more reason for going alone, sir. A single man can escape notice more easily than a party. Besides, I shall have to make haste to reach Goliad by to-morrow evening, and I do not believe there is another horse in the command that could keep up with my Tawny."

"Very well, lieutenant, act as you think best, and remember that the success of our expedition will probably depend upon the information that you can gain. You may start when you please, and if I do not see you in the morning, I shall know that you are already on the road. Good-night, and good luck to you."

The stars were still shining the next morning, though there was a gray light in the eastern sky, when Rex slipped from his blankets, gave Tawny a feed of corn, and made for himself a cup of coffee over the still glowing embers of a camp-fire. Long before sunrise he had left the still sleeping camp and was off on his dangerous mission. At starting, he shivered with the chill of the morning air; but before noon the sun was pouring down a heat that caused him to welcome a slender line of timber that he knew must border a stream.

Reaching the little river and taking a refreshing drink of its clear waters, he rode a short distance down its bank to a place that afforded grass for his horse and was at the same time well hidden from the road. Here he relieved Tawny of saddle and bridle and turned him loose with only a picket rope trailing from his neck. He knew the horse would not stray far and could be recovered at any moment. In fact, they had become such firm friends that Tawny would now obey his call if he were anywhere within hearing.

Having thus provided for the comfort of his horse, Rex threw himself down in the shadow of a great pecan tree, the ripe nuts from which covered a wide space of ground, and began to eat the frugal lunch he had brought with him. He had ridden so hard that morning that he believed he could well afford an hour of rest, and was prepared to enjoy it as one only can enjoy a pleasure that has been honestly earned.

As he lay there munching a cold corn pone, and lazily admiring Tawny, he noticed that every now and then the animal lifted his head to sniff the air uneasily and always from the same direction. He also imagined that he heard a murmur of voices, but the sound was so very faint and indistinct that he could neither decide its nature nor the direction from which it came.

Suddenly a cry of mortal terror, shrill and piercing, evidently in a woman's voice, caused our lad to gain his feet at a bound and dash recklessly through the timber towards the startling sound.

CHAPTER XIII

A WOMAN IN PERIL

SCREAM after scream for help rang out on the still noontide as Rex ran through the timber in the direction of the startling sounds. He had snatched up his rifle, and now he cocked it as he ran. Emerging from the trees, he came in sight of a small log house standing on the prairie two hundred yards away. It was surrounded by a wide fence, to which were tied two horses. Near them was a man uttering unintelligible cries, and acting in the most erratic manner. He would throw himself to the ground, leap up again, fling his arms in the air, cover his face with his hands, run this way and that, and behaved like one bereft of his senses.

Much nearer at hand were two other human figures upon whom our lad's attention was instantly and wholly centred. One was that of a young woman, evidently an American from her white skin. She was flying with outstretched bare arms, streaming hair, and shrill screams, toward the timber from which Rex was just emerging. In close pursuit of her was a man clad in the tawdry red and blue uniform of a Mexican soldier. His swarthy face was devilish in its expression of cruelty, and in his right hand he bore a naked bayonet. So nearly had he overtaken the woman when Rex came in sight of them that his weapon was lifted for a lunge into her body.

Our lad had no time for thought, and only a second in which to act. Without taking aim, he threw forward his rifle and fired, when to his amazement both the woman and her would-be murderer plunged forward and fell to the ground.

For a moment Rex stood horrified at the apparent result of his shot. Then hearing a groan that proved at least one of his supposed victims to be alive, he ran to where they lay. The groans came from the Mexican, who was apparently wounded, though how severely or where, our lad could not determine in the single glance that he gave him. His sympathy, and for the time being his whole attention, were directed to the woman, upon whose person he could discover no signs of a wound, though she lay motionless and apparently dead. Running to the stream for a hatful of water, he dashed it by double handfuls in her face, and was at length rewarded by seeing her open her eyes. Then, with his assistance, she sat up and stared about her, frightened and bewildered.

As she did so, Rex talked soothingly to her, saying that her enemy was powerless to do her further injury, and begging her to believe that danger no longer threatened. After a few moments of convulsive sobbing, caused by exhaustion, and a reaction from her recent terror, the young woman controlled herself sufficiently to murmur something about father and mother, at the same time striving to regain her feet.

In this, Rex lent his assistance, and then he supported her as they walked slowly towards the house. She gave a shudder as they passed the prostrate Mexican, whom she evidently believed to be dead; but her eyes blazed with a feeble fury, as they fell on the other man, who still continued his strange actions, in front of the house, and who, as Rex now saw, was also a Mexican soldier. As this man realized their approach, he hesitated for an instant, and then scrambling clumsily to the back of one of the horses, he rode rapidly away, greatly to the young lieutenant's relief.

The woman paid no attention to him, after that first glance, but appeared doubly eager to reach the house, and seemed to gain new strength as they drew near to it. At the door, she pulled away from Rex, and entered in advance of him, uttering a fervent " Thank God ! " as she did so.

Pressing curiously forward, the lad was filled with horror and rage at the sight that met his eyes. An old man and an old woman, whose white hairs should have protected them from outrage, even by such brutes as Mexican soldiers, were standing at the foot of a tall bedstead, securely bound to two of its posts.

Their clothing was torn, and they were covered with blood from many wounds, seemingly made with knife points, that appeared on all parts of their bodies. Beyond them was a table, set for dinner, and beside it lay an iron skillet with a broken handle. It had evidently been filled with frying bacon, bits of which, together with a quantity of grease, were scattered over the floor.

Without waiting for an explanation of this strange scene, Rex sprang to cut the lashings of the old people. The old woman at once sank helplessly to the floor, but the old man managed to reach a chair unaided.

With others dependent upon her, the young woman recovered her own strength wonderfully, and, aided by Rex, succeeded, after a while, in restoring the old people to a certain degree of comfort. Then, little by little, and with frequent interruptions, she told the lad the story of their sufferings.

From it he learned that the old people were her own father and mother, and that they three, together with her husband, Alvin Yardley, constituted the entire family of this isolated ranch. They had only learned the day before, of the Texas uprising, and of the advance of General Cos, with an army, to over-run the country. That morning her husband had ridden to the nearest neighbor's, ten miles away, to borrow a wagon, in which to remove the old folk to a place of safety.

Soon after his departure the two Mexicans, who, as she learned from their conversation, had been impressed into the army from the Monterey chain-gang, appeared before the house. They forced an entrance, and with dire threats of what they would do in case of resistance, bound its helpless inmates to as many bedposts. Then they ransacked every room in search of valuables, and tortured the old people with knife pricks to make them disclose where such things were hidden.

Having collected whatever seemed to them desirable and fastened their bundles of plunder to the saddles of two horses that they stole from the Yardley corral, they loosened the bonds of the younger woman and ordered her to cook a dinner for them, declaring that if she refused they would kill her parents. As she moved slowly to obey them, hoping with each moment for the arrival of her husband, one of the wretches hastened her movements by threatening the old folk with his knife while the other kept watch from the door.

When the meal, prepared under these circumstances, was finally served, the brute with the knife gave each of the old people a parting cut with his knife as he moved towards the table. This so enraged their daughter that she lifted a skillet of sizzling bacon that she was taking from the stove, and brought it down with all her strength on his head. The man was horribly burned, and very nearly blinded, by the scalding grease ; but without waiting to note his condition the woman sprang through the doorway, hoping for time to secure one of the guns that hung from the Mexican saddles.

The unwounded man pursued her so closely, however, that she was unable to accomplish her purpose, and could only fly, screaming for help, towards the timber. The Mexican rapidly overtook her, and but for the opportune appearance of our young scout, she and her parents would certainly have been killed.

The young woman had hardly finished her story and was trying, in broken tones, to express her gratitude to Rex for his gallant rescue, when there came a clatter of hoofs ; a horse was reined sharply up before the door, and a man, whom the woman greeted with a cry of joy, flung himself into the house.

It was Alvin Yardley, returned without the wagon he had gone to borrow, but with news that rendered the present abandonment of his home unnecessary. Cos had marched to San Antonio with an army of nine hundred men, leaving a small garrison at Goliad, under Colonel Sandoval. This had been surprised, and the place captured, only the night before, by a band of Texans from the Guadalupe, led by a Captain Collingsworth.

While Sandoval and his officers had been taken prisoners, most of the garrison had effected their escape. Alvin Yardley had undertaken to ride to Gonzales and notify the Texans at that place of what had happened, in order that they might cut off these stragglers before they could reach San Antonio. Now, learning of the peril from which his own family had just been delivered, and realizing that there was still danger from other prowling Mexicans, he had no mind to leave them unprotected again.

"I could go in your place as well as not," said Rex, reflectively, "if I could only get word to Colonel Moore, for he will not now need me at Goliad."

"I will guarantee to let him know what you have done!" cried Yardley, eagerly. "If he has gone to Victoria, he probably knows by this time that your present errand is useless, for Collingsworth captured that place before coming to Goliad. If you only will let me out of this Gonzales trip, I shall be mighty grateful."

Rex required but little persuasion to be the bearer of such glorious news to his comrades of Austin's army, the more especially as he was eager to join them in their attack on San Antonio, before which place he believed he should find them rather than at Gonzales. So, after partaking of a hearty meal, prepared by the young woman whose life he had saved, the boy was ready for his eighty-mile ride up the river.

Alvin Yardley went with him to learn what had become of the wounded Mexican who had so nearly taken his wife's life, but when they reached the spot where Rex had left him, he was nowhere to be seen.

"Lucky for him," muttered Yardley, "for I would surely have killed him if I had found him alive. However, he's sure to meet with his deserts before long, for such scoundrels can't go far in this country unpunished."

The ranchman's prophecy was startlingly confirmed a few minutes later, for when they went to secure Tawny they found him quietly feeding not far from the dead body of that very Mexican, whose skull had evidently been crushed by a powerful kick from a horse's hoof.

Rex was shocked, but the ranchman only smiled grimly as he remarked:

"That horse of yours is surely a true Texan, for he not only wears the lone star, the same as his master, but kills any greaser that tries to ride him. Take care of him, lad, for he's a good one."

With this they parted, and Rex, turning his face again northward, galloped away on fleet-footed Tawny, the avenger.

The sun was within three hours of its setting when he started, and he had not ridden many miles before a gathering dusk warned him that it was time to make camp. Thus far he had travelled over an open prairie, with an unobscured view in every

direction.   Now he must seek the thick timber of
the river bottom.   He had no sooner entered this
than his eye caught a distant gleam of firelight, and
he heard the sound of voices.   His first impulse was
to retreat to the prairie.   Then he reflected that
while those whose camp-fire he saw were probably
enemies, they might prove to be friends, and that at
any rate, as a scout, he was bound to gather all possible information concerning them.   Thus thinking,
he tethered Tawny to a tree, and crept cautiously
towards the firelight.

CHAPTER XIV

REX IS CONDEMNED TO BE SHOT

THE bivouac on which Rex had thus stumbled was that of a score of Mexican soldiers who, having escaped from Goliad, were leisurely travelling towards San Antonio. That they had made successful forays on the several ranches of that sparsely settled country was shown by the plunder, provisions, and forage scattered about their camp, while, by occasional flashes of firelight, the young scout could make out a number of horses and mules fastened to surrounding trees. As our lad noted these, he became possessed of an idea that he determined to carry out if possible.

"If I could only run off that stock," he said to himself, "and so leave those fellows to make their way up the river on foot, I could reach Austin's camp in time to bring back a party that would capture the whole gang. I'll have to wait, though, until they settle down for the night. Then we'll see what can be done."

Thus thinking, the lad crept back to where he had left Tawny, fed him from a small sack of Alvin Yardley's corn, ate his own scanty supper, and sat down to wait until the quiet of the Mexican camp should indicate that it was buried in slumber.

He did not mean to go to sleep, of course ; but he was dead tired, and after a while was so overcome by drowsiness, that it seemed as though to close his eyes for just one minute would be the most blessed thing in the world. He reasoned, too, that his hearing would become more acute if his eyes were shut, and as he could not see anything even with them open, there could be no possible harm in closing them for a single minute. He would open them and move about to shake off his drowsiness, if there was any real danger of going to sleep, for he was in too perilous a position to even think of such a thing.

What a relief it was to close them, though; and how decidedly his sense of hearing was quickened. At the same time it was queer that certain of the voices coming to him in a confused murmur should resemble those of his sister Mabel and Nelita Veramendi. What dear girls they were, and how fond he was of them ! So much so that it was difficult to tell which he liked best ; though, of course, it must be Mabel, for she was his sister. Still it was very pleasant to dream of Nelita. So the tired lad slipped happily away into dreamland, and Tawny, standing motionless beside him, also drooped his head drowsily.

For hours they slept. The camp of Mexicans, not more than a quarter of a mile away, was also buried in slumber, with even its guards nodding at their posts, and the only sounds to be heard were the ordinary night voices of the wilderness. A wolf howled from across the river, and was answered from the nearer side. Others took up the weird cry and repeated it until it seemed as though the beasts must be exchanging a regular code of signals. Certainly their voices approached each other, until with a final yelping bark they too became silent.

At the very first wolf cry Tawny lifted his head, pricked forward his ears, and sniffed the heavy night air suspiciously. He was decidedly uneasy, for though his wild life on the Texas prairies had made him well acquainted with many kinds of wolves, from the great lobo down to the sneaking coyote, the language of those now calling to each other on all sides of him was so different from any with which he was familiar, that he could not understand what they were saying. Even after they became silent he continued nervously alert and watchful.

All at once the peaceful quiet of the night was shattered by such a whirlwind of sound, yells, shots, terrified screams, and a thunderous rushing that bedlam seemed to have broken loose in that narrow strip of timbered river bottom.

Thus rudely awakened, Rex sprang up, still dazed with sleep, and instinctively started to fly from the impending terror. Then bethinking himself of Tawny and his rifle, he turned to where he had left them. The next moment he was hurled breathless to the ground, while a veritable cyclone of madly galloping horses and fiercely yelling men swept over the spot where he lay. That he was not killed outright, was owing to a fallen tree that partially protected him; but when the wild riders had passed, and he painfully gained a sitting posture, he felt as though he had been pounded with clubs on every portion of his body.

He could not imagine what had happened, but from the shots that still flashed through the timber in every direction, he believed himself to be in the thick of a battle. It also seemed as though every gun were pointed directly at him, and that if he remained where he was another moment he would certainly be killed.

So he attempted with slow and painful movements to crawl out of range; but he had not gone a rod when a Mexican soldier in fruitless pursuit of the yelling horsemen who had just passed, stumbled over his crouching body and fell headlong. As this leader was closely followed by a dozen of his comrades, Rex was instantly seized and jerked rudely to his feet.

The red flash of an escopetta, fired close to his face, revealed the fact that he was white, and consequently an enemy.

"The heretic!"

"The gringo!"

"Kill him!"

"Cut him in pieces!"

"The dog of a Texan!"

"His vile comrades have stolen our horses and escaped, but he shall suffer for all!"

"Kill him, then!"

"No. That would be too easy. Let us take him to camp and have some sport with him."

These cries, and many others of similar import, uttered to an accompaniment of fierce Mexican oaths, revealed to Rex the imminent danger of his position, and showed him how little mercy he had to expect from his cruel captors. He was, however, wise enough to conceal his knowledge of their language, and paid no attention to the questions showered upon him as to the character of those who had just run off with the Mexican horses. Of course he did not know any more than did they who questioned him, though from the yells that still came faintly back from the open prairie, he shrewdly suspected the raiders to be a party of Comanche Indians.

At the same time, from having found this white lad directly in the track of their recent assailants, where he was supposed to have fallen from his horse, his captors believed the attack to have been made by a force of Texans whom it would not be wise to pursue too far or too closely.

So they made their way sullenly, and with many fierce threats of what they would do to the thieves if they caught them, back to their ravaged camp, driving their prisoner before them with blows and curses. The poor lad was so battered and bruised that every movement gave him sharp twinges of pain, and he could scarcely lift one foot after the other. His wrists were tightly bound behind him, and a picket rope knotted loosely about his neck was constantly jerked by the brute who held it, until the unhappy captive was wellnigh strangled.

When the camp was finally reached Rex was so nearly used up that he sank with a groan at the foot of a tree to which he was immediately secured. There he was left to await the coming of daylight and whatever fate his captors might hold in reserve for him.

Oh! how he ached, and how he was tormented by thirst, for it was hours since he had tasted a drop of water. Now he could smell the river close at hand, and the knowledge of its presence added to his distress. He had begged for water, and even admitted a certain knowledge of his captors' language by repeating over and over again the single word *agua;* but they had only mocked at his distress and left him to suffer.

Besides his aches and his thirst, Rex was filled with gloomy forebodings as to his fate, and with self-accusations at having been so weak as to fall asleep while on duty. He also began to wonder if he had not done wrong in undertaking an independent mission without orders from his superior officer. Until now it had not seemed to him, any more than it did to others of the Texas volunteers, that they formed part of a real army and were as much bound as are all soldiers, to abide by orders. At that very moment the troops comprising Austin's little army were coming and going as they pleased, refusing to mount guard, perform necessary camp duties, or obey unpopular officers unless they chose. In many other ways they were behaving with the folly of independent citizens who had yet to learn by bitter experience that their real strength and only hope of success lay in united action and implicit obedience to those chosen to lead them.

In the light of his present experience Rex could see all this clearly enough, and one of the bitterest regrets of his situation was that he would probably never be able to point out the folly of their course to his recent comrades. He feared that he would never even see them again, for he had overheard one of his captors say to another who proposed giving him a drink of water :

"Why make a trouble for yourself? The gringo will not thirst for long, since he is to be shot at daybreak."

So sentence had been pronounced; and Rex, believing that his life was nearly ended, strove to reconcile himself to the awful thought. And yet how cruel it was ! He was so young, and life seemed so sweet.

He had committed no crime, nor had he been captured in battle against the Mexicans. He only wished he had. If he could have struck even a single telling blow for Texas, he would be willing to die. Or if he could die in such a way as to afford an example to others. But to have his life thrown away and his fate unknown. To be shot down in cold blood like a worthless cur. Oh! it was too hard!

What would his mother imagine had become of him? What an agony of suspense she would suffer! But he must not think of her, nor of the other dear ones, who would wait in vain for his coming, for such thoughts would unman him and he would disgrace the name of a Texan by breaking down in the hour of his supreme trial. No, he must think only of Texas and be proud that he was chosen to die for her.

With this the poor lad tried to fix his thoughts on noble themes, but in spite of his efforts they always came back to his own bodily sufferings and to the consideration of mad plans for escape. He could not believe it possible that he was really to die. Some miracle would surely intervene to save him. He was too young to be reconciled to death, too sanguine to relinquish hope.

In the meantime his captors discussed his fate with brutal laugh and coarse jest about the campfire until daylight. Just at sunrise two of them approached their prisoner, roughly assisted him to his feet, led him a short distance from the camp, and bound him securely to a sapling. Then they deliberately pinned a bit of white cloth over his left breast, and pointing significantly to a file of their comrades who, with loaded muskets, were drawn up in line facing him, gave him to understand that the hour for his execution had arrived.

At the spasm of anguish that swept across the lad's face, they laughed, and one of them said, " He is but a coward, after all, like all these Texas rebels."

As he heard these words, Rex nerved himself with a mighty effort; and, though his face grew white and rigid, he gazed with unflinching eyes straight at the black muzzles of the levelled muskets.

"Ready! Fire!!"

The cruel order was instantly followed by a leaping flame and a crashing report. At the same moment the young Texan's proudly lifted head fell forward on his breast, and, but for its supporting bands, his body would have sunk to the ground.

CHAPTER XV

SAVED BY COCHITO THE COMANCHE

THE Mexicans had not intended to kill their prisoner, at least, not just then; for they had decided that he could be made useful as a guide, and also as a protection for their own worthless bodies against the rifles of any Texans whom they might encounter on their road. They could kill him at any time; and so it might be just as well to save him while there was a chance of his proving useful. Still, with the innate cruelty of all brutal natures, which is the same whether shown by civilized boys in the torture of helpless animals, and the needless infliction of pain upon their weaker comrades, or by savages in their treatment of captives, these cruel servants of a still more cruel master could not forego the exquisite pleasure of witnessing human suffering. So they had conceived the plan of a sham execution, and watched, with amusement, the mental agony of the poor lad, who, firmly believing that the hour of his death had arrived, nerved himself to meet it as became one of his race and breeding.

His strength was already weakened, and the strain

of the last few minutes was so terrible, that, when a volley of blank cartridges was fired directly at him, he all at once lost consciousness of his situation as surely as though every gun had contained a bullet.

As the Mexicans noted this unexpected effect of their experiment, their mirth was silenced, and they ran forward to discover what had brought their anticipated pleasure to so abrupt an end. Cutting the thongs that bound the boy, and so letting his body slip limply to the ground, they began to examine it in search of wounds. But there was none, and at length one after another declared, with strange oaths, that the coward gringo had simply died of fright.

With this they lost all interest in the prisoner who had so disappointed them, and leaving the motionless form to be disposed of by wolves or buzzards, they set forth on foot for San Antonio. Being deprived of their cattle, they were obliged to leave behind them a great stock of provisions, clothing, and other spoil of looted ranches, and were able to carry away but a small portion of their plunder.

This was exactly what Cochito, a young Comanche, who had planned the raid of the night before, had hoped they would do. Although the Comanches were at that time nominally at peace with both Americans and Mexicans, this young Indian, eager to win the laurels of a warrior, had persuaded three lads of his own age to leave their village by stealth and accompany him in search of adventures.

From the very outset their enterprise had been successful; for, reaching the vicinity of Goliad just after its capture, each of them had acquired the scalp of a Mexican straggler without difficulty or danger. Then they ran across the trail of those who, laden with the plunder of outlying ranches, were hastening northward. Like a pack of those wolves, whose cries they imitated in signalling to each other, the four young Comanches followed closely after this party until they encamped, and then withdrew to a safe distance for consultation. The Mexicans were too strong to be attacked and too well mounted to straggle, or to abandon any of their plunder.

"But," said Cochito, "if we could dismount them, then would they leave behind many things that they could not carry. Also, if we had their horses, we could, without trouble, remove to the lodges of our people, that which would make us the envy of every Comanche warrior."

The others agreed that the words of their brother were very pleasant; but how were they to obtain the coveted horses, without risking their own precious scalps?

"Wait, thou here," answered Cochito, "while I cross the river. When I call to thee, it will be made plain how the thing we wish for may come to pass." So the three waited, while their young leader crept noiselessly about the Mexican camp, estimated its strength, located its cattle, and decided the direction in which they should be driven. All this so occupied his attention, that he failed to discover the presence of Rex Harden, who had also planned a raid on the Mexican cavallado, but had fallen asleep while awaiting a favorable opportunity to carry out his design.

When quiet at length reigned in the camp, and its drowsy guards were almost as oblivious to threatened danger as their sleeping comrades, Cochito uttered the wailing bark of a wolf, that summoned his comrades and aroused Tawny's suspicions.

Soon after the utterance of that signal, the young Comanches were gliding like shadows among the Mexican cattle, loosing tethers and cutting picket ropes. Within two minutes, every animal was free, and the young warriors, mounted on four of the fleetest, were driving the stampeded herd, with fiendish yells, towards the open prairie. Rex and Tawny were directly in their path, and, while the latter, snapping his picket rope as though it had been a pack thread, was swept away in the mad rush, his master was overwhelmed by it, and trampled beneath a score of flying feet.

The young Comanches, exulting over their glorious coup, kept their stolen herd in motion until daylight, when they corralled it on a narrow point of timber that projected into the river. Here they rested, prepared food, and waited patiently until the Mexicans should depart.

They were startled by the sound of the volley that was fired at poor Rex; and Cochito, taking one companion with him, rode in that direction, to learn its cause. This time, the Comanche leader was mounted on Tawny, whom he had selected at first sight, as being the finest animal of the captured herd. Although the spirited animal had fought savagely for his liberty, he could no more dismount the young Indian who now bestrode him than he could have shaken off his own head; for Cochito was one of the best riders in a tribe noted the world over for horsemanship.

Cautiously making their way towards the Mexican camp, the Indian lads soon discovered that it had been vacated, and caught sight of its recent occupants just disappearing on the northern trail. When they were wholly lost to view, Cochito sent his companion back to summon the others and bring up the animals. Then he rode boldly into the deserted camp, and dismounting, began eagerly to examine the spoils that his skill had won.

His eyes glittered and his heart swelled with pride as he gloated over the quantity and quality of the treasure that was now his, and which would make him rich, famous, and envied, could he but convey it safely to his distant home on the Nueces. Engrossed as he was with this pleasing occupation, he did not wholly forget the splendid horse which would, after all, be his proudest trophy, nor loosen his hold on Tawny's bridle. All at once the fretting animal tossed his head, sniffed the air keenly, uttered a shrill neigh, gave a sudden leap that freed him from the young Indian's detaining grasp, and bounded away.

For a moment Cochito was overcome with chagrin at having his chief prize thus slip through his hands; but, to his surprise, the horse, instead of galloping out of sight, only went a few rods and then stopped. He was partially concealed behind a clump of bushes, and, with lowered head, seemed to be feeding.

Seeing a chance of recovering him, Cochito crept cautiously in that direction, and, to his unbounded amazement, discovered that the horse was standing over a prostrate human form. A single glance showed this to be a white lad of about his own age, and apparently dead. Excited as he was by this discovery, he did not neglect to secure the horse that had led him to it, and which now refused to move away from his beloved young master.

As Cochito gazed curiously at this his newest find, something caused him to suspect that the white lad might not be dead, after all, and, hastily fastening Tawny to a tree, he ran to the river for water. When he returned, his comrades had also reached the camp. They were equally excited as himself over the finding of Rex, and promptly suggested that his scalp would be more highly appreciated in their village than any other trophy they could carry in.

" But he is not dead," objected Cochito.

" Let us then kill him," said one of the others, drawing a keen-edged knife as he spoke.

" Not so ! " cried Cochito, putting out a detaining hand as the other leaned over Rex to execute his purpose. " It would be foolish to kill him while there is a chance of reviving him and taking him in as a prisoner. Think of the glory that will then be ours. We have already scalps, horses, and much booty. If we can also carry home a prisoner, and an American at that, are there any four warriors of the Comanche nation who could do more? Let us then revive this young man if it be possible, and lead him captive into our village. Then shall the warriors greet us as brothers, the old men will admit us to their councils, and the maidens will sing of our brave deeds in every Comanche lodge."

With this plea was Rex Harden's life saved ; for so alluring was the picture thus presented by Cochito, that his comrades immediately agreed to his proposal, and lent willing aid to restoring the consciousness of their prisoner.

The bringing back to life one who has approached the very confines of death is always a tedious task, and the present case proved no exception to the rule. For more than an hour did Cochito work

over the motionless form of the white lad who, he had determined, should grace as a captive his triumphant home-going. As to what might happen to the prisoner after that, he did not care to consider. He would probably be put to death in such manner as the council of warriors might decide, for that was the fate of all prisoners. To get him to the village alive and strong was the great thing.

So Cochito worked over Rex long after his comrades had given up the task of restoration as hopeless, and turned their attention to the plunder that lay scattered on all sides. He brought water and dashed it in the lad's face. He stripped him, and was amazed to discover no sign of a wound other than innumerable bruises on all parts of the body in which he strove to restore circulation by means of friction.

At length his efforts seemed about to be crowned with success. A faint color came into the white lad's face, a movement of his heart was distinctly perceptible, and he began to draw gasping breaths. Cochito was confident that in another minute the captive would open his eyes, and he watched for this to happen with a curious interest. During his short career he had seen many a man killed; but this was the first apparently dead person whom he had watched return to life. He bent low over Rex to catch a sound of the heart-beats that were becoming stronger with each minute, and as he did so, a rifle-ball whistled close above his head.

In an instant the young Indian had sprung to his feet, leaped on Tawny's back, and was off like the wind ; while behind him, with ringing shouts and fierce yells, half a dozen mounted Texans charged the camp.

CHAPTER XVI

Two of Cochito's comrades were almost as quick as he to gain their ponies and take instant flight at the crash of rifle-shots that was their first intimation of danger. The third lay motionless where the fatal Texas bullet had overtaken him. Satisfied with their easily gained victory, the Texans did not pursue the surviving Comanches, but turned their attention to the contents of the camp they had just captured. Their leader, a grizzle-bearded man of middle age, sprang from his horse beside the white lad, whom he believed Cochito, bending over him, had been about to kill. He was amazed to find a youth, naked and bruised, but apparently unwounded, who lay motionless, staring at him with dazed eyes.

" Well, young man, you surely had a close call," began the Texan, " for that Injun had you foul and would have knifed you inside of another second. What in — "

" Water ! " whispered Rex.

" Eh ! What's that ! "

"Water!" repeated the boy, making a great effort to speak louder.

"Oh, water! To be sure, you do look dry. Hi, Zile! Bring some water, will you? while I get this chap to rights."

With this the big man lifted Rex into a sitting posture, and had partially reclothed him by the time the longed-for water arrived. How delicious it was, and how it sent new life pulsing through every vein! Is there anything on earth so blessed as water? With a single draught of its magic Rex could speak aloud; and, by the time he had drunk all they would allow, his strength was so restored that he could question his rescuers.

"Who are you?" he asked, "and how did you manage to save me from the Mexicans?"

"Injuns, you mean, lad, though it's much the same. My name is Milam, Colonel Ben Milam, just escaped from Monterey prison and got back in time to help the boys take Goliad. Now we are on our way to San Antonio to take a hand in driving the last greaser out of Texas. But how did you chance to fall into the hands of these cursed Injuns?"

"You mean Mexicans, of course," replied Rex, with a faint smile. "I haven't seen any Indians, but was tied up to be shot by a party of Mexican soldiers. I don't see why I wasn't shot and why I'm not dead at this minute," he continued, with a perplexed air, "for I can remember seeing the guns pointed right at me, and hearing the order to fire. Then there was a stunning roar, and all was over. So I am certain I must be full of bullet holes. Can't you see them, sir?"

"Nary hole," answered Colonel Milam; "you look as though you'd been pounded a right smart, but otherwise you are as sound as a bottle. What did you say your name was?"

"I don't believe I said. But it is Harden, Rector Harden, and I belong to the Texas army."

"Not a son of Squire Harden of the Herrera?"

"Yes, sir; he is my father."

"Good enough! Old Ben Milam hasn't come back to Texas for nothing, after all. Why, boy, Squire Harden is one of my dearest friends, and I'd gladly risk my life any time to save a son of his from the Injuns. But how did the bloody—"

"Mexicans," interrupted Rex. "They were Mexicans, colonel, and not Indians at all."

"Look here, son," rejoined the other, sternly, "it's lucky for you that you are weak and light-headed, for I don't like being told than I can't make out an Injun from a greaser, far as I can see them. Say, boys, what were the chaps that we jumped out of this camp?"

"Injuns, of course," promptly responded one of the men who had listened to this conversation, "and one of 'em's lying dead over yonder now."

Before Rex could frame an answer to this direct statement a rush of galloping hoofs caused the Texans to spring to their rifles. Ere they could use them, a single horseman, reeling in his seat and struggling weakly to retain it, appeared among them. Beside Rex Harden the horse stopped so suddenly that its rider was flung heavily to the ground.

"Why, it's Tawny!" exclaimed Rex, in amazement.

"An Injun!" cried Colonel Milam, springing up with levelled rifle, "and, as I live, the very one that was bending over you when we came. Take that, you red devil!"

As he spoke, he fired, aiming point blank at Cochito's head, and holding the muzzle of his rifle not more than a yard away.

With an effort of strength, that one moment before would have been impossible, Rex threw himself forward and struck the rifle. It was a feeble blow, but it deflected the murderous barrel a couple of inches, and the bullet intended for the young Indian buried itself harmlessly in the ground.

"He is my prisoner, for my horse has brought him to me," cried the boy, almost choked with excitement. "As such I am responsible for him, and I forbid you to harm him, sir."

"Upon my word!" exclaimed Colonel Ben Milam, "when he was about to kill you not more than five minutes ago, and would have done it too, if we had not come along just at that time."

"If he was bending over me, as you say, colonel, it is my belief that he was trying to save my life and not to take it, for they were Mexicans who tried to kill me, and even now I can't understand why they didn't succeed.   At any rate, this horse is mine, lost to me since last evening, and whether the Indian has brought him back to me, or Tawny has brought the Indian, I don't know; but in either case I claim them both."

"Well," laughed Colonel Milam, "the horse certainly seems to recognize you as a friend, and he, at least, is worth having.   As for the Injun, I suppose we must allow your claim to him too, if you want him, though I can't imagine what use any white man can have for a live Injun.   If you'll take my advice, you'll let me put him out of his misery, for he's badly wounded and 'pears more'n half dead anyway."

"So he is wounded," agreed Rex, glancing pityingly at the young Indian, who lay where he had been flung from Tawny's back.   He was bleeding freely from the bullet hole in his thigh, and it seemed as though his very life were ebbing away with the crimson flow.

"He mustn't die, though, if we can prevent it, and for the sake of your friendship with my father, you will help me fix him up, won't you, colonel?"

"Well, lad, if you put it that way, I suppose I must

do what I can for the young whelp," answered Milam; "though trying to bring back to life an Injun, that ought by rights to be dead, will surely be a new experience for yours truly."

Cochito's wound, though bleeding profusely and ugly to look at, was not otherwise serious nor did it carry any broken bones. After the flow of blood was staunched, and it had been dressed with rude skill, the young Indian was placed on an outspread blanket near Rex, and both lads were left in quiet to renew their strength as best they could.

The Texans were well content to spend a day and a night where they were; for, besides having plenty to do in collecting the thrice-scattered herd that both Mexicans and Indians had destined to carry their plunder, and which the new-comers now proposed to use for the same purpose, they were not anxious to overtake the strong force of the enemy that Rex assured them was but a short distance ahead. He compiled this information partly from what he knew, and partly from what Cochito, who could speak Mexican fairly well, told him as they lay near each other on their blankets.

From the young Indian, too, Rex gained a clear idea of much that had happened to himself since the preceding evening, though how he had been shot by his Mexican captors without being killed or even wounded was still a mystery. So the white lad and the Indian learned much concerning each other that day ; for the latter, knowing that he owed his life to Rex, talked to him with the freedom of a brother.

With the coming of night the Texans did not deem it necessary to secure the young Indian, for they believed him to be too severely wounded to make even an attempt at escape. So he was allowed to lie near Rex, unwatched and apparently buried in profound slumber. Wolves howled about the camp from greater or less distances, but this sound was then so common in all parts of Texas that the guards who relieved each other every two hours paid no attention to it. Only Tawny, securely tethered close by his young master, occasionally tossed his head and moved uneasily.

With earliest daylight the man then on guard replenished the camp-fire and taking a kettle went to the river for water. As he passed the spot where Rex and his prisoner lay, he noticed that the latter had drawn the blanket over his head so as to entirely conceal it.

" Curious," reflected the guard, " how Injuns and greasers hate to breathe fresh air."

He lingered at the river long enough to plunge his face in its cool waters and perform a rough toilet. Then, noting the advance of dawn, he said to himself that it was high time to turn the stock out to grass. At the same moment there came to him a sound of movement among the horses, a snorting and a trampling of hoofs.

"Some of the other boys must have woke up and are turning out the critters," said the man, and thus thinking, he strolled leisurely back to camp. He wondered at not meeting the herd on its way to the river as he went, and was still more surprised to see that his comrades still slept. Only Colonel Milam was sitting up and yawning.

"What have you done with the horses, Bill?" he demanded at sight of the guard.

"I haint done nothing with 'em, colonel. Didn't you turn 'em loose? If you didn't, who in thunder did?"

"No, I did not," rejoined the leader, springing to his feet. "But I thought of course that you had. Hello, men! Tumble out! Something's gone wrong!"

CHAPTER XVII

IN THE ANCIENT MISSION OF LA ESPADA

IT was quickly evident to the occupants of the camp that something had very decidedly gone wrong, as they ran excitedly to where their stock had been secured for the night, and found no trace of them, save a broad trail leading towards the prairie. Every horse but one, including those of the Texans, had disappeared. The one remaining was Tawny.

Several of the men had started on foot to follow the trail, and Rex, awakened by the confusion, was wondering what it was all about when Colonel Milam hurried over to him.

"Our stock's been run off, Harden," he said, "and I want to borrow your horse to follow the thieves at least far enough to find out who they are."

"All right, colonel, you are welcome, if you can ride him."

Without replying to this insinuation, save by a contemptuous snort, the man attempted to spring on Tawny's back. He was not an expert horseman, judged from the Texan standpoint, and as Tawny always objected to any authority save that of his

young master, the colonel at once found himself
engaged in a struggle that bade fair to last all day.
So fierce was Tawny's attitude that, after several
futile attempts to mount him, the Texan was glad
of an excuse to withdraw from the contest.

He found it in glancing at Cochito's sleeping-
place, which was apparently still occupied by the
young Comanche, lying motionless, partially concealed by an overhanging bush, and with a blanket
drawn over his head.

"Hello! What has happened to your prisoner?"
cried Colonel Milam. "He must be dead, not to
wake up with all this racket."

Thus saying, he desisted from his struggle with
Tawny, stepped over to the place and pulled down
the blanket. Beneath it lay a log of wood.

"Euchered, by thunder!" exclaimed the Texan.
"Euchered by a half-dead Injun, and a boy at that.
Seems to me, Ben Milam, you'd better take to pick-
ing huckleberries for a living, or doing something
else more in your line than setting up to be a leader
of Texas rangers. Euchered by an Injun kid!
'Nough to make a dog sick! Ugh!" Here the
humiliated soldier spat fiercely in token of his disgust.

"Would you like to have me follow them, sir?"
inquired Rex, sympathetically. "The horse is used
to me, you know, and —"

"Follow nothing!" interrupted the other, angrily.

"You ain't fit, to begin with, and 'twouldn't do any good, if you were.   No, son, we'll just swallow our medicine like little men, allow we're beat, and mosey along toward San Antonio on foot the same as others have had to do before us.   Don't you wish now you'd let me kill the young devil, though?"

"No, colonel, I don't," replied Rex, stoutly.   "I am glad he's alive, and I'm glad he has got away too, for I know he saved my life, and so I should have been responsible for his as long as he was a prisoner. Of course I'm awfully sorry that your stock has been run off, and if you will ride my horse, he is at your service until we reach San Antonio."

"Thanks," returned the other, with a quizzical glance at Tawny, who was gazing steadfastly at him, evidently in expectation of renewed hostilities.   "I don't believe I care to ride your critter under the circumstances.   The other boys might think I was proud, and as long as they have got to hoof it, I guess I'll do the same.   It isn't the losing of the stock I mind so much, you understand, — for there's a plenty more horses to be had in Texas, — but it's the idea of an old Injun fighter like me being euchered by a single Comanche, and him a boy, wounded at that."

"Of course he couldn't have done it alone," suggested Rex, anxious to offer consolation.   "The two who escaped must have met friends and led them back here.   For my part, I think we are mighty lucky to be wearing our scalps at this minute."

"I guess you are right, son," rejoined Colonel Milam, brightening visibly. "Of course that young whelp couldn't have done it alone, as you say. In fact, I don't see how he got away with himself. Sure you didn't hear anything during the night?"

"Not a sound," replied Rex.

"Well, it is certain they must have been a strong party. Same time, it was shameful for us to let 'em run off our stock, and I should like to kick myself all the way from here to San Antonio."

The other Texans were in much the same mood as their leader, and when, after destroying everything in the camp that could not be carried away, they started northward on foot, — a method of travel that all Texans abhor, — they formed a very crestfallen company.

For three days they marched, and on the evening of the third reached the lonely mission of La Espada, about nine miles south of San Antonio. Not a soul was to be seen in its vicinity. Priests and converts, soldiers and laborers, Spaniards and Indians, all had vanished. The beautiful church, with its chime of bells, its frescoes, and its grilles of wrought iron, was open and empty. The long ranges of arched colonnades were dark and silent, and the strong bastion towers were without defenders.

But everywhere were evidences that the old mission had recently been occupied by an army. Had it been a force of Mexicans, or had Austin's men rested here ?   Had one driven the other out ? and if so, which side had been victorious ?   These were the questions asked of each other by Milam's little party as they prepared to pass the night in the deserted plaza of the old mission.

While the others prepared a supper of venison killed that day, Rex strolled through the long rows of deserted buildings, wondering at the thickness of their walls, admiring the beauty of their arches, and trying to picture to himself the many strange scenes they had witnessed.   As he walked he was attracted by a soft rustling above his head, and, looking up, saw that it was caused by the wings of innumerable bats that were swarming from an aperture high up in the wall of one of the ruined buildings.   Curious to see where they came from, he sought an entrance, and stepped inside.

The interior was filled with gloom, but he was able to see his way into a lofty hall along two sides of which opened ranges of small cell-like rooms. Overhead the bats were flitting in incredible numbers and with sharp mouse-like squeakings.   Having satisfied his curiosity, and shivering with the chill of his gloomy surroundings, Rex was about to retrace his steps, when he was startled by the unmistakable cry of a babe coming from close at hand.   It was checked so promptly as to suggest that a hand had been clapped over the child's mouth ; but the alarm had been given.

"Who is there?" challenged the boy, speaking in Mexican and at the same time feeling decidedly nervous.

There was no answer.

"Who lives?" he demanded. "Answer quickly, or I will bring men with torches and guns."

"Oh, señor," cried a trembling voice, "have pity on an unfortunate woman, and do not betray her to the cruel Tejanos."

"Who are you? and how many are with you?"

"I am alone, señor, except for my little one, and it was through him that I could not fly with the others, for he is ill. I am the wife of Sebastien Tejada, who was left in charge of the mission by Padre Tomasso, but the General Cos compelled him to go into Bexar to serve as a soldier. He would not fight the Tejanos, indeed he would not, but that he is compelled."

"But why do you hide?" queried Rex of the still unseen woman. "The Texans do not make war on women or children, nor harm them."

"Ah, señor, if you had but heard what has been told us of them. It is even said that they eat infants as do los Indios. Thus when an army of them came to this place, we of the mission fled and remained in hiding until yesterday, when they marched away. Then some of us returned, but when we saw more of the Tejanos coming this very evening, the others again ran away; but I could not, fearing that my little one would die.   So I hid myself in this place, hoping that the devourers of infants would speedily depart.   Now, therefore, if the kind señor will but show pity and go away, leaving me and the little Sebastien in peace, I will never cease to pray for him to Our Lady of Guadalupe."

For a moment Rex was puzzled as to what he ought to do.   Those cells might swarm with Mexicans only awaiting a favorable opportunity for attacking Milam's little company.   Then, again, the woman might truly be alone and in trouble, in which case she must not be left to pass the night in that gloomy place.   Finally he said :

"If you will prove the truth of your words, by going with me to the captain of the Texans, I will pledge in the name of my father that you shall not be harmed.   I am the son of Squire Harden of the Rancho Herrera."

"The Señor Harden I know by report to be a good man," replied the voice, "and so I will trust you and do as you request, for I am indeed hungry and frightened, while my little Sebastien is so ill that I am distracted."

With this a shadowy form stepped forth from one of the black arches, and as Rex gladly left the building, it followed him.   He led the way directly to Colonel Milam's camp-fire, where his arrival aroused the greatest curiosity.

The chivalrous Texan not only believed the

woman's story, but was more than willing to aid her because of kindnesses recently shown him by the women of Monterey.   So the wife of Sebastien Tejada was fed and treated with all possible courtesy, while the sufferings of her child were greatly relieved by the kindly care of several rude nurses, who were also parents and treated it with the skill gained from experience.

In return for this kindness, the grateful woman told them that Austin's army, having camped for several days at La Espada, had just advanced to the Mission Concepcion, seven miles nearer to the city, and that a battle between them and the troops under General Cos was expected to take place very shortly.

"Hurrah for Texas!" shouted Milam's followers when this was translated to them.   "That's what we want.   Let's push on to-night, boys, so as to be on hand when the fun begins!"

But their leader advised them to spend the night in resting, saying that in a fight, one fresh man was worth four fagged with weariness and loss of sleep.

So the little company remained where they were until the following morning.   Then, shortly after daylight, a dull booming sound from the north, unlike anything most of them had ever heard, caused them to spring to their feet with eager questions as to its cause.

CHAPTER XVIII

A THICK fog veiled the landscape of that morning, and through it the ominous sounds that had aroused Rex Harden's companions were borne to them with startling distinctness.

"It is musketry in volleys," declared Colonel Milam, listening intently with practised ear. "And that is the note of a field-piece, a six-pounder, if I'm a judge. Boys, the war is on, the first real battle for Texas is being fought over yonder, and it is my fault that we are not in it."

"We can get there in a hurry, though, colonel," cried one of the men; "and if the greasers make any sort of a stand, we'll be in time to polish 'em off yet. Come on, men."

With this every Texan, including Colonel Milam, seized his rifle and, forgetful even of breakfast, started on a run up the road. Only Rex was left behind, but the lad knew that, with Tawny's aid, he could allow them nearly an hour's start, and still overtake them ere they reached the Mission Concepcion.

So, in spite of his excitement, he gave Tawny a feed of corn and mended the fire, over which he proposed making himself a pot of coffee, besides cooking, for the benefit of his comrades, such venison as had been left from the meal of the evening before. But he was not allowed to do this; for while he was still engaged with the fire, the woman whom he had befriended appeared beside him.

Sebastien Tejada's wife was very slight and girlish in appearance; but with the confidence gained from matrimony she did not hesitate to assume immediate charge of the present culinary operations, only bidding Rex fetch her a vessel of water from the river, as she feared the well was polluted. This our lad willingly undertook, and as the river flowed at some distance from the mission, he was gone for several minutes. On his return he was startled to find, sitting and lounging about the fire, a dozen or so of Mexicans, four of whom were men armed with bell-mouthed escopettas and rusty sabres, while the others were women and children.

Rex came upon them so suddenly that he was within a few paces of the group before seeing it. It was then too late to retreat, so he stood where he was, returning with interest the scowling glances cast at him.

"Come and eat without fear," said the mother of the little Sebastien, as she noted his presence. "These are my neighbors, who, having watched the departure of los Tejanos, have returned again to their homes. After what I have told them of thy kindness, they will not harm thee."

Although the looks of hatred cast at him by the four scowling men were anything but reassuring, Rex put on a bold face, and, still standing, hastily disposed of the simple breakfast prepared for him.

Then, desiring the woman to put the remainder of the meat into a wallet, he walked steadily and without looking back, to where Tawny had just finished his corn. To move with deliberation on that occasion required all his nerve, for he knew that he was followed by murderous eyes, and expected with each moment to be shot at from behind. So intense was this feeling, that when he reached Tawny's side, he was bathed in a cold perspiration, and trembling in every limb. He could barely command strength to saddle the horse, and started as though he had indeed been shot, at the sound of a voice close beside him, for he had not noted an approach.

He smiled at his own weakness as he recognized the woman of whose friendship he was assured. She had brought the package of food for his comrades, and with it she gave him a small silver amulet that had hung by a thong from her own neck.

"If thee shall meet my Sebastien," she said hurriedly, and in a low tone, "give him this in token that his wife and child are safe. Until then it will protect thee from harm. Now fly with speed, for I fear that evil is intended. May the saints protect thy journey!"

She had barely ceased from speaking, when Rex, with hurried thanks for her kindness, leaped on Tawny's back, and was off. A single backward glance showed him that the four men had disappeared, and he believed they would try to waylay him. In this he was not mistaken, for he had not gone a hundred yards beyond the mission gate, when he saw the scowling quartette drawn up in line across the road that he must traverse. Four rusty escopettas were levelled directly at him, and though he was rapidly learning that firearms were comparatively harmless in the hands of Mexicans, he realized that accidents may always happen. So he reined Tawny to a walk, and then threw up his hands.

Believing that the young Texan was wholly in their power, and knowing that he would be of more value to them alive than dead, the swarthy bandits withheld their fire until he had approached to within a few paces of where they stood. Then two of them, lowering their weapons stepped forward to seize Tawny's bridle.

At that moment Rex dropped his hands, dug his heels into his horse's flanks, and gave a yell that caused Tawny to launch himself forward like a thunderbolt. The two nearest Mexicans were overthrown in a twinkling and hurled breathless to the ground. The others fired their old blunderbusses with a prodigious roar into empty space, and Rex, with an exultant shout, disappeared in a cloud of dust raised by Tawny's flying feet.

Filled with joy at this escape, and telling Tawny what a clever horse he was becoming, the young Texan pressed rapidly forward until at the end of three miles he dashed through the crystal waters of a ford and passed the ruined buildings of the Mission San Juan. Here not a soul was to be seen, and he knew that his comrades were still in advance.

Two miles further on he found them just arrived at San José, oldest and most beautiful of the Texan missions. Here they were so close to the scene of conflict towards which they were hastening that they could now hear the shouts and screams of the combatants mingled with the roar of guns. As yet, however, they could see nothing, being unable even to distinguish the smoke of battle through the screen of timber standing between it and them.

As he overtook his comrades, Rex handed them the meat that he had brought, and which they seized with famished eagerness. While they ate, the new-comer followed Colonel Milam up into the belfry tower of the mission church. To gain it he skirted the façade of the building with its massive doors of carved cedar surrounded by exquisite stone sculpture, and entered a narrow doorway at one side. Here a quaint spiral stairway formed of hewn blocks of live-oak led him to the first floor of the belfry, from which a curious ladder made of single logs deeply notched on their upper side, gave access to the lookout above.   From this platform sprang four graceful arches supporting a square pyramidal roof.

Here Rex found Colonel Milam gazing eagerly northward at certain smoke clouds that less than a mile away mingled above the tree-tops with the thinning fog and drifted slowly westward.

" It's almighty hard to tell smoke from fog," muttered Milam, " and it's a deal harder to tell greaser smoke from Texan. Still, we've got to find out somehow which is which before we take part in yonder scrimmage, and we want to know all about it in a hurry too."

" Why can't I ride ahead, sir, and pick up the information you want ? " suggested Rex.

" Hello ! are you here ? " exclaimed the colonel. " I'm glad you've come ; but do you know the danger of what you have just proposed to do ?   You'll have to ride much closer to those chaps than is either pleasant or safe, in order to discover which is which, how many there are on each side, how they are posted, and what they are doing. But those are the very things I want to know. You must go and get back within fifteen minutes too, for we won't wait longer than that before pushing to the front. Do you still want the job ? "

" Yes, sir ; and if I'm not back within fifteen minutes, I'll not come back at all.   Good-by."

Thus saying, Rex sprang down the rude stairway of the belfry tower, ran to where he had left Tawny, and rode away. When he got so near to the scene of conflict that the rattle of musketry seemed to come from all sides of him, and he could plainly see the leaping flashes of fire between the trees, the young scout dismounted and crept still closer. Crouching low, he moved swiftly from one shelter to another, until at length he reached an opening from which he commanded a partial view of the battle.

For it was a regular pitched battle between his own countrymen and the soldiers of the tyrant who sought to rob them of their liberties. In a horse-shoe formed by the winding river, and from behind a slight natural embankment, rang out the Texas rifles. But those deliberately aimed and deadly shots were very few as compared with the volleys of musketry that crashed almost without interval from close at hand. It needed not a second glance at the tawdry uniforms and swarthy faces of the troops who were thus burning such quantities of powder with so slight effect, to know that they were Mexicans. Beyond them Rex could see still other flashings of fire and clouds of smoke.

"How we could astonish these fellows by making an attack on them from this side," he thought. "It would simply scare them stiff, and this is the very place, too. A dozen rifles here will be as good as a regiment, and I'll have them here, too, inside of ten minutes."

What he had to do was very plain, and the result appeared so certain that Rex seemed to see the battle already won, and largely through his efforts.   But suddenly something happened.

He was just beginning to creep away from his dangerous proximity to those dark-skinned soldiers, when all at once there came a roar of artillery from a new direction, and a whirlwind of grape mowed a ghastly lane through the Mexican ranks.   At the same moment a line of yelling Texans, rising apparently from the ground not ten paces away, leaped at them with such ferocity that the terrified soldiers broke and fled, rushing with frantic haste directly towards the place where Rex lay concealed.

CHAPTER XIX

REX BECOMES A MEXICAN SOLDIER

IT was all so sudden and so unexpected, that by
the time Rex realized what had happened, and
started to run, he was surrounded and swept away
by a mob of panic-stricken men. These, flinging
aside weapons, and everything else that impeded
their movements, sought only to escape by flight
from the terrible knives of los diablos Tejanos. So
oblivious were they to everything save their own
danger that for a time the presence of a white lad
among them passed without notice, and Rex, finding
himself unmolested, still entertained hopes of escape.
If he could only work his way to the outskirts of the
flying throng, he felt certain that he could slip away
unnoticed.

He made the attempt, but so dense was the mob,
that, in spite of his efforts, he was borne along for
more than a mile before finding himself comparatively free, and in company with but half a dozen
soldiers. The exultant yells from behind had died
away, and even the most badly frightened of the
Mexicans were beginning to realize that their

dreaded enemies had ceased from pursuing them. So their headlong pace was slackened, they began to glance furtively at one another, and even to excuse themselves in panting gasps for having run.

"It was so sudden," explained one, "that I fled without reflection."

"We could not have saved our lives otherwise," growled another, "for the Tejanos were five to every one of us."

"Los diablos!"

"Los heriticos!"

"Let us meet them on even terms, and we will sweep them from the face of the earth. Is it not so, amigo?"

This last remark was addressed to Rex by the man who ran nearest to him. As he made no reply, the man glanced curiously beneath the sombrero that, pulled well down over the lad's face, very nearly concealed it.

"Holy Virgin!" he cried; "here is one of them! Seize him! Help! Do not let him escape!"

With this he flung himself upon the stranger, only to be met by a stunning blow that caused him to measure his length on the ground.

During the whole of that involuntary flight, Rex had expected an attack of this kind and had held himself in readiness to meet it. Now he sprang to one side, and might have escaped had there not been one more soldier still beyond him. This man grappled with the lad ; there was a moment of fierce struggle, and then they rolled to the ground together, but with the young Texan on top. With one free hand he tried to draw a knife from his belt; but ere this could be done, half a dozen soldiers rushed at him, and further resistance became useless.

When the poor boy, breathless, begrimed, bare-headed, with torn clothing and pinioned arms, was finally allowed to regain his feet, he gazed helplessly about him. On all sides were the scowling faces of those who not only thirsted for his life, but would feel that in killing him they would be performing a meritorious deed. From all mouths there was but a single verdict.

" Kill him ! "

" Death to the heretic ! "

" Tear the heart from the Texas rebel ! "

" And make haste, for we have no time to spare."

A dozen knives flashed in the sunlight, and a dozen arms were uplifted. Rex closed his eyes, and his brain seethed with its tumult of thoughts. Of them all, one stood clearly forth — was any one ever put to death twice in one week before ? The idea was so absurd that the lad actually laughed aloud.   It was a ghostly hysterical laugh, to be sure, but so unmistakably a mirthful sound that the uplifted arms were paralyzed with amazement. What sort of a youth was this who actually laughed in the face of

death?   Was his act one of bravado or madness?
Others pressed forward for a look at him, and one of
these uttered a loud cry.

"Mother of God save us! It is a miracle, and the
dead can return to life.   You cannot harm him, and
he laughs because he has knowledge of the fact.   We
killed this same lad a week ago, near Goliad.   With
my own eyes I saw him pierced by a dozen bullets.
We left him where he fell, dead I tell you, dead!
Now he stands yonder, alive, and mocking us with
laughter.   Let him go before he casts upon us the
eye of evil; for I tell you he is a devil in human
form."

"No, he is not a devil," said another.   "He is one
whom the saints protect.   See you not that he bears
upon his bosom the holy symbol of Our Lady?   We
could not harm him if we would, for the arm that
struck at him would be withered.   It is no wonder he laughs, knowing how little he has to fear.
Let him go, then, before the Holy Ones become
angry at us."

"But he is surely a Texan, and a spy," murmured
other voices, "and to let such a one escape would be
a crime."

"It is a case for the Church to decide, since he
wears a charm that the Church has blessed," argued
one who seemed to possess authority.   "Let us then
take him to the priests.   If he is protected by the
saints, they will recognize the fact.   If he is of a

weak mind, as his merriment in the face of death would seem to indicate, they will find it out. If he is an impostor, who can discover it more quickly than they? Let us carry him to the holy fathers, and so shift from ourselves the responsibility of either his life or his death."

This advice seemed so good that it was instantly adopted, and so, within five minutes after discovering him among them, the still retreating Mexicans were hurrying Rex Harden towards San Antonio.

Although he had heard and understood their conversation regarding him, he had not uttered a word nor given a sign of comprehension. He recognized the fact that his life had been spared for the time being, on account of the amulet that the Señora Tejada had hung about his neck that very morning, and which, during his recent struggle, had been pulled from its place of concealment beneath his shirt. He also knew that by his present captors he was regarded as being in some way mysterious, or at least of an unsound mind, and he determined to profit by the knowledge if possible. Above all, he realized that he had just escaped death by the narrowest possible margin of safety, and was humbly grateful for his wonderful deliverance.

In vain did the Mexican officers attempt, by commands, threats, and even by pleadings, to check the retreat of their demoralized troops. The latter had had enough of fighting for that day, and nothing could induce them to again face the terrible Texans in an open field.

"How could we fight if we should return," they argued, "since we have burned all our powder and thrown away our guns?"

As even the most ferocious of the officers could give no satisfactory answer to this question, the retreat was continued. By noon all who remained alive of the four hundred troops sent out to destroy a force of ninety Texans had thankfully regained the comparative safety of the city.

General Martin Cos with one thousand troops held San Antonio and was preparing to defend it until his brother-in-law, the Mexican President, should arrive with an army strong enough to sweep Texas from end to end. Already had he sent to Matamoras for reënforcements, and while awaiting them was strengthening his defences in every possible way. Thus, as Rex was hurried through the narrow streets, he saw on all sides parties of soldiers constructing barricades, digging trenches, planting batteries, and turning such of the thick-walled houses as commanded important positions into temporary fortresses.

Although the streets were thronged with people, soldiers, priests, vaqueros who had come in with cattle for the garrison, and other civilians, they were all Mexican, and not a single white face was to be seen among them. Every American, except three or four held as prisoners, had fled or been driven out, and amid all who stared or scowled at Rex as he passed, the lad could not discover a single friendly face or one that was even familiar. His heart was very heavy, but he laughed aloud and uttered childish words of pleasure. At this, those who guarded him looked at each other and touched their foreheads significantly.

Finally they brought him to the well-remembered Veramendi house in which the Mexican general had established his headquarters. Here, after a few minutes of waiting at the entrance, Rex was ushered into the presence of a stout, smooth-faced man, who, clad in a gorgeous uniform, sat in an easy-chair, rolling cigarettes, and angrily receiving reports from those officers whom the Texans had just defeated. Near by was a table littered with papers at which two clerks were busy. Several officers, all smoking cigarettes, but looking very miserable, stood about the room.

At this juncture the appearance of a prisoner was hailed with relief, and the several persons present regarded the young Texan curiously.

"Who are you?" demanded General Cos, savagely; "and why are the people of Texas in rebellion against their President?"

"You can talk," replied Rex, in English, "because your hands are not tied. If your hands were tied so that they hurt like mine, you could not remember anything else. No one could."

As the general understood English very well, and had been informed that the prisoner did not seem to be quite in his right mind, he ordered the bonds of which the captive complained to be loosed. This was no sooner done, than the lad picked up the commander's plumed chapeau from the table, and with a silly smile, placed it on his own head, saying as he did so:

"It is fine to be a soldier and wear feathers."

"How dare you, sir!" thundered the general, starting from his chair. At the same moment an officer snatched away the chapeau and returned it to the table, with a low bow.

The prisoner looked from one to another with a grieved and puzzled expression, while the general, sinking back in his seat and lighting a fresh cigarette, began to question him farther, this time speaking in broken English.

For a moment Rex seemed to be paying most gratifying and intelligent attention to what was said. Then, with a cry of delight he started in pursuit of a kitten that had just entered the room and was walking demurely across the floor.

Instantly there ensued a scene of direst confusion. The frightened animal fled wildly from side to side, with the prisoner in hot chase, while the officers, nearly choked with suppressed laughter, either leaped out of the way or made futile efforts to detain him. The general swore, furniture was upset, and for a minute pandemonium reigned.   Then the kitten took refuge under the general's chair, where Rex, trying to follow, was captured and dragged to his feet.

"He is an idiot, a raving lunatic!" roared the commander, furiously. "Take him away, or turn him loose beyond the lines, or shoot him, I don't care which; only let me not be pestered with him again."

As Rex was being hustled from the room, Martin Cos cried: "Hold! I have another plan. Put him in uniform, make a soldier of him, and place him where the Texans themselves can shoot at him. In the meantime let him dig in the trenches; only at night confine him with the convict troops, and see that he does not escape."

CHAPTER XX

"THAT'S a cheerful prospect for me," thought Rex, as he was led away towards the guard-house. "It is better than being shot, though, or placed in solitary confinement in one of their rotten old dungeons. So I might be worse off, and as the idiot racket seems to be working pretty well, I guess I'll keep it up until something better offers. Ha-ha! Ha-ha! See the birdie, pretty little birdie. When I catch him I'll put him in a cage, and hear him sing. Ha-ha! Ha-ha!"

As the " birdie " toward which he pointed was one of the city scavengers, a huge turkey buzzard, tearing at a bit of carrion in a gutter, the soldiers looked at him curiously, and then broke into coarse laughter. By this time the character of the handsome young Tejano was established with all classes, and every one, from the general down, was speaking of him as El Tonto (the fool).

According to orders, Rex was conducted to the guard-house, where he was stripped of his own clothing, and compelled to assume a dirty uniform of coarse blue cloth, with red facings, and a stiff cap in which was stuck a green pompon. He was not given shoes, stockings, nor any underclothing except a gray flannel shirt. These garments were not only so large as to hang loosely about the lad's slender form, and make him appear more like a scarecrow than a soldier, but they were so filthy that mere contact with them turned him sick. Of his own belongings nothing was left to him except the amulet that the Señora Tejada had slipped into his hand, and which the superstitious Mexicans would have deemed it profanity to remove.

When the transformation had been effected, amid much heartless laughter, and many coarse jests on the part of the guard, and when Rex had been given a number (names being unknown among the convict troops), he was turned loose in a large, walled enclosure like a great corral. This was the camping-place of the convicts, and here, when not at work, they were penned like so many animals. A soldier with loaded musket was stationed on a raised platform beside the entrance. From here he commanded a view of the whole enclosure, and could call any individual in it to order, in case of a disturbance. He was even empowered to fire into the mob, in case of any riot that commands and threats could not quell.

As the convict soldiers were unarmed, while their warder was backed by a score of picked troops stationed in the guard-house close at hand, it seldom happened that his words were not listened to with respectful attention.   At the same time he rarely interfered with the ordinary quarrels that were of frequent occurrence among this scum of Mexican prisons.

On the present occasion, as our poor lad was ushered into this horrible enclosure unannounced, and its gate was swung to behind him, he felt as though he had descended into a place of lost souls, and that all hope must be abandoned from that moment.

Lining the walls on three sides were low, open sheds, having rough board floors sloping outward, that formed the sleeping-places of the convict soldiers.   Across one corner of the camp flowed an acequia or ditch of clear water from the river. Several hundred men, with the faces of murderers, and the furtive air of thieves, sat or lay beneath the sheds, strolled aimlessly here and there, gambled, quarrelled, smoked corn-husk cigarettes, or squatted apathetically about the smouldering embers of a small fire.   All wore the honorable uniform of the Republic of Mexico, which Santa Anna had thus degraded.

At the entrance of the new-comer a murmur of languid interest ran through the entire camp, and all eyes were turned towards him.   At first they only noted that he wore the same uniform as themselves; but in another moment some one called attention to his fair skin.   With that there came a general movement in his direction, and he quickly formed the centre of an eagerly questioning throng.

Rex had determined that even here he would sustain the character of an idiot, in which he believed lay his only hope of safety and ultimate escape. So, as the convicts gathered about him, he smiled foolishly, jabbered at them in English, and even threw his arms about the most ill-favored cut-throat of the lot, as though inviting him to dance. The man pulled away with an oath, while the others roared with laughter.

Slowly the jeering mob forced the lad to the opposite side of the camp, and when well removed from the guard, who had watched their proceedings with a mild interest, they began a series of petty persecutions, that would have taken the form of open violence had they dared use it. So they only shoved their victim violently from one to another, pinched him or thrust thorns into his legs, all the while shouting with laughter at his involuntary starts and cries of pain. Most amusing of all was to watch his rising anger, and his fruitless efforts to single out the most active of his tormentors.

By the time Rex had grown so desperate, that he was just about to attempt a rush back to the gate, where he proposed demanding protection from the guard, the rattle of a drum caused a general movement of the convicts in that very direction, and in less than a minute he was left standing alone. His late tormentors, drawn up in double file, were marching slowly past the open gateway, where each one appeared to be receiving something. Attracted by curiosity, the unhappy lad strolled that way until he could see that several camp cooks, standing beside great kettles, were handing to each man a small wooden dish or trough containing his supper.

Catching scent of the food, Rex became aware that he was faint with hunger, and determined to secure his share of whatever was to be had. So he took position at the very rear of the column, and at length, after a weary delay, reached the place where the cooks were standing. A petty officer with a file of armed soldiers superintended their movements, while the regular camp guard also watched them from his platform.

As Rex came up, one of the cooks handed him a dirty wooden platter, containing a meagre quantity of boiled beans and a cube of meat about an inch square. Another gave him a single tortilla, or thin cake of corn meal, and then the gate was closed, for the task of feeding the convicts was ended for that night. In the morning every one of them would be expected to present his greasy little trough unbroken to the cooks, failing to do which he would get no breakfast.

Of course Rex knew nothing of this, and his only thought was whether or not he could bring himself to eat the disgusting-looking mess just given him.

Finally concluding that he was hungry enough to try, he was raising the tortilla to his mouth when it was snatched from his hand. At the same time a man on the other side grabbed the bit of meat that had fallen to our lad's portion, and another, seizing hold of the wooden bowl, attempted to wrest it from him.

With a cry of rage, Rex jerked away his property, and fetched the man who was trying to take it from him such a blow on the head that the trough was split in two pieces, and its contents streamed down over the convict's face. Wheeling on him who had snatched the meat, the lad dealt him a right-hander under the ear that felled him to the ground; then he sprang after the thief who was making off with the tortilla. Ere he could reach him, a by-stander stuck out a foot, over which Rex tripped. Quickly recovering himself, he turned with a blind fury upon this new aggressor, and in another moment was lost to sight in the vortex of a yelling, struggling mob, who fought like wild beasts maddened by the scent of blood.

In vain did the soldier on guard shout commands and threats. He even fired his musket over the heads of the infuriated throng; but with no more effect than if it had been a breath of wind. Seeing that the fight was already beyond his control, and bade fair speedily to involve every convict in the camp, the sentry summoned his comrades from the guard-house. These charged the mob with such lusty blows from their clubbed muskets, that within ten minutes it had taken to howling flight, leaving poor Rex bruised, dazed, and wellnigh smothered, lying on the ground.

At command of a sergeant he was picked up, carried to one of the sheds, laid on its sloping floor, and there left to recover as best he might. Having thus done their duty by all concerned, his rescuers, impatient to resume their own interrupted supper, marched back to the guard-house. Only the sentinel lingered behind to take a final survey of the field of battle, and to him Rex heard the retiring sergeant say:

"Take care, Tejada, that no more fights occur while you are on duty."

"Tejada!" Where had he known that name? It certainly sounded familiar. Oh, yes, the mission of La Espada, the woman and the child, the little Sebastien. Perhaps this soldier was the very one of whom she had spoken; and if so — well he would first find out, and then think what to do. So he called softly:

"Tejada! Sebastien Tejada!"

The sentinel started and gazed about him inquiringly.

Again came the murmured sound of his own name. To his amazement it was uttered by the wretched youth lying at his feet, who had just caused so much trouble.

"Why do you call me?" he asked shortly.

"Do you know the mission of Espada, and a muchachito of thy name who dwells within its walls?"

"And if I do, what then?"

The soldier was now bending curiously over the lad, and his tone was full of eagerness.

"I bring this token from the mother of your child," answered Rex, drawing the amulet from his bosom, "and by it I beg of you to aid me now, even as I was able to aid them but a few hours since."

The soldier snatched the bit of silver, and kissed it passionately. Then, whispering, "Lie quiet till I come again," he rose and exclaimed harshly :

"No, dog. I will not bring thee water nor aught else, but will beat out thy idiot brains if thou but lift a hand to make further disturbance."

This was for the benefit of several convicts who were drawing near, and whom Sebastien also threatened if the quiet of the camp was again broken that night. Having thus disarmed suspicion, the sentinel resumed his place beside the gate, and a little later the inmates of the convict camp were ordered to their sleeping-places.

As Rex had been laid at the extreme end of one of the sheds, he was spared the misery of being crowded on both sides by his filthy companions. Even so, after an hour of breathing the foul air of the place, and listening to the vile conversation of the wretches about him, he began to think that he should in truth lose his mind unless speedily released from the well-nigh unendurable situation.

While he was thus thinking, and wondering if Sebastien Tejada would indeed prove a friend, a harsh voice from outside the shed called: "Two hundred and one is ordered out for punishment, and must come quickly. Which is he?"

"Two hundred and one is the gringo! El Tonto the gringo!" cried a score of eager voices, while, as Rex stiffly rose, and stepped forth from that den of iniquity, he was followed by a torrent of jeers and loudly expressed hopes that he was about to be flayed alive.

CHAPTER XXI

FEELING that fate was indeed dealing very harshly with him, and yet glad of any change, Rex quietly submitted to be led away by the soldier who had summoned him. He wondered vaguely, and indeed felt mortified that it had only been deemed necessary to send a single man for him instead of a file of soldiers. Then he remembered his assumed idiocy, and acknowledged that it sufficiently explained the contempt that sent a messenger instead of a guard to escort him to the place of punishment.

What was he to be punished for, though, and how? With half a chance to escape, or even to fight in his own defence, he would show these miserable greasers that they could not ill treat a free-born Texan with impunity. The lad grew hot with anger as these thoughts surged through his brain, and defenceless as he was, meditated an attack upon the armed man by his side as soon as they should reach a favorable place.

They had left the convict camp, and were passing the guard-house as this possibility presented itself. A band of light streamed from its open doorway, and, as they crossed this, Rex glanced curiously at the face of his escort. To his surprise the man who held his arm, and was leading him to punishment, was the same whom he had believed to be a friend; for he was Sebastien Tejada.

The soldier noted his prisoner's start of recognition, but checked the words that rose to his lips, with a warning pressure of the arm. A minute later they entered a tiny jacal, or hut, that stood but a short distance beyond the guard-house, and in which Tejada made his temporary home.

Although the interior was in inky blackness, the Mexican led his guest to a corn-husk bed, that, rude as it was, seemed to our aching lad delightfully soft and comfortable.

"Here also is food," said Tejada, handing him tortilla after tortilla, until he had eaten as many of the thin cakes as would have served two Mexican soldiers for a full day's ration of food.

"Now if you could give me a drink," said the lad; and in reply Tejada handed him a jug of fresh milk, that Rex drained to the very bottom.

"There!" he exclaimed, as he set the jug down, with a great sigh of satisfaction, "I feel like a new man, and ready for anything that may turn up. What comes next, Tejada? Do you deliver me to the tormentors, or aid me to escape?"

"Neither," replied the Mexican. "There is no punishment in store for thee that I know of, and I only threatened one to throw yonder dogs off the scent. If one was intended, however, I could not save thee from it. Neither can I aid thee to escape, without putting in peril the lives of my wife and child, as well as my own, for I am held responsible for thy safe keeping. I must even gain thy promise not to attempt an escape during the night, or else return thee to the camp of convicts."

"I am willing to promise, that from now until daylight I will make no attempt to leave this place," said Rex, "for I can imagine nothing more awful than to be taken back among those wretches."

"They would surely kill thee before morning," said Tejada; "but tell me, art thou truly of sound mind, and reasonable?"

"Perfectly, having only played the idiot for a purpose."

"And thou hast recently seen my wife, together with the little Sebastien?"

"As I told you, I saw them only this morning, if the hour is still before midnight, or yesterday, if it be passed," answered the lad. Then he gave a full account of his recent adventures in the mission of Espada, including the part borne in them by the Señora Tejada, to all of which his companion listened with breathless interest.

"For thy goodness to them I will serve thee with my life!" exclaimed the grateful soldier, when Rex had finished. "Without it I would still serve thee for the sake of thy most excellent father, the Señor Harden, whose kindness is known to all the poor dwellers in the missions. I am not able to do much; but what I can, that will I do gladly. From among the convicts I am permitted to take one as a servant; but when he is with me alone I must be responsible for his safety with my life. In this way only could I remove thee from the others, who, as I have said, would surely have killed thee this night. Now, therefore, while in reality I am thy servant, bound to obey thy every wish, to all others thou must appear to be mine. Sleep then in safety on this poor bed till daylight, when I will wake thee and instruct thee in thy semblance of duties. Also, I think it would be safer if thou do not put off thy idiocy too suddenly."

"Trust me for that," laughed Rex, restored to good spirits by this unexpected friendship. "The trick has proved too valuable to be cast aside before a better offers. To-morrow you will see that I am more of a fool than ever."

"Then, until the morrow. Buenas noches!"

"Buenas noches! and may Heaven bless you for a true friend in time of need," answered the young Texan.

So Rex Harden, after a day of turmoil, exciting adventure, many dangers and narrow escapes, was left to a night of peaceful quiet, and slept soundly on Sebastien Tejada's corn-husk bed until morning.

Then he was awakened by his swarthy host, who respectfully requested that, for the sake of appearances, he would assist in the preparation of coffee.

Not only did the young Texan willingly accede to this request, but he still further carried out the idea that he was Tejada's servant by cleaning the soldier's musket and performing such other duties as came to his hand. He also submitted in silence to the volleys of abuse and harsh language which, also for the sake of appearance, his supposed master showered upon him when within the hearing of his comrades. Our lad's indifference to all this was commonly supposed to be owing to his ignorance of the Mexican language, for only Tejada knew that he was master of it.

Soon after sunrise Rex was driven with a party of convicts under guard, to work in the trenches. Here, although he performed fully as much labor as any of his fellow-slaves, who shirked in every way possible, he did not neglect to make certain exhibitions of idiocy that excited great mirth among the spectators, and confirmed the impression that he was a fool. So from that day he was known to all the city as El Tonto; and while his supposed infirmity gained for him certain privileges, it also exposed him to many cruel tricks, that the brutal soldiers thought it great sport to play on one mentally incapable of defending himself.

Having been thus introduced to a life of captivity

N

and slavery, the unfortunate lad was compelled to
endure it for an entire month without finding his
condition materially changed.

During this time the Texan army, under Stephen
Austin, advanced closer and closer to the city until
it was regularly besieged, and communication with
the surrounding country was cut off. Provisions became so scarce that the daily rations of the soldiers
grew smaller and smaller, until actual starvation
stared them in the face. What with scanty food,
hard work, anxiety, and the mental strain of sustain-
ing his assumed character, Rex grew so pitiably thin
that it is doubtful if his own parents would have
recognized him.

Towards the end of this month the garrison made
several sorties, generally at night, after provisions for
themselves and forage for their horses; but they
were always driven back empty handed, and generally with ranks sadly thinned by Texas bullets.

All this time it was noticeable that, while the
Mexican soldiers were suffering from hunger, and
the diseases caused by an absence of nearly every
necessity of life, their officers still seemed to have
plenty to eat and drink. They still smoked their incessant cigarettes, gambled, danced, and made merry,
as though there were no such things as anxiety or
sorrow or suffering within their horizon. Even
their horses remained sleek and high-spirited while
those of the troopers were reduced to skeletons.

Seeing these things, and despairing of the reën-forcements that General Cos declared would surely come to their relief, the common soldiers muttered curses that grew louder each day, plotted rebellion, and threatened to desert in a body to the enemy.

Knowing this state of affairs, and believing that it must also be known in the Texan camp, Rex could not understand why the besiegers did not attack the city and seek to carry it by assault. Night after night, he lay awake on his wretched pallet, listening for sounds of the attack, which he constantly expected would be made, and fretting himself into a state of feverish nervousness over its unexplainable delay.

At length it happened that, one afternoon, he with a party of convict troops was sent to strengthen a breastwork across one of the streets leading from the main plaza. While they were wearily performing their hated task, a group of officers rode into the plaza to exercise their horses. With them came two soldiers leading a steed so high-spirited that he would have been unmanageable had he not been choked into submission by two halters about his neck.

At sight of this horse, Rex dropped his spade and, uttering an inarticulate cry of amazement, stood staring at him, forgetful of all else. As he looked, he saw man after man of those skilled Mexican riders leap into the saddle, only to be so promptly and ignominiously flung from it that he had no desire to repeat the attempt. So intensely interested were all the spectators of this struggle that even the convicts were allowed to neglect their work unheeded.

Step by step the young Texan drew near to the scene of contest, staring with fixed gaze at the horse, until he too began to share the general attention. His fellow-slaves jeered at him with mocking shouts of " See El Tonto! See the gringo scarecrow! He, too, wishes to ride! Let him try. He has never been in a saddle, and should take his first lesson on a nice quiet horse like this one."

Finally one of the officers, attracted by these shouts, and thinking to extract some amusement from the wretched appearing lad, ordered him to mount the furious horse, and ride him twice around the plaza, under a penalty of flogging if he failed.

A chorus of approving shouts greeted this proposition, and in another moment the young Texan was hustled forward, picked up by the mocking soldiers, and flung into the saddle. At the same instant the men clinging to the halters let go their hold and jumped aside.

As though in an agony of terror, Rex fell on the horse's neck, and clasped it with both arms. As he did so, he managed to whisper a single word in the animal's ear, at sound of which Tawny — for it was indeed he — stood for a moment quivering. Then he sprang away and dashed furiously around the plaza, with Rex still clinging to his neck, as though in abject fear.

The spectators screamed with delight as they scampered out of the way, and redoubled their shouts of derision at sight of that most contemptible of beings to a Mexican — a timid horseman. As the splendid brute flew for the second time around the plaza and drew near the barricade at which the convicts had been at work, his scarecrow rider suddenly sat erect in the saddle, seized the bridle in his hand, and uttered a shrill cry. At sound of it the horse threw up his head, charged straight at the breastwork, cleared it with a superb leap, and, dashing like a whirlwind up the narrow street beyond, was lost to the view of the amazed spectators, before they clearly realized what had happened.

CHAPTER XXII

WHO WILL GO WITH OLD BEN MILAM?

WHERE Tawny had been during the month of his
young master's imprisonment in San Antonio, and
how he fell into the hands of the Mexicans, Rex
could not imagine, nor did he ever discover. All he
ever learned was, that during the night before he
made his wonderful escape, his old enemy, the soldier named Domingo, who had been absent for some
weeks on a mission to Matamoras, returned, bringing
with him the animal in question. He had offered to
sell his prize, which he described as the finest horse
in all Texas, to General Cos, who agreed to purchase
him if he proved to be well broken to saddle, and the
animal had been sent to the plaza for trial, with
what results we know.

All this Rex learned a long time afterwards, but
at the moment when he found himself dashing up
Flores Street on the back of his own incomparable
Tawny, he only knew, or cared to know, that he was
free. The thought filled him with a wild exhilara-
tion, his blood coursed like fire, and as he flew up
the narrow roadway, scattering its occupants like
chaff before a gale, he uttered yells of exultation as

wild as Comanche war-whoops.   To the few who recognized him as "El Tonto," his aspect, together with these wild cries, were only added proofs of his demented condition, and they piously crossed themselves as he swept past.

The Texans, who were at this time encamped on the west side of the city, and within a mile of its plaza, had exhausted every effort to draw General Cos from behind his breastworks, and induce him to fight them on the open plain.   When they found that this could not be done, and that their own commander would not attempt an assault, they, too, grew dissatisfied and mutinous.

As they were volunteers, serving without pay, and free to come or go as they pleased, hundreds of them returned in disgust to their homes, and their numbers dwindled daily.   Among those who remained an expedition was planned for the invasion of Mexico; and on the 4th of December it looked very much as though the besieging force was about to melt away without making an effort to capture the stronghold before which they had sat so long.

Austin, their chosen leader, had been taken from them, to be sent as a commissioner to the United States, and his place had been filled by Edward Burleson.   Sam Houston, the idol of Texas, and commander-in-chief of her slender forces, was detained, fretting like a caged lion, by the squabbling factions at San Felipe.   Men of influence and presumed patriotism were trying to lure the besieging force to its destruction in Mexico, and exaggerated reports of the enemy's strength were spread through the camp daily. All minds were filled with suspicion and uncertainty. Only a handful of brave men, among whom were Milam, Bowie, and Deaf Smith, stood firm in their determination to capture San Antonio, or die in the attempt.

On the afternoon of that memorable 4th of December, Milam and Bowie stood before the latter's tent, gloomily watching a scene of riot and confusion that was throwing the whole camp into an uproar. General Burleson had just issued an order to raise the siege, and prepare for a retreat that very evening. By some, this order was received with approval; by others, with grief and bitter anger. The latter declared they would not obey it, and denounced as cowards and traitors those willing to do so. Hot words led to blows, until it seemed to the onlookers that war was about to break out between the opposing factions.

The two officers, gazing on the scene of tumult, were torn by conflicting emotions. For the sake of example, they desired to obey the order of their superior, and yet they believed that to do so would be to deal a death-blow to Texas liberty.

"My God!" cried Bowie, in a tone of anguish; "is this the end of all our hopes and boasts and struggles? Must we slink away like whipped curs, and lick the hands of the tyrant who will grind us into the dust?"

To this cry Milam could find no answer. His heart was too full for utterance, and he only turned his gaze toward the city he had hoped to win. Now, bathed in the glory of sunset, it seemed to be fading away, and with it all hope for Texas.

As he looked towards it, he started, and gazed more eagerly. A moving object coming from the city had caught his eye. "Look, Bowie!" he cried. "A horseman comes this way, riding like the wind! Is he a deserter, a messenger, or an escaping prisoner? Did ever you see such speed? He must be mounted on the immortal Pegasus! Great Cæsar! How he rides! as if Death and all the Furies were in pursuit. And yet I cannot see that any follow. See him wave his arms, and hear him yell! He must be a madman, just loosed from Bedlam."

"He is a Mexican, and consequently a deserter; for I can make out his uniform," replied keen-eyed Bowie, after a long look at the approaching horseman. "But what a glorious brute he is riding! Too noble an animal by far to be burdened with so worthless a carcass. I shall make it my business to see that he enters a better service."

"You surely would not rob the poor greaser?" questioned Milam, slyly; "especially in face of the order respecting the property rights of those enemies who are won over to our cause."

"A fico for your orders!" cried Bowie. "Who values an order since the issue of this last one? But the deserter is making straight for us, and I will toss you for his horse. By Heavens, colonel, he is a white man!"

As Bowie uttered this exclamation, the wild horseman reined his steed to a sudden standstill within two paces of the officers, and after a moment of eager staring at them, slid limply to the ground, muttering as he did so:

"Bowie and Milam! Thank God!"

Both men sprang forward to support him, and in spite of his tattered uniform, his emaciation, and the general wretchedness of his appearance, both recognized him.

"Rector Harden, by all that's good!"

"Rex and Tawny, as I'm a sinner!"

In another moment they had borne him into the tent, where with stimulants and food they fought away the weakness into which the strength lent by his recent excitement had been merged.

Within fifteen minutes he had so recovered strength and voice that the men bending over him had learned the outline of his story. They knew also of the starvation and threatened mutiny in the Mexican ranks, they knew that no expectation was entertained in San Antonio of a Texan assault, they knew that all the hopes of Martin Cos rested upon the coming of reënforcements, and they knew that now if ever was the accepted moment for storming the city.

In the meantime, a curious throng of those who had noted the arrival of the supposed Mexican deserter, were gathered outside the tent, clamoring for news.   To these came Colonel Milam.

"Boys," he shouted with a voice that reached every quarter of the camp, "men of Texas, give me your attention for just one moment."

The appeal was heeded, and from all sides the volunteers, dropping their personal quarrels, crowded forward to hear what this man, whom they all knew, and whose personal bravery all respected, had to say.

Milam waited for silence ; and then, in ringing tones, told them of what had just happened ; of the wonderful escape from San Antonio of Rector Harden, whom many of them knew and whose supposed death they had mourned. "The lad is a keen observer and knows what he is talking about," continued the speaker. "He says that now or never is the time to make an assault on yonder town.   I, for one, believe him, and am willing to risk everything on this chance.   Fellow-soldiers, who of you will go with old Ben Milam into San Antonio?"

For answer there came a mighty yell from the assemblage. Officers and men pressed eagerly forward to offer their services. Bowie sprang from the tent and stood beside his comrade.

"I move that we capture San Antonio, and that Colonel Benjamin Milam be chosen to lead the assault!" he shouted.   "All in favor will say 'aye!'"

"Aye!" yelled hundreds of the eager troops as with a single voice; and with that outcry the fate of San Antonio was sealed.

Colonel Milam, who believed in striking iron while it was hot, accepted the responsibility thus thrust upon him, and ordered all who were willing to join in the attack to meet him at an old mill half a mile away as soon as the night was sufficiently dark to conceal their movements.   Then he reëntered the tent and held an earnest consultation with the lad whose opportune arrival had wrought this sudden change of plans.

"I must go with you, sir," declared Rex, when this talk was ended.   "Indeed, I must."

"My dear boy!   You must rest where you are until you regain your strength," replied Milam.

"All right, colonel; I will lie right here until you are ready to start, but then I shall join you," rejoined the young soldier; and from this decision nothing could move him.

At length Rex adroitly changed the subject by saying, "Oh, colonel, can't you find something Texan for me to wear?   It doesn't seem as though I could stand this vile uniform a moment longer."

"Of course we can, son.   You just lie still, and I'll have you rigged out in no time."

With this Milam left the tent, to which he returned a few minutes later, laden with an assortment of clothing, including boots and a sombrero, from which Rex might select whatever suited him best.

That night, at the old mill, three hundred picked men were detailed for the assault, and all arrangements were perfected. A separate company was ordered to cross the river and make a feint against the Alamo, that should divert the enemy's attention from the main expedition. The remainder of the little Texan army, under command of General Burleson, were to guard camp and cover the retreat of the assaulting columns in case they should be driven back.

By the time all preparations were made, it wanted but an hour of daylight, and James Bowie went to waken Rex. A hasty breakfast was washed down by cups of strong coffee, and then they were off.

The three hundred men were divided into two columns, headed by Colonels Milam and Johnson. As they began their silent march towards the mist-enshrouded city, a distant volley of rifles and an answering roar of artillery told that the feint against the Alamo was begun.

So completely did this divert the enemy's attention, that Milam and Johnson entered two of the principal streets of the city, that ran parallel with each other to the plaza, without discovery. Down these streets the shadowy columns advanced in swift silence, until they were within one hundred yards of the great square. Here a shot from a Mexican sentry rang out its quick alarm. It was answered by a volley and a yell, as the Texans flung themselves into the nearest houses. Then the streets they had just vacated were swept by a storm of cannon-balls from the plaza batteries, and the battle was begun.

CHAPTER XXIII

FROM HOUSE TO HOUSE

THE struggle for the possession of San Antonio quickly resolved itself into a house-to-house fight, in which every foot of ground was stubbornly contested. The first two buildings occupied by the Texans were the Veramendi house, in which both James Bowie and his young friend, Rex Harden, had passed so many happy hours, and the Garza house, on the opposite side of Soledad Street. The space between them was so incessantly swept by one of the plaza batteries which Rex had unwillingly helped place in position a few days before, that, for many hours, all communication between them was cut off.

Against these two buildings was rained so furious a storm of bullets from adjacent roofs, that for a long time no Texan dared show himself beyond the thick walls, or even near the wooden-shuttered windows. At length, after hours of labor, a few loop-holes were pierced close up under the eaves and a rude platform, on which men could stand, was erected. Now the deadly Texas rifles began to pick their victims from roof and battlement with noticeable effect.

Almost immediately the Mexican fire began to slacken, and soon the Texans, in turn, were able to gain the house-tops, beneath which they had thus far found shelter. To these they dragged bags of sand, and were soon as securely fortified as they had been in the rooms below. Now they fired with such terrible effect that no Mexican dared expose the smallest portion of his body within a radius of one hundred yards, and two of the more advanced batteries were reduced to silence. At the same time the Texans found, to their cost, by attempting to send messengers from one party to the other, that their foes were as watchful for human targets as they themselves were.

So the long day wore away, and night found the weary assailants still penned in their two buildings like rats in a trap. The low-ceiled rooms were filled with sulphurous smoke, and the groans of wounded men rose from all sides. As no provisions had been brought along, and none could be found in the empty houses they had occupied, the Texans were ravenously hungry, but still the storm of bullets swept the street with unabated fury. In the Veramendi house eight wounded men lay on the bare floors, and the position of the entire party seemed so critical that men began to curse their folly in joining so reckless an expedition, and to make gloomy predictions of the fate that must ultimately overtake them.

"Where is Rex Harden, the young fool who

brought us into this fix, by pretending to know more than his elders?" cried a voice; but there was no reply, nor could the lad be found in any part of the building.

"Looks like he for one had paid for his folly with his life," said a grizzled veteran, who, having sons of his own, felt more tenderly towards all boys than did some of the younger men.

At thought of the brave youth, who had so cheerfully shared all their sufferings of that day, lying dead in some dark corner, even the most uncharitable were softened towards his memory, and admitted that his many good qualities more than compensated for his boyish follies.

While they were thus discussing him, there came a sudden pounding on the floor beneath them, and a muffled shout caused them to spring to their feet in terror. Their one thought was, that the building had been undermined, and that they were to be attacked from below, as well as from all sides. Some seized their rifles, while others stood in sullen despair. Then a bit of the floor was slowly lifted, a twinkle of light showed through the aperture, and a voice called up:

"Don't shoot, men; we are friends."

With this the trap-door was flung back, and the very lad whose fate and character they had just been discussing, appeared among them. He bore a lantern, and was followed by half a dozen others, who were recognized as having been left in camp that morning. These were laden with sacks of provisions, and a supply of ammunition to replenish the nearly exhausted Texan stock.

In answer to the questions of his bewildered friends, Rex told them of the passage leading beneath the Veramendi gardens to the river. He had conceived the idea of slipping out through it about sunset, and, if possible, making his way to the camp under cover of darkness, for he knew that without provisions the Texans could not long maintain their position.

Realizing the dangers of his proposed expedition, he would not ask for company, nor would he even mention his plan, for fear of further disheartening his friends in case of. failure. So he had gone away unnoticed, and had finally reached camp in safety. On his way he made the important discovery, that Mexican cavalry were guarding the further end of the very street by which the Texans had entered the city. Thus they were prepared to cut off a retreat, should the latter be rash enough to undertake one through the merciless fire by which their route would be swept.

In spite of these dangers, which Rex clearly explained in General Burleson's camp, half a dozen brave fellows volunteered to return with him as bearers of supplies. Their trip had been made without a challenge, and here they were.

"DON'T SHOOT, MEN; WE ARE FRIENDS."

This was the substance of the story told by Rex Harden, while his famished comrades ate of the food he had brought them. They were very grateful to him, and very proud of what he had done, but it did not occur to them just then to say so. Nor did the young soldier feel that either thanks or praise were called for by his simple performance of a duty. "Any one of them would have done the same thing if they had known what I did about the passage," he said to himself, and there the matter ended so far as he thought of it.

But the results of his daring act were by no means ended with its successful completion. The food that he had brought, and the knowledge that a way of retreat was open to them, so inspired his comrades with new courage, that they had no longer a thought save to continue the struggle until the city should fall into their hands. They also remembered their friends across the bullet-swept street, and determined to open communication with them, that they, too, might share the welcome supplies just brought in. Above all, they rejoiced that there was now a chance of removing their wounded to the comparative comforts and safety of the camp.

While some undertook this humane but arduous and dangerous task, others set to work with a will to dig a trench across the street, through which they might crawl to the Garza house. About midnight it was completed, communication was established, and to Milam's men was extended the relief from hunger and despair that Rex had brought.

On the following day, both sides maintained a steady fire from daylight without accomplishing anything of importance until towards night, when the Texans rushing from the Garza house, stormed and carried a small building some twenty yards away, and thus took an important forward step.

Another night found the situation comparatively unchanged, and was passed by both sides in strengthening their positions. The morning of the 7th of December found a new intrenchment thrown up on the Alamo side of the river, from which a hot fire was poured into the rear of the Veramendi house. This, and the strong batteries commanding the direct route to the plaza, caused Colonel Milam to cast about for a change of base, and a more favorable direction of attack. He sent for Rex, and together they ascended to the house-top, where, by lying flat, they could, with comparative safety, overlook the scene of conflict.

" Which are the strongest of the plaza batteries? " asked Colonel Milam.

" Those commanding the streets by which we entered town," promptly replied Rex.

" And where is its weakest point? "

" At the northwest corner near the priest's house."

" Can you see the priest's house from here? "

" No, sir. Zambrano Row is in the way."

"Which is that?"

"The long building from which comes that steady firing."

"Then we should have to capture it first?"

"Yes, sir. And the houses of Navarro and of Yturri as well."

"But you think they can be taken?"

"I do, sir. The convict troops will never stand for a hand-to-hand fight."

"Good! That settles it. Those houses shall be taken, and the plaza shall be carried from the point you name, or I will die in the attempt; for I am determined to lead every charge between here and there. Come with me, and help explain this new plan to Johnson."

So the commander and his young lieutenant walked together across the bullet-swept street. As the former disdained to stoop behind the sand-bags that had only been piled breast high, Rex followed his example, and both walked with proudly lifted heads. At the very entrance to the Veramendi house, within reach of safety, Colonel Milam, whose face was turned with a smile towards his companion, gave a convulsive spring and fell headlong, his brain pierced by a Mexican bullet.

Rex was instantly on his knees beside him, but already was the dauntless spirit fled, and the name of Benjamin Milam had become a memory to be fondly cherished by all Texans from that day.

Colonel Johnson, instantly summoned, was quickly beside his dead friend; and, across the motionless form, Rex outlined to the new commander the plan of attack that Milam had just decided to adopt.

"It shall be carried out to the letter," cried Johnson. "With Ben Milam's spirit to lead us, and working on the lines he has laid down, we cannot fail."

Twenty men were left to guard the dead, and the others were ordered across the street. When the attacking force was thus consolidated in the Garza house, Johnson announced their leader's death, and told of the plan he had formed. "What say you men?" he cried. "Shall we carry out Ben Milam's last wishes, and follow the lead of his brave spirit to victory?"

For answer there came a yell so loud and fierce, as to be heard above the din of battle even in the Mexican plaza. At the same moment a private soldier named Henry Karnes, snatching a crowbar, sprang forth into the storm of bullets, and with mighty blows crushed in the door of the first of the four buildings Milam had decided to capture.

For a moment the Texans stood aghast at the man's audacity. Then a score of them dashed after him, and in two minutes the house was taken, with every Mexican who had defended it dead or put to flight. An hour later the Navarro house was stormed and captured in a similar manner. On the following morning Zambrano Row fell into the hands of the Texans, after a fierce struggle for possession of each thick-walled apartment of its long range.

The Mexicans were appalled by this steady advance, and sent out their cavalry to attack Burleson's camp, in the hope of drawing off Johnson's men to its defence. But the camp was able to care for itself, and the cavalry were driven back, some of their pursuers even entering the city, and joining their friends in Zambrano Row.

Thus matters stood on the evening of the 8th of December, or at the close of the fourth day of fighting.

CHAPTER XXIV

As darkness settled over the stout little town, that for four days had been the scene of heroic assault and stubborn defence, the din of battle died away, the hot batteries became silent, rifle and musket were laid aside, while fierce-eyed men, smoke begrimmed, and haggard with weariness, flung themselves down in their places to rest. A sullen quiet, intensified by the recent uproar, brooded over the place, and in it those who could not sleep took anxious thought for the morrow. They knew that the crisis had been reached, and that within a few hours more the fate of the city must be decided. On one side the Mexican general, nervously smoking cigarettes, weighed the chances of defence and retreat; while, on the other, a group of stern-faced Americans talked in low tones of the final assault that they hoped would lead to victory. Near them Rex Harden, stretched at length on the blood-stained floor of beaten clay, lay in dreamless sleep.

As the hour approached midnight one of the wakeful group rose and looked at him. "The lad is completely done up," he said, "and no wonder. It seems cruel to disturb him, and I hate to do it; but no one here knows the haunts of the greasers so well as he, and we dare not go without him." So the man, who was a grizzled and battle-stained veteran, touched the sleeper's smooth forehead lightly, and the latter sat up, wide awake.

"Has the time come already? It doesn't seem as though I had more than closed my eyes."

"I don't suppose it does, son," answered the man, "and yet you have slept like the dead for nearly five hours, and in as many minutes more we must start. Take a bite and a sup first, though; for we've keen work to do between this and daylight."

Others of the group who had kept watch were waking other sleepers, and one hundred dim forms were quietly gathering in the black shadows of Zambrano Row. All were heavily armed, and some carried picks, iron bars, or axes. James Bowie was with them, and Johnson. They were to lead this midnight assault.

"Remember Ben Milam, boys! He died for the liberty we still must fight for," said the former in low, but thrilling tones.

Then, without a whisper, and with guarded steps, the company of picked men moved out into the night. Guided by Rex Harden, they took their noiseless way towards the priest's house that stood in a walled enclosure facing the plaza. The low wall was reached without an alarm; but as Rex surmounted it and dropped lightly to the other side, he lighted squarely on the body of a man who lay asleep in its shadow, and who uttered a yell of terror at this rude awakening.

The spell of silence was broken, and, with fierce answering yells, the Texans swarmed over the wall regardless of a heavy fire from the building they sought to gain.

"Give them a volley, boys; then charge!" shouted Bowie, and in a moment Rex, crazed with excitement, found himself in a line of yelling men, all of whom were racing across the enclosure directly in the face of those blazing muskets—five minutes, or it might have been an hour, for all the lad knew, of curses and crashing blows, lightning flashes and thunders, shrieks and yells, and then all was over. The convict soldiers who had filled the house poured from it in hurried flight, while the Texans hastened their steps with a final volley and a great shout of victory. Then they set to work barricading doors and windows, piercing loop-holes through the thick walls, and in other ways preparing to defend their prize.

The fire of the enemy had by this time become general; and so terrific was the uproar that it seemed as though every Mexican gun must be in active play. Artillery thundered, musketry rattled incessantly, and though but few shots struck the building for which they were intended, the air was filled with screaming missiles. Unmindful of this uproar, the Texans labored steadily at their barricades, until, with the coming of dawn, their fortress was practically impregnable. And it commanded the plaza in which the enemy's strength had been concentrated.

Since capturing the building the Texans had not fired a shot; and now they stood with ready rifles, awaiting the daylight that should direct their aim.

Gradually the Mexican fire slackened until it finally ceased; and with the growing light the Texas riflemen looked in vain for a foe. The plaza was deserted, not a gunner manned its silent batteries, not a soldier wearing the hated uniform of Santa Anna was to be seen.

Yes, there was one slowly crossing the plaza in their direction, and he bore the white flag of surrender. General Martin Cos, brother-in-law to the Mexican President, had retreated to the Alamo with fourteen hundred men ; and from there he sent in a flag of truce. The fight was ended; brave Ben Milam's plan had been crowned with success, and San Antonio, the stronghold of Western Texas, was won to the cause of freedom.

At first the three hundred Americans, hollow-cheeked, with the terrible strain of their four days' fight, unkempt, and powder-stained, could not believe the evidence of their senses, and each sought in the faces of his comrades the assurance that what he saw was true. But there was no mistake about that white flag; no enemy was in sight, and his silent batteries were clearly deserted. Yes, the city was certainly theirs to enter at will and do with as they pleased.

Their moment of doubt was succeeded by a wild rush into the empty plaza, where in mad jubilation they embraced and danced, yelled themselves hoarse with cheering, caused the church bells to ring peals of joyous music, and, for a short space, acted more like crazy men than rational beings. Some one procured a white blanket, rudely chopped out a great star from a blue flannel shirt, and for the first time in the history of San Antonio, a lone-star flag floated from the tower of the cathedral. At sight of the glorious emblem, the mad uproar of jubilation broke out afresh, and no voice sought to stay it.

Soon afterwards the troops from camp came streaming into the city, gazing with eager curiosity at the manifold signs of the recent struggle, and looking with envious eyes upon the heroes of the assault, every one of whom walked with a free stride and proudly uplifted head.

The inhabitants of the town peered fearfully at the stalwart victors from behind closed doors and shuttered windows, but gaining courage, as they saw no sign of pillage, they finally ventured forth, until swart-faced men, women, and little children were mingling freely with the victors and even sharing their rejoicings. In the Mexican throng, Rex found his friend, the little 'Rillo, and made the child supremely happy by going with him to his father, whom he assured that he might resume his business without fears of molestation from the Americans.

That same morning brave Ben Milam was buried with all the honors his comrades could bestow, in the Veramendi garden, close to the spot where the fatal bullet had overtaken him. A great company assembled to see him laid to rest, and among the foremost at his grave was the lad to whom, more than to any other, was due the capture of San Antonio. Tears stood in his eyes, and his heart was very heavy when the final volley rang across the soldier's grave; but as he turned sadly away, his grief was changed to a sudden joy. Loving arms were flung about him, and he heard as in a dream the voice of his own dear father, uttering fervent thanks for this, his boy, who had been lost, but was found.

" They sent me to New Orleans on a mission, son, and only upon my return to San Felipe did I learn that you had disappeared so absolutely that it was not known whether you were dead or living. I came to unravel, if I could, your fate, and find you, not only alive, but a hero. From all sides I hear words of praise for my boy, and my cup of happiness is indeed running over."

Impatient as the Hardens now were to leave the city, they could not do so at once, for they must wait to witness the final triumph, and three days later it came. Martin Cos, having pledged his word that neither he, his officers, nor the troops under his command, should ever again take up arms for the subjugation of Texas, was allowed to depart with such of his army as chose to follow him.

So, on the 14th of December, the flag of Mexico was hauled down from the Alamo. The flag of free Texas took its place, and the glittering but humbled army of General Cos marched away towards the distant Rio Grande. Three hundred of his soldiers had chosen to remain behind and cast their lot with Texas, while there also remained to the victors, twenty-one pieces of artillery, one thousand muskets, a great quantity of ammunition, besides clothing and stores of all kinds.

Having obtained this signal victory, and driven the enemy from the fair land that they claimed as their own, the Texas volunteers dispersed to their homes, leaving Colonel Johnson with a small body of troops to hold the city he had won.

"Now, son, let us go," said Squire Harden, as, with full hearts, he and Rex watched the disappearance of the last Mexican troop. "There are others who, though they doubtless know ere this of your safety, are longing to greet you. I left your mother and the girls at San Felipe, but with permission to come on as far as Gonzales, where they must now impatiently await us."

So Squire Harden and his son, James Bowie, Deaf Smith, and several others, whose homes lay in that direction, rode merrily eastward, along the Gonzales trail. Rex was, of course, mounted on his beloved Tawny, who seemed to know as well as any one that he was going home.

"We will stop at the old ranch for the night," said Squire Harden, "though I fear we shall find it but a melancholy camping-place. It looked desolate enough as I came past on my way west, though I hadn't the time to stop, nor the heart to enter the house."

The short winter day was fading into twilight when the party came in sight of the Rancho Herrera, and for a moment it seemed as though they must be mistaken in the locality. Instead of the gloomy, deserted building they had expected to find, every window in the great house was ablaze with light. Even the outlying quarters appeared to be occupied, and cheery camp-fires glowed in every direction.

"Some scoundrels have dared take possession and make themselves at home," cried the squire, angrily ; "but we'll quickly rout them out. Come on, boys, and help an old man regain possession of the home his son has fought to save."

Thus saying, he dashed forward, and the others followed him ; but Tawny outstripped them all.

Thus when the irate squire reined sharply up before the entrance to his own house, it was to find Rex clasped in his mother's arms, with Mabel, Nelita Veramendi, Aunty Day, and a dozen servants clustered joyously about them.

CHAPTER XXV

"WE could not wait at Gonzales, Ellis, when we heard the glorious news," explained Mrs. Harden, when the tumult of greeting had somewhat subsided. "It seemed as though we must come on, at least as far as our own home, and prepare a welcome for our boy. Besides, such a fine escort was offered us that we really couldn't find an excuse for refusing to accept it."

"Did you try very hard?" laughed the squire.

"Yes, of course. But we couldn't, because it was— Why, where can he have gone? Oh, here he is!"

At that moment a graceful, soldierly appearing young fellow, apparently but little older than Rex, stepped from the porch, and advanced with outstretched hand.

"Will Travis!" shouted Rex, springing to meet him. "Dear old Will! Oh! how glad I am to see you!"

"Colonel William Barret Travis, of the Texas regulars, if you please; at present, superintendent of the recruiting bureau," said the young soldier, with assumed pomposity, as he grasped the hand of his old schoolmate and well-loved friend. "I believe," he continued, "I have the honor of addressing Lieutenant Rector Harden, also of the Texas regular army."

"Not exactly," laughed Rex. "It is true that some of the fellows at Gonzales did elect me to an office in a moment of enthusiasm. As they were only volunteers, though, who have already given up soldiering and gone home, I expect my military position has gone with them, leaving me only a high private in the home guards."

"Not if you will accept this," rejoined Travis, holding out an official-looking paper as he spoke.

As Rex examined the document with a puzzled air, his friend continued :

"It is all right, old man, and you needn't look at it as though it were a sentence of banishment back to school. It is a genuine O. K. commission as lieutenant in the regular army of Texas, signed by Samuel Houston, Commander-in-chief. The recommendation came from Colonel Milam, and was written the very evening before you all started in to capture San Antonio. How I wish I had been with you ! but with good luck I'll have a chance to do some fighting yet. General Houston wrote out the commission at once, and requested me to offer it to you. Therefore, Lieutenant Harden, I have the honor, etc., etc."

"But what is the use of an army, now?" asked Rex. "We have driven the Mexicans out of Texas, and General Cos has given his parole not to fight against us any more."

"Ho, ho!" laughed Travis. "And they won't come back again with an army ten times as strong, and Santa Anna won't lift a finger to recover Texas, and old Cos won't forget all about his parole as soon as it is convenient to do so, and we haven't got a bitter fight ahead of us before winning our independence, — oh no, not at all! But all those things are going to happen, old man; and we've got to prepare for them while we are given time for preparation. To begin with, we want every son of Texas who has had any sort of a military training to help us work up our splendid fighting material that now exists in the shape of raw recruits. So, my boy, you'll please accept this commission without another word, and walk in to supper with such dignity as becomes an officer in the regular army of Texas. If I can't enlist my best friends, why am I chief of the recruiting service, I'd like to know?"

During this conversation, these two had drawn a little to one side, while the remainder of the joyous company had either gone to the corrals with their horses, or entered the house. At the supper-table, where all were shortly afterwards assembled, Travis announced the young lieutenant's acceptance of his commission, which was loudly cheered, and made a short address upon the present condition and future prospects of Texas. He repeated what he had said to Rex, and made an earnest appeal to every man present to hold himself in constant readiness for a call to the field. Squire Harden and James Bowie talked in similar strain; and thus while this gathering was still the most joyful that the Rancho Herrera had ever witnessed, its mirth was tempered by sober thought for the future.

On the following morning, while those of the party who were to continue their journey were collected before the house bidding farewell to those who were to remain, there came a striking confirmation of the warning words spoken the evening before. A very humble appearing group of wayfarers, consisting of a man on foot leading a donkey on which was seated a woman holding a child, had halted in front of the ranch. They were Mexicans, and, as they looked irresolutely at the horsemen, apparently afraid to approach them, and yet anxious to do so, one of the latter rode out to inquire what they wanted.

A moment later he returned looking puzzled. "The man first said that he wished to see El Tonto," he announced, "but when I told him there were no fools about here, he apologized, and said he meant the son of the Señor Harden. At that I came mighty near knocking him down, and will do so now if the lieutenant gives the word."

"Not on any account," Rex said. "El Tonto is the name I have answered to for the past month, and probably that chap never heard me called by any other. I wonder, though, how he knew who I was? I thought only Tejada was aware of my real identity."

"Suppose you go and ask him," suggested Travis.

"A bright idea that was flashing through my own mind at that very moment," laughed Rex, starting towards the waiting group by the roadside.

As he drew near to them, those who watched were amazed to see him advance eagerly, and shake hands in the most cordial manner, first with the man and then with the woman. Then they talked earnestly together for several minutes, after which he started back, bringing the strangers with him.

"Father," he cried as they approached, "this is Sebastien Tejada, who not only saved my life, but did everything in his power to make me comfortable while I was a prisoner in San Antonio. And this is his wife, who also did me a good turn at Espada, you know, and the baby is the little Sebastien."

"For your sake they are more than welcome," said the squire, heartily; "but what fetches them here?"

"To seek safety for themselves, father, and to bring us a warning. Sebastien was one of the troops who preferred to remain a Texan rather than go with Cos to Mexico. The night after their surrender the Mexicans camped at the mission. There this woman overheard the general say that, as a promise made to heretics was not binding, he should speedily return with another army. Then he should make it his especial business to kill every Mexican who had chosen the cause of freedom, as well as every Texan who had borne arms against Santa Anna. After the troops had left and her husband reappeared at the mission, the woman told him what she had heard, and begged him to fly to some place of safety. As Tejada believes that Cos really will return and carry out his threats, at least so far as the Mexicans who have joined our cause are concerned, he readily consented to do so, and remembering me, has come to us for advice and assistance."

"Both of which they shall have," said Squire Harden, giving the Mexican's brown hand a friendly grasp. "They shall stay here for the present, and if Cos ever is so forgetful of his plighted honor as to attempt to carry out his threat, then will I endeavor to provide for their further safety. But I cannot think that even he will descend to such baseness."

"He will, though!" exclaimed Travis, "and this man's story only goes to confirm what I said last night. So, my friends, I beg of you to be on the alert, and remember that those who would win Texas have still to fight for her. Now, squire, I must be off; so, au revoir, for a time. Rex, be sure that you report to Houston early in the new year. Good-by, men, till we meet again."

Thus saying, the dashing young officer clapped spurs to his horse and rode away, while those who watched him out of sight had little thought that, in a few short weeks, he would have passed from among them forever, leaving behind him a fame as undying as history itself.

The breaking up of that company was quickly followed by the assembling of another at the same place, for the Christmas festivities of the Rancho Herrera never lacked for guests. In spite of the anxieties of that year, or perhaps on account of them, the fun and frolic of the season had never been so enjoyed or kept up with such spirit. Will Travis was there, and James Bowie, the first coming from his recruiting-station at San Felipe, and the other from Goliad, where he was raising a force for the invasion of Mexico. All the hard-riding Texas youths from fifty miles about, with their sisters and sweethearts, were gathered under the hospitable roofs of the great ranch. With them came many strangers from the States, who had volunteered to aid in the struggle for freedom, and to whom the occasion was a fascinating novelty.

The days were filled with shooting-matches, hunting, horse-racing, and feasting ; the nights with music and dancing. Nor did our young lieutenant neglect this opportunity for enrolling a number of his festive friends into a military company, and preparing them, with daily drills, for the emergency of war that all felt might arise with the coming year.

After this happy season was ended the ranch had hardly settled to its everyday routine, before it was again thrown into a flutter of excitement. This time the cause was a visit from the most famous of Texans, General Sam Houston. As commander-in-chief of the army, he was on his way to Goliad to direct the movements of the forces gathering in the southwest for an invasion of Mexico. This future President of the Republic was at that time a man in the prime of life, possessed of a well-informed mind, a clear brain, great physical powers, and a commanding presence. A single glance at his resolute, clean-shaven face showed him to be a natural leader of men, and Rex Harden, who now met him for the first time, at once yielded him the homage of implicit confidence and honest admiration. He in turn was so well pleased with the young lieutenant that he appointed him a member of his staff and took him away to Goliad.

After that, for another month the peace of the ranch was only disturbed by rumors and counter-rumors brought by passing travellers. Then, about the middle of February, the quiet household was startled late one night by the sound of rapidly galloping hoofs. Evidently a horseman was approaching who rode with urgent speed. They had barely time to exchange glances of anxious inquiry when the door was flung open, and Rex, flushed and trembling with hard riding, stood before them.

Ere they could utter the joyous welcome that sprang to their lips, he announced his news. "Santa Anna himself, with an army of six thousand men, has crossed the Rio Grande, and is marching toward San Antonio!"

CHAPTER XXVI

NEVER had Texas been so ill prepared to resist an invasion, as when Santa Anna, most able, most vindictive, and most merciless of Mexicans, led an army across the frontier to make a terrible example of the people who had dared declare for liberty. The provisional governor of the state was engaged in a bitter quarrel with the Council of Safety — each countermanded the other's orders until none knew which to obey. Sam Houston, the strongest man in Texas, had been recalled from the southwest, temporarily relieved from command of the army, and sent off to make a treaty with an Indian tribe.

In the southwest a few hundred armed men at Goliad, San Patricio, Victoria, and Refugio, under leadership of Johnson, Fannin, Bowie, and Grant. each of whom aspired to the supreme command, proposed invading Mexico. Only eighty men were left at San Antonio, and these, stripped of horses, provisions, ammunition, clothing, blankets, and medical stores by their comrades who had gone south, were in a pitiful state of weakness and destitution.

The post was so defenceless and ill prepared to resist an attack that one of General Houston's latest acts as commander-in-chief was to send James Bowie and thirty men to that point, with orders to demolish the fortifications, and transfer the artillery to a place of safety. For want of teams with which to remove the guns, this order could not be obeyed. So Bowie remained in command of the city, impatiently awaiting the aid that he urgently requested, and doing everything in his power to inspire his scanty garrison with confidence as well as to provide for their more pressing needs. Finally even his splendid constitution broke down beneath a crushing weight of anxiety, disappointment, and overwork, and he lay in the Veramendi house tossing with fever. At this juncture Colonel Travis was relieved from his recruiting duties at San Felipe, and despatched with a score of men to San Antonio to take command in place of fever-stricken Bowie.

All this time there were no funds available for the payment of troops, or the equipping of an army. The people were paralyzed by the quarrels of their chosen rulers. The men dared not leave their homes unprotected, and so declined service in the field. They also seemed to think that there would be enough volunteers from the United States to fight the battles of Texas, and win her freedom. This was the hope of those who admitted the possibility of an invasion from Mexico, and a necessity for further fighting. As many more declared that there would be no war, and that Santa Anna would never dare cross the Rio Grande.

Holding these conflicting opinions, the people still awaited hopefully the meeting of a convention that had been summoned to assemble at Washington on the Brazos by the 1st of March. This convention was to declare the independence of Texas, adopt a constitution, and under it elect officers. When this was done, all would be well, and Texas would set forth on a career of unexampled prosperity. So the majority of Texans believed, and they also looked to this convention to provide by some means for the safety of the state.

In the meantime the Mexican President, knowing nothing of conventions and caring less, was straining every nerve to assemble a powerful and well-equipped army whose first act should be to regain possession of San Antonio. At the Rio Grande he was joined by General Cos, and his paroled troops. Santa Anna at once ordered these to face about and march back into Texas, which order, in spite of his pledged word, Martin Cos obeyed without a protest.

A friendly scout riding night and day across the desert lying east of the Rio Grande carried news of the invasion to Goliad, and as he entered the little town, reeling from exhaustion, his horse fell dead beneath him. The same messenger brought word that General Urrea, with one thousand men, was

ordered to advance from Matamoras upon San
Patricio, Refugio, and Goliad.   After the small
forces at these places were wiped out the Mexican
armies were to unite, and sweep across Texas like a
devastating flood.

This was the startling news that Rex Harden had
brought from Goliad, and which he was commissioned to carry with all speed to San Antonio.
Mounted on Tawny the tireless, he had covered
ninety miles in less than ten hours.   Now with one
hour for rest and refreshment, he must again be off
so as to reach his destination by daylight.

"I don't believe that there is another horse in
Texas could have done it, father," said the lad, with
honest pride.

"I don't believe there is, son.   But what are you
going to do after you reach San Antonio?"

"Ride on whatever errand Travis may send me,
or stay and fight beside him if he so desires."

"But with his handful of men he hasn't a ghost
of a chance against Santa Anna."

"Behind the walls of one of the missions he might
hold the Mexicans in check until the country could
be aroused and a force raised for his relief, since
Santa Anna would never dare come on leaving
Travis in his rear.   Don't you think so, sir?"

"There is some sense in that.   But who is going
to arouse the men of Texas, and collect this army
you speak of?"

"You are, sir, or at least I hope you will make the attempt. Fannin and Johnson and all of them are agreed that if it can be done, you are the one member of the council who can do it. So they beg of you to make the effort. Part of my present errand was to tell you this, and that is why I was allowed to come by the longer road."

"I'll do what I can, son; but I fear it won't be much, for I don't believe the angel Gabriel could rouse our people to action before the meeting of the convention. I was going to leave for Washington next week, anyway; but now we'll start in the morning. You and the girls can be ready by that time, can't you, wife?"

"I didn't know you intended us to accompany you to Washington, Ellis!" exclaimed Mrs. Harden, who with Mabel and Nelita had been eager listeners to this conference.

"I did not, my dear; but I do. What use should I be in Washington if I had the thought of you left here in the face of danger to distract my mind?"

"But, Ellis, I can't leave my home again. I did not believe it was necessary before, and now I am confident it is not. Santa Anna surely does not war with women, and no Mexican would harm a daughter of the Veramendi. So with Nelita here, our home will certainly be safe; while if we should desert it, the first vagabond who came along might destroy it. Besides, the Mexicans may never pass

San Antonio; and if they do, we shall have warning in ample time to escape.   Rex will be close at hand, and so will Bowie, to say nothing of Will Travis and his brave fellows.   No, dear, you will do your part much better without us, and we shall be safer here without you ; for you would want to defend our home with your strength, while we shall do it more effectively with our very helplessness."

With these and similar arguments the resolute woman finally carried her point, so that, by the time Rex was ready to resume his journey to San Antonio, Squire Harden was also on horseback and ready to start in the opposite direction.

Even as they were bidding farewell to the dear ones who were to remain behind, a sound of hoof-beats from the direction of Gonzales announced a new arrival, and all waited with anxious interest to see who it might be.

In another moment a middle-aged stranger, who by the light streaming from an open doorway was seen to be clad wholly in buckskin, rode up and in-quired if this were the Rancho Herrera.

" It is, sir," replied the proprietor.

" Then mebbe I have the pleasure of speaking to Colonel Harden ? "

" Squire Harden is the title more generally be-stowed upon me, though I have not the shadow of a claim to it."

" Squire or colonel, it's much the same, for no man

gits a handle to his name without arning it one way or another. Now, I never riz to be rightly more than a cap'n under old Hickory, but the boys will have it that I'd ought to been made colonel, and so Colonel Crockett is what I answers to from the Arkansaw to the Potomac."

"Not Colonel David Crockett of Tennessee?"

"The same, sir, at your sarvice, and as hot now for a scrimmage as ever I was. That's why I'm down here in Texas ; for they say up in the States that there's a right smart chance of old Santy Ann coming this 'er' way, though there's a plenty to bet he won't dast do it."

"Colonel Crockett, I am proud to meet you, sir," exclaimed Squire Harden, urging his horse to the other's side and extending his hand. "I've long known you by reputation as an honest man and a brave soldier. If you have come to aid Texas in her time of need, she has every reason to be grateful to you. Nor could your arrival have been more timely; for my son here has just brought word that Santa Anna has already crossed the Rio Grande at the head of an army with which he first intends to retake San Antonio. At this moment my boy is about to ride west to notify Travis of the Mexican advance, while I am about to travel east by way of Gonzales to rouse the country. Under the circumstances I know you will excuse my apparent lack of courtesy in leaving you ; but if you will accept the hospitality of the Rancho Herrera as extended by my wife, you will be made more than welcome."

"Squire, you do me proud, and I thank you same as if I'd camped in your ranch for a month. But if Santy Ann is really travelling towards San Antonio, it's high time I was making a trail to the same place so as to be on hand to say 'howdy' when he gets thar. So if you've no objection, squire, 'stead of lighting as I had intended, I'll just ride on in company with your boy, and not detain you another minute from the duty you have undertaken. Evening, ladies! So long, squire! Come on, young man."

Thus saying, this quaint character, then at the height of his fame as a stump orator, a backwoods politician, a fearless fighter, and the deadliest rifle shot in America, put spurs to his horse and rode away into the darkness from which he had emerged but a minute before.

With a quick "Good-by, mother! Good-by, father! Good-by, girls!" Rex leaped on Tawny's back and followed him; while, after listening a moment to the hoof-beats of the two steeds, the brave old squire also bade his dear ones farewell and started to bear onward through the night the momentous message brought by his son.

Q

CHAPTER XXVII

THE OATH OF NO SURRENDER

In spite of Tawny's long journey from Goliad, one hour of rest and feeding had put him in such condition that he speedily overtook the horse ridden by David Crockett.

"You're sure, son, thar's no mistake about old Santy Ann being headed this 'er' way?" asked the latter, as Rex slackened Tawny's pace to ride beside him.

"There is no doubt of it, sir; and unless he changes his plans, he will certainly appear before San Antonio within three or four days."

"Then I'm in luck at last," rejoined he of the buckskin suit, "though I must say I was beginning to think I should be disappointed after all. Back in Arkansaw everybody was sartin thar was going to be the biggest kind of a fight down here; but, the further south I come, the less I heard of it. Lately, right here in Texas, I've been told the war was all over, and the greasers would never dare show their faces this side the Rio Grande again. So I began to think perhaps I was barking up the wrong tree after all. I'll confess I was mighty low spirited when I pulled up at your paw's place awhile ago; but now I'm all right again in my mind."

" Are you, then, so very fond of fighting, sir? "

" Son, I'm the peaceablest man you ever see, 'cepting when it comes to a question of right or wrong : then I'm a fighter for the right every time. I always say to the boys, ' Be sure you're right, then go ahead and never mind the consequences.' That's been my motter ever since I can remember, and I expect it'll be the death of me some day."

" How so, sir? "

" Because, boy, thar's so many wrongs to be fought agin and whipped into rights, that I can't expect to live long enough to see 'em all settled. So I'll probably die fighting for some one or the other of them. I hope it'll turn out that 'er' way, too, for I couldn't a bear to die peaceful long as thar was necessary fighting to be done."

" That sounds very much like Don Quixote," laughed Rex.

" Don't think I'm acquainted with the gentleman. I reckon, though, he must be some sort of a greaser, from the name."

" He was a Spaniard," admitted Rex, " who went about in search of wrongs that he might set right."

" That don't sound like a greaser," reflected Crockett; " for I never heard of one of the breed going into a fight 'cept 'twas on the wrong side."

"But there have been good Spaniards," argued Rex.

"Mebbe thar has been some with good intentions, son, but always mistook in their ideas of right and wrong, — leastways I never met up with any other kind, nor do I think I'm likely to on this particular hunt."

In listening to the quaint conceptions of this strange man, Rex found time pass so quickly that the distance to San Antonio had never seemed so short. By sunrise the little city lay before them seemingly as peaceful as though no sound nor threat of war had ever disturbed its serenity.

The sun shone brightly, the air was deliciously mild, the timber of the river bottom was clothed in the green gauze of earliest spring, and the whole scene was one of such quiet beauty, that the tall hunter from Arkansas declared it to be one of the likeliest places to fight for that he had ever run across.

Both travellers received the warmest possible welcome from Travis, — Rex on account of the strong friendship existing between them, and Colonel Crockett because of his wide-spread reputation. At the news brought by the former, the young commander's face grew very grave, and he said at once :

"If Santa Anna comes now, there is no possible chance of holding the town against him, since we have neither men, powder, nor provisions. Colonel, you have just crossed the entire state; what hope is there for reënforcements?"

"A mighty slim chance, colonel, I'm afeared, till after convention meets. You see the whole country is plumb crazy over politics just now, and they won't think of a thing else till after the first of March. Then, if the convention does the right thing, and puts Sam Houston back as commander-in-chief, thar'll be some show, for that man will bring help if he has to come alone. Then thar'll be fun too; for when him and old Santy Ann gets into a scrimmage, one of 'em is going to be almightily licked, and that one ain't going to be Sam Houston, nuther."

"Then you think that if we can hold out until the first of March, aid will be sent us?"

"I do, colonel; and moreover, if you can check Santy Ann's advance till then, you will not only give Texas time to wake up, but you will give hundreds of defenceless families a chance to escape to places of safety."

"Then, gentlemen, I pledge you my word that, so long as I live and an enemy remains in sight, I will never surrender this place nor leave it."

As he uttered these words, the face of the young commander took on an expression of fixed resolve and high purpose, that was never forgotten by those who saw it.

"Colonel!" exclaimed Crockett, "you've spoke like a man, and expressed sentiments that is likewise mine. Such being the case, I'll back you up till death in maintaining of 'em, and thar's my hand on it."

In the firm hand-clasp that followed, a friendship was cemented between those widely differing specimens of western civilization, that was not dissolved during the remainder of their lives.

"Now let's go in and tell the news to Bowie," said Travis. Then, for the first time Rex realized that their slow walk had led them to the Veramendi house; and that the compact he had just witnessed had been made on the very spot where brave Ben Milam gave up his life in the cause of freedom.

They found Bowie still in bed and nursed by a Mexican woman who was indebted to him for past kindnesses. Although slowly regaining strength, he was filled with the impatient irritableness of a convalescent, and bewailed his helpless condition. At sight of his friends he visibly brightened, and he expressed a sincere pleasure at again meeting with David Crockett. But the best tonic that could have been given him was the great news brought by Rex.

"Santa Anna across the Rio Grande!" he cried. "Then, boys, I mustn't lie here an hour longer." With this he sat up in bed and continued excitedly, "Travis, you won't let him have San Antonio without fighting for it, will you?"

"No, James, I will not," answered the other. "Nor then, if I can help it; for I have just pledged my word never to surrender nor retreat, and friend Crockett here has promised to stay with me to the end."

"You must let me in on that, boys," exclaimed Bowie, his pale cheeks flushed with excitement, "for I couldn't retreat if I would, and I wouldn't if I could; while as for surrender, the word is not allowed in the Bowie family. So give me your hands, you two, and let me swear the same oath you have taken."

Thus those three brave hearts stood pledged to die together, rather than surrender or betray the trust reposed in them, and each instinctively felt that the spirit of Ben Milam was witness to their compact.

"But, Will! Bowie! Colonel Crockett! Am I to be left out?" cried Rex Harden, in grieved tones. "Do you doubt that I too am ready to die for Texas?"

"Not for an instant, my dear fellow," rejoined Travis, earnestly. "You have already faced death for the cause oftener than any one of us, and so proved your devotion beyond words. We know that you are with us soul and body; but I can't allow you to take oath never to leave this place so long as an enemy remains in sight, for that is the very thing I am most likely to want you to do. None but you can ride Tawny, no horse in Texas

can cover ground as he can, and consequently there
is no one else prepared to render such splendid
service as a courier. In that capacity I shall rely
upon you, and I hope not only to have you leave
San Antonio, but return to it again, more than once,
before the result of the impending struggle is decided. So, old man, though we count you as one of
us, you must not assume a pledge that might interfere with your greatest usefulness."

The others agreeing that Travis was right, Rex
was forced to submit to their decision, and so was
kept from taking an oath that would have ultimately
cost him his life.

Bowie having been persuaded to remain quiet and
save his feeble strength until the Mexican army
should actually appear, and Rex having earned a
long sleep, Travis and Crockett started off to see
what could be done towards strengthening the fortifications. Although, after their inspection, both
agreed that much ought to be done in the way of
preparation, and could be done with adequate means,
Travis quickly convinced his companion that nothing
would be done. He did this by calling a sergeant
and ordering him to turn out his squad for work in
the trenches, telling him at the same time of the
Mexican approach.

" Of course I'll order the men out, colonel, if
you say so," replied the sergeant; " but not one
of my squad, nor yet of the whole detachment,

will lift a hand to work on the fortifications, or do anything else except fight. That's the only thing they'll do without pay; and I don't believe they'll stay here and starve much longer on the chance of that, if it doesn't come mighty quick. There's not a night that I don't expect to see the whole command desert, and I'm not sure but what I'll go with them. So, colonel, if you want to have a fighting man left in the town to-morrow morning, I would advise you not to insist upon that order."

"Very well, sergeant," said Travis, smiling grimly, "I withdraw it; but for the sake of Texas, use your influence to induce the men to stick it out a few days longer."

"You see how matters stand," he added bitterly, turning to Crockett. "I have only one hundred and fifty men, all told, for the defence of this, the most important post on our frontier. Many of them are sick, and they have not received one cent of pay since enlisting. They have not drawn a single full ration of anything, are poorly supplied with ammunition, and are actually suffering for want of clothing, blankets, and medicines. I know they will fight like devils when the time comes for fighting; but I know also that what the sergeant has just told us is true, and that to compel them to work would be to give the signal for a general dispersion to their homes."

"Colonel," replied the rugged backwoodsman,

"I appreciate the situation, and sympathize with you. At the same time, it is comforting to remember that desperate men make desperate fighters. Out of just such hopeless situations as this have come the most glorious results. Valley Forge was one of them."

Four days after this, Rex and his stanch friend, Colonel Crockett, who had been on a short scouting expedition on the Leredo road, dashed breathlessly into town shortly before noon, with the thrilling announcement that they had seen and been fired at by the advanced guard of the Mexican army.

This news was received by the Americans in grim silence, and by the Mexican population with ill-concealed exultation. An hour later, a group of plumed and glittering horsemen appeared on the crest of a low ridge a mile west of the town. There they halted for a survey of the scene before them. Santa Anna had indeed arrived, and the struggle for Texas was to be renewed with greater fury than ever.

CHAPTER XXVIII

AN EXPRESS FROM THE ALAMO

No reënforcements had reached San Antonio; and, as it was evidently impossible to hold the town against the army gathered before it, Travis gave orders to retire to the Alamo, the semi-ruinous old mission across the river. There he had succeeded in partially repairing the walls, and in mounting on them fourteen of the Mexican guns left by General Cos.

Obeying this order, the little band of Americans filed across the only bridge spanning the San Antonio, up the gentle slope beyond, and disappeared within the Alamo as the enemy's advance entered the opposite side of the town. Some of the Texan sick were borne on litters; but James Bowie insisted on rising from his bed, dressing, and riding on horseback at the head of his own company.

The retreating force had so little in the way of provisions to carry with them, that they were forced to raid every house within reach, and take what they could find. In this way they secured a small quantity of corn and a herd of thirty beef cattle.

This was all; and when it should be exhausted, the end must speedily come.

In striking contrast to this pathetic outgoing of the Texans was the gorgeous incoming of Santa Anna and his troops. Most of these were the flower of the Mexican army; and as regiment after regiment of dashing lancers, heavy dragoons, and sturdy infantry swept into the plaza, while batteries of artillery rumbled through the narrow streets, the awe-stricken spectators held up their hands at the audacity of the Texans in daring to await the onslaught of such a force.

"To defy El Presidente is to war with Heaven itself. It is the same thing!" they exclaimed, piously crossing themselves. Then they turned away to prepare for the fiestas, such as cock-fights, horse-racing, eating, drinking, and dancing, that would surely follow the coming of the Mexican army.

Besides men and guns, the invaders brought with them hundreds of mule loads of baggage and provisions; while their camp followers, fully one-half of whom were women, formed an army by themselves. Thus in one short hour San Antonio de Bexar was transformed from a stagnant frontier town, garrisoned by a handful of ragged, hungry men, into a bustling metropolis, thronged with people, and full of glittering activity. No wonder its Mexican population hailed the change with rapture, and anticipated with pleasure seeing the white-faced gringos driven away forever.

Only three of the dark-skinned race had accompanied the Americans into the Alamo, and two of these were women in attendance upon the sick. The third, a man, was no other than Manuel Peralta, the zapatero, now so recovered of his lameness as to dispense altogether with crutches. Believing that the Texans who had driven Cos from San Antonio were strong enough to hold the place forever as an American town, this man had trimmed his sails according to what appeared to him the most favorable breeze.

He had loudly welcomed the victors to his pulqueria and professed himself an ardent Texan patriot to whom no name was so hateful as that of Santa Anna. He scorned to associate with those of his own race and treated them with such contempt as to win their bitter enmity. Thus he succeeded in making his saloon a favorite resort for bibulous Texans, and in acquiring a very tidy sum of money.

Great was Manuel Peralta's consternation when another Mexican army appeared before San Antonio. To save himself from his jubilant neighbors, who threatened to have not only his money but his life, he fled with his American friends to the Alamo, leaving only the brave little 'Rillo, who was so generally liked that none would harm him, in charge of the pulqueria. In the Alamo, Peralta especially attached himself to Rex, as representing the master whom he had formerly served; and our lad, never doubting the man's sincerity, good-naturedly tolerated his presence.

Entering San Antonio at noon of February 23d, 1836, Santa Anna at once sent an officer to demand the unconditional surrender of the Alamo; but to him Travis only made answer with a cannon-shot of defiance.

Furious with rage and burning to avenge this insult, the Mexican commander ordered a blood-red flag to be displayed above the Cathedral as a sign that in the coming struggle no quarter would be allowed and no mercy shown to rebels. At the same time such batteries as could be brought to bear on the Alamo opened fire. As these guns were only light field-pieces, they did no particular damage,. and the defenders of the old mission were content to reply to them with occasional shots at favorable opportunities.

That night a small party of Texans, led by Lieutenant Harden, sallied out and succeeded in setting fire to a number of straw and wooden huts that had afforded concealment to the Mexican sharp-shooters. As the blaze lighted the heavens, the Mexican camp buzzed like a beehive and a storm of bullets swept across the illuminated space. Battery after battery joined in the harmless uproar, which was continued until the last flame of the brief conflagration had expired and long after the incendiaries had gained the shelter of their walls.

On the following day the bombardment was kept up from daylight to dark, but always from such a safe distance that Crockett was led to declare he didn't believe the greasers meant to fight, or dared to fight, or had any fight in 'em.

On the morning of the 25th, however, Santa Anna himself crossed the river at the head of a strong battalion, for the purpose of planting a battery within three hundred yards of the main gateway of the Alamo. They approached under cover of a heavy fire, which Travis forbade his men to answer until the Mexicans had advanced as far as they would. Then the guns of the Alamo, double-shotted with grape, and the long-barrelled Texas rifles rang out together, with such terrible effect that the battalion of Matamoras, torn to ribbons, broke, and fled panic-stricken to the bridge. The battalion of Ximines was hurried to their support, and a second advance was ordered; but again the Mexicans were swept back by the deadly fire of rifles.

Santa Anna, black with passion and raging like a madman, called out battalion after battalion of fresh troops, but with no avail. The unerring precision of the Texan fire, for which every rifle was carefully aimed, and in which every bullet found its mark, was so demoralizing that finally the Mexican troops could no longer be forced within its range. So the attempt to plant a battery on the desired spot was abandoned, and one was established at the garita instead. At the same time Mexican cavalry patrols were so posted, that Santa Anna believed he had effectually cut off all communication between the Alamo and the outside world.

In spite of these precautions, the Texans made successful forays night after night, for fuel and forage. In this way they also ascertained that a way of retreat from their perilous position was still open to them, should they care to avail themselves of it. But they did not, for all were now animated by the spirit of their fiery young leader, and shared his determination never to retreat. Besides, they could not leave their sick and wounded behind. And so the question was never even considered. Among those whose helplessness called forth this noble self-sacrifice was Bowie, whose recent exertions had brought on a relapse of his fever.

The defenders of the Alamo were sustained in their devotion to duty by an ever-present hope of relief. Surely their countrymen would rush to their aid by thousands, the moment their situation became known, and Travis had taken measures to have it known, by sending out two messengers on the second night of the siege. One of them, a fearless rider named Bonham, had gone with an urgent letter to Fannin at Goliad. The other was Rex Harden, who was despatched to the eastward, with orders to lay the situation before the delegates at Washington. Under cover of darkness he had slipped out from the Alamo mounted on Tawny, and, after several narrow escapes from the Mexican patrols, had finally found himself pushing, at a swinging gallop, along the familiar Gonzales road.

At the Rancho Herrera he only halted to make sure of the safety of its dear inmates, and tell them of his errand. Daylight found him relating his thrilling story at Gonzales, and two days later he reached Washington on the Brazos. To his intense disappointment, his father was not there, being absent on a strenuous effort to rouse the country to immediate action. So Rex reported to General Houston.

"God knows, boy, that I would set forth with you this very minute!" exclaimed that whole-souled patriot, in a voice broken with emotion, "did I not believe I could do more good by remaining here two days longer. Now I am but a private citizen, possessed of but little influence. In two days the convention will meet, and I may be in command of an army. So ride back, and tell that band of heroes to hold out for a few days more. Then I will either come alone to die with them, or will bring the relief for which they pray."

Everywhere Rex received the same answer to his pleadings and demands. "You must wait until the convention meets. Until then we are powerless to help you." Finally, discouraged and heart-sick, he turned his face westward, and began to retrace the weary way he had come.   At Gonzales he found a ray of hope in shape of thirty-two resolute men, ready to march to San Antonio under his guidance.

Again was Rex granted only a few hurried minutes at his home.   He found its inmates terrified by the constant and unmistakable rumblings that came to them from the direction of San Antonio, but otherwise they had gained no direct intelligence since he passed.   Every Mexican on the ranch, saving only Sebastien Tejada and his wife, had disappeared.   What was taking place?   What should they do?   Why could Rex not stay with them?   Surely one more or less could not make any difference in the ultimate result, at San Antonio.

So they wrenched his heart with their appeals, but could not turn him from his clearly defined duty.

"I must go, mother, for I have promised.   Besides, I am carrying help and hope to the very bravest fellows in all the world.   I should be worse than a traitor if I disappointed them, or caused them to lose heart for a single minute.   So you must let me go, and I will come again if danger threatens you. No horse ever ridden by a Mexican could catch Tawny, you know, and I shall keep him always ready.   Listen for the sound of cannon.   So long as you hear it, the Alamo is holding out, and you are safe.   If at any time it ceases for more than half a day, then fly to Gonzales.   There at least you will find stout protectors."

"But Rex dear—"

"But mother dear, I must not stop another moment. By daylight I must be with the brave fellows who are waiting for me in the Alamo. So good-by, dear, dear mother."

"Good-by, my darling boy, and may God hold you in His omnipotent keeping. Good-by."

CHAPTER XXIX

A HANDFUL WITHSTANDS THOUSANDS

On through the night rode the brave men of Gonzales, exchanging few words as they went, but with every sense keenly alert. At sunset they had heard the far-away roar of artillery and knew that their beleaguered countrymen still held out.

It was decided that, after riding as near to San Antonio as they dared, they should dismount and make their way into the Alamo on foot. Their horses would be sent back in charge of two men who had come for that purpose. So, as they came within sight of the Mexican camp-fires, a halt was called, and the horses were turned over to the herders, who were ordered to remain where they were until daylight, and then make their way with all speed back to Gonzales.

Only one horse was retained, and that was Tawny. Believing that he might still be wanted for urgent service, Rex had determined once again to conceal him in Manuel Peralta's stable, where he could be cared for by 'Rillo.

As the dismounted volunteers began their cautious

advance, with Rex, leading Tawny, at their head, our lad was perplexed at the number of lights, denoting either camps or batteries, that twinkled on all sides. Certainly they had not been nearly so numerous five days before. Could the Mexican lines have been extended entirely around the Alamo?

The dark mass of the garita was close at hand, and Rex was whispering to Captain Smith, leader of the Gonzales troop, that as it was unoccupied, it might be passed with safety, when suddenly a tiny flame flared from it and disappeared. A Mexican artilleryman had struck one of the recently invented lucifer matches then just coming into general use, to light his cigarette.

The warning was sufficient, and a wide berth was given the danger thus carelessly disclosed. The edge of the timber was reached in safety, and there Rex begged the others to remain for a few minutes while he led Tawny to Manuel Peralta's stable.

He succeeded in arousing little 'Rillo and getting him out of the house without disturbing any of the neighbors. The child was overjoyed to see his dear friend Rex once more, and readily consented to take charge of Tawny, who, he said, could now have the whole stable since the donkey had disappeared.

"I think the wicked soldiers stole him," he complained, "as they did El Bravo, my beautiful chicken, which the señor must remember. Oh! but he was so — "

"Yes, I remember him well," interrupted Rex, "but why have the soldiers stolen him?"

"Because of their hatred of my father, who is even now in the Alamo. Many times did they come here to kill him, and when they found him not, they carried away whatever they liked. Now that there is nothing left, they come no more, so will El Diablo be very safe in the stable of the donkey."

By plying the wise little chap with further questions, Rex learned that many fresh soldiers had reached the Mexican camp since he left the Alamo, and that every day they had brought new cannon. "So," concluded 'Rillo, "it is time for my father to leave that place also if he does not wish to be killed, for it is said by the soldiers that after two days no man in it will live."

"Perhaps it is so, little 'Rillo, and I will tell your father what you say. At the same time, as you value his life, do not so much as whisper to any one in the whole world that Tawny is hidden in the stable of the donkey."

No, 'Rillo would never let the great secret be even suspected. So the young lieutenant returned on foot to his waiting comrades, and led them by devious ways to where, in the gathering daylight, they could plainly see the gray walls that still sheltered Travis and his men.

At that moment a sentinel challenged, his musket

blazed in their faces, and a score of dark forms, hitherto unseen, rose up directly in front of them.

"Charge them, men! And run for it!" shouted Captain Smith. "It is our only chance!"

With an answering yell and a volley, the men from Gonzales charged the Mexican picket and swept it from their path. Then they ran for the shelter of the friendly walls. Behind them thundered a strong cavalry patrol, that in passing had been summoned by the shot of the outpost sentry.

In a moment they would overtake the flying footmen, and already the cruel sabres were uplifted for the slaughter. But all at once the despairing cries of the Texans were answered by a ringing cheer close at hand. A line of men, who had been lying prone on the ground, beside a tiny canal of clear water, sprang to their feet as the fugitives reached it. Ere the startled horsemen could draw rein they were met by a sheet of flame so deadly that they fled in dismay, taking with them half a dozen empty saddles.

The opportune presence of this force from the Alamo at that place was readily explained. Only the day before the enemy had diverted from its course the direct stream of water by which the old mission was supplied. So the defenders had been compelled to sally forth under cover of darkness to the nearest available ditch, and carry what they could of the precious fluid to receptacles prepared for it within the walls. The last party to be thus engaged were filling their canteens just at dawn when startled by the rush, in desperate flight, of the men from Gonzales.

Now the united bands poured joyfully into the Alamo, heedless of the roaring batteries that had been awakened on every side. Cheer after cheer greeted the new-comers as they passed within the barricaded gateway. Travis and Crockett shook hands with each one of them, and blessed them for their coming. Bowie, from his pallet, called that they should gladden his eyes with the sight of Texans who had risked their own lives to save those of their fellows who were in peril.

Nor was Rex Harden forgotten. Indeed, he was the hero of the hour; for without his guidance this timely aid could never have reached the besieged fortress. Moreover, he had talked with Houston, and brought from him a promise of speedy relief.

The day was the first of March. At that very hour the convention that was to decide the destinies of Texas was assembled. Perhaps Houston was already reinstalled as commander-in-chief, and armed with the authority for which they prayed. If they could hold out for a few days longer, he would be with them, and all would be well. Of course they would hold out. Hunger, thirst, weariness, and suffering all were forgotten, and with stout hearts these heroes of the Alamo sprang to their defences, where,

WITH STOUT HEARTS THESE HEROES OF THE ALAMO SPRANG

with rifle and cannon, they hurled back the challenge of Santa Anna's guns.

Late in the day a fierce norther smote the city with chill breath, and, as though borne on its mighty wings, the men of the Alamo rushed forth with impetuous fury, swept every Mexican from the nearest battery, seized its ammunition, and spiked its still smoking guns.

That night as they shivered over their feeble fires, drawing their tattered garments closer and more closely about them, they discussed hopefully the prospects of speedy relief, and imagined that they heard in the wild blasts of the norther the exulting shouts of armed hosts hurrying to succor them.

About midnight the leader of the Gonzales men left them, once more to seek perilous passage through the Mexican lines, and make his way to the Guadalupe, whence he promised speedily to come again with other volunteers.   He also promised Rex Harden that if the inmates of the Rancho Herrera had not already left when he reached there, he would persuade them to go with him to Gonzales.

Rex had sought Manuel Peralta soon after his return to the Alamo to tell him of his recent interview with 'Rillo.   He also told of Tawny hidden, ready for instant service, in the little stable behind the pulqueria.

Peralta had for some time been convinced that the Alamo must eventually fall into the hands of his countrymen, and he trembled to think of his own fate when that should happen. If he had only been wise enough to cast his fortunes on the stronger, instead of what had turned out to be the weaker side! If he could only devise some scheme, even now, by which to gain favor with Santa Anna! As he listened to Rex, a plan flashed into his mind, — a cruelly treacherous plan, to be sure, but what did that matter? To further it, he asked shrewdly:

"But does the señor expect again to use the horse thus concealed?"

"It is more than likely that I shall," replied the unsuspecting lad. "If an express is wanted to ride in any direction, I shall not hesitate to offer my services."

"And if it so happens that the señor should leave this place of terrors, will he notify his servant, that I may prepare a message for my child?" whined the zapatero.

"Certainly I will, my good Manuel, and moreover, when we have driven these troublesome countrymen of yours out of Texas, I will undertake to see that you have a comfortable berth at the ranch. You will find that we Texans are not ungrateful to those who like yourself have lent us aid in time of need."

Here Rex was called away, and as he departed the Mexican looked after him with an expression of crafty triumph.

Another day of incessant cannonading and unrelieved anxiety dragged wearily by. The feeble garrison was very hungry and very cold, but still presented a dauntless front to the enemy. On the third of March came two events of disheartening nature. One was the successful planting of a new battery within musket shot of the Alamo on the north, and the other was the return of Bonham from Goliad with the bitter news that Fannin had indeed started to their relief with three hundred men and two pieces of artillery, but had been compelled by a lack of teams and provisions to turn back.

On Friday, the 3d, the Mexican lines were drawn a little closer in spite of desperate sallies by the garrison to beat them back, and a feeling of despair began to settle darkly over the brave band who were holding an army in check.

The 5th, which was the tenth day of their heroic defence, brought neither relief nor tidings from the outer world; and when in the afternoon the enemy abruptly ceased their cannonading, Colonel Travis took advantage of the respite to summon his entire garrison to a council of war.

CHAPTER XXX

WHO WILL CROSS THIS LINE?

THE council of war was ordered to assemble in
the church of the Alamo, — where the sick and
wounded were quartered, — that they, too, might
participate in it. Here, then, gathered the battle-
worn defenders, to hear what their chief might say.
Some of them were veterans with grizzled locks,
others were boys; but the majority were sober men
in the prime of life, who fully realized the gravity
of their position, and their slight chance of success in the terrible task they had undertaken.

When the little company was drawn up in single
file, Colonel Travis, young, handsome, and strong,
but pale and worn with weariness and anxious responsibility, took position opposite the centre, and
addressed them as follows:

"My dear comrades, I have taken advantage of
the temporary lull in conflict to gather you for what
may be our last meeting on earth. I want not only
to thank you for your noble support in our struggle
with overwhelming numbers, but to advise you of
my conviction that the end is close at hand. Both

our ammunition and provisions are nearly exhausted. Even should no assault be made upon our position, we could hold it but a few days longer, while our feebleness could not repel a general attack more than a few minutes.

"Except for the noble band from Gonzales, who are now with us, the relief promised by our friends has not arrived. Five days ago the convention met, and if they had realized our extremity, we should have heard from them ere this. Fannin may be on his way to us, or he may not. I shall send out another courier this very night to meet him if he is on the road, and hasten his movements.

"But to come to my main object in calling you together. It is to tell you that, while we have every reason to regard our position as desperate, there yet remains a chance of escape for those strong enough and brave enough to attempt it. Harden and Bonham have successfully passed the Mexican lines, and will probably do so again. What they have done others may do. Only the sick and wounded must remain; and I, for one, shall remain with them to the bitter end. Now I want each of you to choose freely which course he will take. Will you stay, or will you make the attempt to escape? My own choice is to stay, and die for my country, fighting so long as breath shall remain in my body. This will I do, even if you leave me alone. Do, then, as you think best, but remember that no man can die with me without affording me comfort in the hour of death."

Here Colonel Travis drew a line with the point of his sword on the earthen floor of the old church in front of his men, and stepping back, said:

"Now must you make your decision. Let every man who is in favor of retreat or surrender keep his place; but let every one who is willing to remain, and face an almost certain death with me, cross to this side of that line. Who will be the first? Forward! *March!*"

The last word had not left the young commander's lips before Rex Harden leaped across the line and stood by his side. David Crockett was almost as quick to do so; and then, with a ringing cheer, that bade defiance to death, every man, save one, in that extended file, sprang over the fatal line. Every one of the sick and wounded, able to walk, rose from his pallet and tottered to the side of his comrades.

James Bowie, too feeble to move, but loyal to the traditions of his race, even in the face of death, said: "Boys, I am not able to come to you; but I should be very grateful if some of you would help me over that glorious line."

Instantly four men ran to him, and lifting his bed in triumph, bore it to the desired spot.

The young wife of Lieutenant Dickinson, who was the only white woman in the Alamo, stepped proudly over the symbolic line with her babe in her arms, and the men cheered her to the echo.

As the young commander witnessed these proofs of devotion to the cause of Texas and to himself, his eyes filled with tears, and for some moments he could not find voice to express his feelings. When the words came, and he had thanked them in faltering tones, he turned to the one man who still remained with downcast eyes, on the further side of the line, and said kindly:

"Peralta, as a Mexican, you could hardly be expected to feel with the rest of us on this question, and I cannot blame your choice. You are free to leave when and how you will. I am going to send Lieutenant Harden out to-night with another appeal for help, and perhaps you two can aid each other in passing the enemy's pickets.

"Me, colonel! Are you going to send me out?" cried Rex, in genuine distress. "Am I not to be allowed to remain here and share your glorious fate, whether it be victory or death?"

"My dear fellow," replied Travis, with a smile, "while we are inexpressibly grateful to those who are willing to die with us, we shall be infinitely more so to him who is willing to risk his life on the chance of saving ours. My chief, in fact my only, hope lies now with Fannin, whom I cannot believe has willingly deserted us. He is probably trying to drag his cannon through the infernal mud of prairies

and river bottoms.   He may even be near at hand.
At any rate, I want you to find him wherever he is.
Beg him to abandon guns, baggage, everything that
can cause delay, and push on with all speed.   With
his force added to our own I will undertake to drive
Santa Anna and his thousands beyond the Rio
Grande.   Without Fannin's aid we are lost.   Will
you then go on this most important mission, or shall
I send some one else who will be much less likely to
succeed ? "

"Of course I will go, since you put it in that
way," answered Rex.   "But oh, Will! promise to
hold out until I get back."

"I will promise to do all that mortal man can do,
my dear boy ; and if you do not find us here on your
return, you will have no difficulty in discovering the
reason of our absence.   Now try and get a nap, for
I want you to start about midnight."

Rex did as requested, and at the hour named was
ready for departure.   In vain did he search for
Peralta, who was to accompany him through the
enemy's lines, for the Mexican was nowhere to be
found.   So after an affectionate parting from Travis,
Bowie, Crockett, and every other man of the defenders who was awake, he slipped softly out of the barricaded gateway, and was instantly lost to view in
the blackness of that black night.

Before he had gone one hundred yards, he nar-
rowly escaped running into a group of shadowy

forms moving in profound silence directly across his path. A little further on, he heard the muffled tread of another party moving in the same direction. These companies were evidently much stronger than mere patrols, and he began to suspect that some aggressive movement was on foot. He soon found that still other bodies of men were marching in such directions as to entirely surround the Alamo; while the tramp of horses' hoofs showed cavalry to be also on the move.

The young lieutenant decided to return and advise his friends of this movement, but on attempting to do so, found to his dismay that an impenetrable line of troops had been formed behind him. So there was nothing to do but adhere to his original purpose, and gain the place where Tawny awaited him as quickly as possible.

After many delays and several hairbreadth escapes from discovery, he finally stood at the door of the humble stable in which he had left his beloved horse. The worst of his dangers were over, and once mounted on Tawny's back, he could defy the hottest of pursuits. Everything was so quiet about him, and he was so impatient to know if Tawny were still in the stable, that as he reached it he sounded softly the well-known signal whistle, which was instantly answered by a joyful whinny from within.

Relieved from a load of anxiety, our lad laid hand on the door to open it, and at the same instant was seized in a powerful grasp from both sides at once. A moment later a rope had been so tightly wound about his body that he was as helpless as a trussed fowl.

The onset was so sudden and unexpected that Rex had no chance to resist it, nor did he make an outcry. He was dumb and passive in the hands of his assailants, and only wondered vaguely whether he was to be killed then and there, or whether his execution would be postponed until daylight. He was confident that his doom was sealed in either case, for he knew that Santa Anna's order was to shoot all captured rebels and hold no prisoners. His curiosity concerning his fate was somewhat satisfied, and he was at the same time notified of the identity of two of his captors, by a few words exchanged by them within his hearing.

"Have you got him safe?" was asked from the darkness, in a voice which, despite its trembling, Rex recognized with a shock to be that of Manuel Peralta.

" Yes, we've got him safe enough this time," replied one of the men who held him, and whom he now knew to be his bitter enemy, Domingo, ex-herder of the Rancho Herrera.

" Then you now know and can bear witness that all I have done has been for the good of Mexico, and the glory of our noble President," whined Peralta.

"Humph!" sneered Domingo. "We will see what reward El Presidente will pay for this prisoner before making any promises."

"But you would never have taken him had I not told you of his coming ; and as a messenger from the gringos in the Alamo, he is a captive of the greatest importance."

"Come, we will present him to Santa Anna at once," replied Domingo, gruffly ; and without vouchsafing any further answer to the cowardly Peralta, who reluctantly followed them, the men led their helpless prisoner away.

After they were gone, a childish figure that had crouched in a dark shadow of the little stable rose, and, with a choking sob, stole unnoticed in the same direction.

The morning star was shining brightly, and already a faint glimmer of dawn was stealing over the eastern landscape, as this strangely assorted group hurried up the river towards the Alamo, in order to gain the only bridge leading into the city. Ere they reached it a sudden blare of trumpets rang out with a note of startling menace.

At this signal the air was rent by the roar of half a dozen batteries, and the rattling crash of a thousand muskets. Then, with a mighty shouting, thousands of armed men clad in the uniform of Mexico, rushed furiously at the grim Alamo from every side. The long-expected and fearfully anticipated assault was made at last.   The death struggle between four thousand well-fed Mexican troops, and less than two hundred half-starved Americans had begun, and the dawning of that memorable Sabbath day was reddened with its horrors.

CHAPTER XXXI

THE LAST SHOT FROM THE ALAMO

"CARRAMBA!" muttered Domingo, as his little party was brought to a stand by these sounds. "For a while we may not approach El Presidente. He is now busy with other matters, and until this affair is settled we must wait. Let us then seek a place where we three, together with this young gringo, may enjoy the spectacle. Come, Peralta, I know it will be painful for thee to see the heretics assigned to everlasting flames, but it will be a lesson for thy future guidance."

Domingo and his fellow cut-throats were too cowardly to fight, but from a place of safety could regard with savage glee a scene of slaughter. So they made their way to a deserted house, and dragging their prisoner with them, clambered to its flat roof, whence they commanded an unobstructed view of the Alamo.

From here in the reddening light Rex, forgetful of his own peril, gazed with a fearful interest upon the spectacle before him. Through the sullen smoke clouds he could catch a glimpse of dark masses of troops advancing swiftly to the very walls that had so recently sheltered him. Behind them stretched a gleaming cordon of cavalry, ready, with drawn sabres, to drive the infantry back to their horrid work, should they show signs of faltering. Beyond these the Mexican commander, surrounded by a glittering staff, and mounted on a coal-black stallion, issued his orders and personally directed the assault. Near the bridge the combined regimental bands poured forth in mighty volume inspiring strains of martial music, and on all sides, well beyond reach of bullet or ball, the citizens of San Antonio were massed at every point of vantage.

In the grim Alamo reigned a silence as of death, until the foremost rank of assailants, bearing stout ladders, were within twenty paces of the walls. Then the Texan fire leaped forth ; a crashing, withering discharge of grape and canister, musket ball and rifle bullet, that cut down the leading Mexican ranks, as tall grasses are laid low by a sweep of the mower's scythe. Stunned and demoralized, the rear ranks, goaded on by the cavalry behind them, still essayed to advance; but a second volley from the Alamo, equally deadly with the first, put them to headlong flight, that even the encircling cavalry could not restrain.

Dashing among the disorganized masses with shrill curses and flashing swords, that they used to beat the soldiers into place, the Mexican officers finally reformed their lines and sent them again at the deadly walls; but again they were hurled back by that terrible fire, shattered and panic-stricken.

At this sight Domingo stamped with rage. The coward Peralta trembled at the thought that the terrible gringos might after all win the day, and so become masters of his fate; while Rex, pale and almost breathless with alternate hopes and fears, so far forgot his position as to give a great shout of exulting joy. For this Domingo sprang at him, knocked him down with a savage blow, and threatened to tear out his tongue if he uttered another word.

The lad made no reply, but the moment Domingo turned from him he struggled to his feet, and again fixed his gaze on the scene of battle.

After their second repulse, the Mexicans reformed slowly. Santa Anna, foaming at the mouth, and raving with incoherent rage, dashed among them and swore to turn their own batteries against them in case they should dare give way again. Then he ordered up his reserve of picked troops, and having thus concentrated his entire force, again gave the word to advance. Shrill bugles and braying trumpets sounded the charge, the band played a furious quick-step, and again the dark columns hurled themselves against the low walls from which a few score of desperate men had twice repulsed them.

This time the Texan fire was feeble, their supply of powder had given out, and the ladders were placed. Many of them were overthrown, and their swarming occupants were killed by the score; but the defenders were too few in number to guard every point; and in another moment the Mexicans had gained the walls at a dozen places.

Filled with the fury of despair, and now fighting only for vengeance, the defenders sprang at these with clubbed rifles and their terrible bowie-knives. Scores were killed, but hundreds took their places. Step by step, the fighting Texans were overborne and driven back by sheer weight of numbers. Covered with wounds, they fought to the last, each man as he fell surrounded by a ghastly heap of the foes he had slain. At length a scanty remnant, not more than a dozen in all, led by Travis, took refuge in the church that sheltered their wounded.

From its roof, David Crockett, possessed of a horn of powder, still coolly picked of the Mexican officers with his unerring rifle, while the others loaded the single cannon placed at that point for a final discharge. As they finished their task, a volley from the walls tumbled the brave rifleman to the courtyard, from which he was dragged into the church by Travis. By the same volley both of his companions were killed where they stood; but one of them, with an expiring effort, touched a match to the loaded cannon.

As this last gun from the Alamo thundered forth its note of defiance, its unaimed ball sped to the house-top on which Rex Harden knelt in an agony of prayer, and laid beside him the mangled corpse of Domingo the Mexican.

With yells of terror, Peralta and Domingo's surviving comrade leaped to the ground and fled, leaving Rex alone. Even then the lad did not seem to realize what had happened. He still knelt, dumbly gazing, with an awful fascination, at the Alamo and listened with aching ears to the muffled sounds of conflict that still came from it. Finally a crash of musketry echoed from the courtyard, and a dull roar sounded from the reeking interior of the building that had been consecrated to peace and good will. It was the last shot of that bitter struggle, and was fired from a cannon loaded with grape, that had been aimed through the doorway of a small room in which were huddled the Texan wounded. As the smoke-pall of that murderous discharge was slowly lifted, it disclosed only a heap of mangled corpses.

A few moments before, David Crockett and five others, all wounded unto death, but desperately fighting with what feeble strength remained to them, had been taken alive and dragged before Santa Anna. There Colonel Almonte was so affected by the heroism of their resistance that he begged his commander to spare them.

With a contemptuous sneer on his thin lips, the Mexican President turned to a file of soldiers and said:

" Kill for me these rebels! "

As the fatal volley rang out, he pointed to the poor dead bodies, saying harshly, " Those, colonel, are my only terms for the Texas dogs ! "

Travis died defending the room that held his helpless wounded ; but ere he fell he had reared to himself a monument of slain foes.

A Mexican officer taunted gallant Bowie with the defeat of his cause, and handing him a dagger, invited him to kill himself, thus saving his conquerors the trouble. For answer, the blue-eyed giant rallied his failing strength with a mighty effort, sprang, like a wounded tiger at the throat of his tormentor, plunged the dagger to its hilt into his body, and fell back, to be pierced an instant later by a dozen bayonets.

So the Alamo fell, and its defenders died, until not one man of them all was left to tell the heroic story. Mrs. Dickinson was spared together with her babe, and the two Mexican women of Bexar. There was none other ; but ere the noble band who thus died for Texas yielded up their lives they had demanded a tribute from the enemy of five hundred and twenty dead besides a like number unfitted for further service by reason of their wounds.

It was all so quickly done that the morning sun was hardly an hour high when, awed into silence by the tragedy they had just witnessed, the spectators of the battle returned to their homes, and the wearied but exultant troops to their camp.

But Santa Anna would not have his victory passed

over in silence; and, though the dead still lay in ghastly heaps, staring with sightless eyes into the brilliant sunshine, and though the acequias of the city still ran crimson, the Mexican President ordered a general rejoicing. At his command the batteries thundered forth a salute, the church bells rang out joyous peals, while at the altars below priest and acolyte chanted a service of thanksgiving; the whole city was decked with flags and bright colors; there was everywhere feasting, and dancing, and songs of joy.

As soon as the troops were somewhat rested they were set to work to dispose of the slain, which they did by burning them on great piles of timber beyond the walls for which they had fought. Thus, by the hour of sunset on that ever-to-be-remembered Sabbath, nothing mortal was left of the heroic dead save a few handfuls of wind-blown ashes, and of all who had garrisoned the Alamo, only Rex Harden remained alive.

Alone on that housetop he had watched, with bloodless face, the swarming Mexicans scale the walls, the hand-to-hand conflict of tens against hundreds, and had seen the fearful struggle roll slowly back until it was hidden within the church. Of the awful happenings in that narrow space he could then only know by conjecture, though he afterwards learned the bitter details. All this time he had no thought for himself, but only for the gallant comrades who were being done to death before his eyes.

At length he was aroused to his immediate surroundings by hearing a light footstep beside him and feeling a tiny hand laid on his arm. Turning quickly, he looked into the frightened face of his little friend 'Rillo, whose quivering lips betrayed the effort he was making to be brave.

"Why, 'Rillo!" exclaimed the lad, at the same time glancing about him to discover who had brought the child to that place. "How came you here?"

"I came," answered the little chap, "to see what the wicked Domingo was going to do with you and my father, and I could not find where you had gone. Then the shooting began, and I was so frightened that I myself hid. When it was more quiet, I looked out and saw you up here; so I came to you. But why are you tied?"

"Because I can't help myself," replied Rex, with a thrill of hope in his breast; "but if you can undo those knots behind me, 'Rillo, I shall be very glad. So please try as hard as you can."

Eager to be of service, the child gladly undertook the task, and after a struggle, working with teeth and fingers, he finally loosened one of the tightly fastened knots. Rex could now help with the others, and in a few minutes was freed from his bonds.

"Now," he said to himself as he glanced at the still swarming troops, any one of whom would have killed him at sight, "what shall I do next?"

CHAPTER XXXII

"But I cannot find my father," sobbed the child, recalling his original purpose. "I heard Domingo say that he should be killed, and now I am afraid the wicked men have done it."

"No, they haven't, little 'Rillo," said Rex, soothingly. "Domingo has been killed; but your father is safe at home, and if you run back there, you will find him. Besides, Tawny must be very hungry, and wondering why you do not feed him. But, 'Rillo, you must not tell any one, not even your father, that you have seen me; for if you do, the wicked men will kill us all. Will you remember and promise?"

"Yes, I will remember."

"That's right. Now run along, and take good care of Tawny until I come."

With a heart full of gratitude to the child who had loosened his bonds, Rex watched him out of sight, and then proceeded to carry out the only plan of escape that presented itself. It was to assume the uniform of the dead Domingo, and, by passing himself off as a wounded soldier, endeavor to make his way beyond the Mexican lines.

Much as he dreaded to strip the rigid body, he forced himself to the task, and in a few minutes had drawn on the blood-stained uniform over his own clothing. Pulling the soldier's cap well down over his eyes, and smearing every exposed portion of his white skin with moistened gunpowder, he picked up the dead man's musket to use as a staff, limped stiffly from the building, and began his anxious search for some place where he might hide until night.

That the last vestige of resistance in the Alamo had been overcome he knew; for not only did the gaudy flag of Mexico float above its walls, but the throngs of people passing in both directions were eagerly discussing the final scenes of the struggle. Thus from fragments of conversation he learned of Bowie's gallant death, of how Travis fell, of Almonte's fruitless effort to save Crockett, and of the butchery of the helplessly wounded, so that no man was left alive.

As he heard these things, he could hardly breathe for the horror and rage with which they filled him; and he trembled as though he were indeed the sorely wounded man he appeared. Fortunately for him, wounded soldiers were hobbling from the scene of battle on all sides, and attracting but slight attention from the excited townsfolk, who ran to and fro exchanging thrilling items of news. To be sure, he was several times accosted, and begged for information; but he only groaned, and passed on without answering.

He had not thus proceeded far when Peralta and another brushed by him so closely that he could have touched them, and he overheard the former say: "Yes, we must find him, for he was too securely bound to escape"; at which Rex ground his teeth and quickened his steps.

He knew that his situation was now more critical than ever; for when those men found that he had disappeared, they would give an alarm, and the whole city would be searched for him. To enter it, then, would be to enter a trap from which there would be no chance of escape. But which way should he turn? What should he do? Where should he go?

Why not to the very house of him who had betrayed him? Peralta was away, only loyal little 'Rillo would be there; and surely the last place to be searched would be the premises of the man most interested in his capture.

The thought was an inspiration, and, yielding to it, Rex hobbled in the direction of Manuel Peralta's pulqueria. He had the good fortune to find it so absolutely deserted that not even 'Rillo was to be seen. Feeling that he would be safer outside the house than in it, and also desiring to be as close as possible to his horse, Rex entered the little stable, where Tawny, chafing at his confinement, was overjoyed to see him, though he sniffed suspiciously at the blood-soaked garments worn by his young master.

Believing that he should have no further need of these, Rex stripped them off, and hid them. Then, arranging a place of concealment beneath a scanty pile of forage, he prepared to pass a weary day, and await with what patience he might the coming of darkness. Tawny was munching the corn with which 'Rillo had recently supplied him, and the sound of his eating caused Rex to realize his own hunger. As nothing better offered, he, too, ate raw corn, and turned heartsick, as he thought of the brave fellows whom he had seen doing the same thing in the Alamo only a few hours before.

The horror of his thoughts so overcame him that, to change them, he began with his pocket-knife to enlarge a chink in the mud walls, so that he might look out. Although the view thus obtained was very limited, he could see gay banners replacing the symbol of death, that for two weeks had streamed ominously above the Cathedral. He could also hear the saluting guns, the jubilant bells, the triumphant music, and the glad shouts with which the Mexicans celebrated their victory, and the sounds filled him with an impotent rage. This was succeeded by a despondency so deep that it seemed as though his whole beloved country lay beneath a pall of destruction and death. Who now could hold Santa Anna in check, or who would dare oppose his victorious march?

Then he thought of the dear ones waiting fearfully by the beautiful Cibolo. Perhaps even now the brutal soldiers of the tyrant were marching in that direction. It seemed as though he must mount Tawny that very minute and fly to them. So strong was his longing for action that he might have attempted this, had not the sound of approaching voices warned him of the folly of such an attempt, and caused him to crouch in his hiding-place.

It was only a party of peons on their way to join in the festivities of the city, and laughing noisily as they passed. A little later some soldiers came and ransacked the pulqueria for liquor. Rex heard them swear because there was none, and rejoice that the keeper of so wretched a place would never return to it. The lad wondered what they meant, but it was some weeks later before he found out.

Then he learned that the comrade of Domingo, furious at the latter's death, the disappearance of their prisoner, and the loss of his expected reward, had denounced the zapatero as a traitor who had served the rebels in the Alamo, and assisted one of them to escape. With this Peralta was taken before Santa Anna, who, upon hearing the charges against him, had ordered the wretched man to be shot. So he was dragged away, already nearly dead with fright, and from that moment the places that had known him knew him no more.

Little 'Rillo, in the meantime, ignorant of the tragedies that were overshadowing his young life, had gone into the city with some other children, and was enjoying to the full the unwonted festivities of the day. He was reassured as to his father's safety, for he had seen him in the pulqueria, when, by the desire of the Señor Rex, he had returned to it that morning. At that time Peralta had been in such a terrible temper, that the child fled from him, and so had wandered into the city.

It was dark when, tired and hungry, the little chap reached the cheerless place that he called home, and was terrified to find in it a party of soldiers who were searching its every corner with lanterns. When he saw them he started to run, but they caught him just outside, and demanded to know where the young Señor Harden was hidden.

"I do not know," answered the terrified child. "He is not here, but only his horse."

"Where is his horse?"

"In the stable of the donkey, where I am to feed him."

"We will take care of him for you, muchacho," said one, and then all started towards the place where Rex and Tawny were hidden.

The fugitive lad had heard their arrival, and

knew from their conversation that they were in search of him.   He grew faint as he realized the imminence of his danger, and his knees trembled so that he could hardly stand.   Still he made out to prepare for it; and when approaching voices together with tiny gleams of lantern light announced the coming of those who sought him, he was ready to make a final effort for freedom.

Tawny had been turned about so as to face the entrance, and Rex, with arms clasped about the animal's neck, lay on his back.   There had been no time for saddle or bridle, and he had not more than assumed this position when the door of the stable was wrenched open.

At that instant the hunted lad uttered so fierce a yell in Tawny's ear, as caused the horse to bolt through the doorway with the force of a catapult. Half of the soldiers were hurled to the ground, their lanterns were extinguished, and a veritable cyclone seemed to sweep over them.   Ere they realized what had happened, only the beat of galloping hoofs told of the passing of El Diablo.   Even then they knew not if he were riderless or bore with him the fugitive whom they sought.

As Rex burst from the timber and gained the open country beyond, a cavalry picket let fly their escopettas at him, and started in hot pursuit.   But they might as well have chased the wind.

The guard at the garita, startled by the sound of

on-rushing horses and men, formed in line across the
road, and shouted for them to halt; but dared not
fire until the last moment, for fear they might be
friends. As they were on the point of doing so, a
black form reared itself in their faces, took a great
flying leap over their heads, and vanished in the
further darkness amid the flashing roar of their
muskets. Directly afterwards a squad of cavalry
charged furiously through their broken line, and
disappeared in the same direction. Half an hour
later these returned sullen and crestfallen, declaring
that they had chased no horse of flesh and blood,
but El Diablo himself, who had vanished in a cloud
of flame and smoke, leaving no trail by which they
might follow him.

So Rex Harden had again escaped a deadly peril
by Tawny's aid, and it was fortunate for him that
his pursuers gave up the chase when they did. He
had gone but a few miles from the garita when the
pace of his splendid steed began to slacken; and a
little later, in spite of all efforts to urge him forward,
he came to a full stop. Leaping to the ground, and
feeling carefully over the animal's body, Rex quickly
found his hands covered with blood, and knew that
his brave Tawny was wounded. Ignorant of what
else to do, he tried to lead him forward; but after a
few faltering steps the horse again stopped, and could
not be persuaded to move.

"Oh, Tawny, Tawny! My dear, splendid,

Tawny! What can I do?" cried the poor lad, in an agony of distress. "To remain here would mean death not only to me, but perhaps to many others. To leave you will break my heart; but I must go on, Tawny. — I must. There is no other way. Good-by, dear old horse. In giving you up for Texas, I sacrifice one of the things I love best on earth."

Then, tearing himself away with a mighty effort of will, and a sob that sounded like a heart-break, Rex clapped his hands to his ears to shut out Tawny's reproachful whinny, and ran as though pursued.

CHAPTER XXXIII

THE spring rains had so drenched the black soil that the road was heavy with mud, through which Rex quickly found that even walking demanded the fullest exertion of his strength. So heavy hearted was he, and so forlorn was his situation, that, but for the dear ones whom he believed to be awaiting him, he would have returned to die with Tawny. As it was, he would not give up, and so pushed on through the clinging mud, wading the shallow prairie streams, and floundering through quagmires until it seemed as though he must drop from sheer exhaustion.

The darkness merged into daylight, the sun rose, the morning was filled with the song of larks, and the verdant prairie was sprinkled with the earliest blooms of spring flowers; but the weary lad noticed none of these things. He only plodded stolidly forward, like one in a daze, with his eyes fixed on the far-away timber line marking the Cibolo.

It was high noon before he reached the Rancho Herrera, and, as he approached it, the hope that had thus far sustained him was dashed by its appearance of utter desolation. There was no sound of voices, no sign of human presence. Doors and windows were closed, and over the whole place brooded an unbroken silence. What had happened? Had its inmates been murdered or had they fled?

Sick with fear, Rex forced an entrance, and explored the silent rooms. To his unspeakable relief he found no signs of violence, but only those of hurried departure. In the cook-house he discovered food, which he devoured ravenously. Then, making his way to his own room, he flung himself on the bed, and instantly fell asleep.

So utterly weary was the lad that he lay for twenty-four hours motionless, and without waking. When he finally did so, he lay for a while wondering how long he had slept, and whether it were yesterday or to-morrow, but his hunger finally decided the question, and he sprang up with a sudden activity. A bath, fresh clothing, and a hearty meal made him again fit for any undertaking, and anxious to push on to the eastward.

First he visited the corral and stables, with the hope of finding an animal to ride, but all had been turned loose or driven away. He saw several distant bands of horses, but they were far too wild to allow a man on foot to approach them, and after a number of futile efforts to do so he returned to the house.

Night was already falling, and Rex was wondering

whether he ought to start at once on his weary walk to Gonzales or wait until morning, when he was amazed to see a light shining from one of the windows of the building. His first impulse was to fly, since it was more than probable that the house was occupied by enemies. Still, it might be in possession of friends, either his own people or another relief party for the Alamo; and if so, the sooner he made himself known to them, the better.

Thus thinking, he crept cautiously forward and peered in at the lighted window. Three Mexican soldiers were seated at a table, greedily devouring what remained of the food he had cooked a few hours before. They were evidently in great haste, and would finish their meal within a few minutes.

Having learned these facts by a single glance, Rex ran noiselessly to the front of the house, where, as he had hoped, he found three horses fastened. To undo their halters, leap into the saddle of one, and gallop away, leading the other two, was but the work of a minute. As he thus dashed out on the Gonzales road, it was all the young lieutenant could do to restrain a yell of exultation at having thus gained from his enemies the very means for defeating their plans. He only regretted that he could not have done them some greater injury; for, with the memory of the Alamo still fresh in his mind, he was full of vengeful thoughts towards all who wore the uniform of Mexico.

He had ridden several miles when suddenly a harsh voice issuing from a clump of chaparral called out:

"Who goes there? Halt, or we fire!"

The young man nearly leaped from his saddle, but he still realized that an English voice must be a friendly one, and reining up sharply, answered:

"Friend! Don't shoot!"

"What is your name, friend? Where are you from? and whither bound?"

"Lieutenant Rector Harden from San Antonio for Gonzales," was the answer. "Who are you?"

"Holy smoke! It's Rex Harden, and in another instant I should have shot him for a greaser!" cried the voice, in accents of horror, as several dimly out-lined forms rose from the bushes and hastily advanced to where Rex was curbing his three horses.

"Thank Heaven, lad, that I've been saved from murder this night!" exclaimed the foremost of these as he gained the road. "I'm 'Rastus Smith, and these two are Henry Karnes and Bob Handy. We are scouting in advance of fifty men marching to the relief of the Alamo, and there are three hundred more in Gonzales ready to start to-morrow for the same place. But what's the news, lieutenant? All's been so quiet the past two days that we've been mightily afeared the Alamo had fallen."

"It has," groaned Rex. "It fell Sunday morning before an assault of four thousand Mexicans led by

Santa Anna in person. Every man in the Alamo was killed and their bodies were burned."

"Good God, man! You don't mean it! It can't be true!" cried Henry Karnes. "Don't tell us that Will Travis is dead, and Jim Bowie, and Davy Crockett, and Bonham, and —"

"Every one of them, as well as one hundred and eighty others, gave their lives for Texas last Sunday morning, and the air of San Antonio recked with the stench of their burning bodies all that day," replied Rex.

While he was relating all that he knew of the awful tragedy and telling of his own miraculous escape, the main body of the expedition came up. His sad news quickly spread through the ranks, and he was at once surrounded by a throng of men clamoring for details, cursing Santa Anna, and vowing vengeance against all of his race. When our lad told of the three Mexican scouts he had just left at the Rancho Herrera, Deaf Smith cried out :

"They must never get back to Bexar alive, boys ! and I'm going after their scalps."

A score of eager volunteers begged for the privilege of accompanying the scout, but he said he meant to go on horseback, and asked Rex for the loan of one of his horses.

This request was readily granted, as were those of Karnes and Handy, who also begged for horses with which to join in the vengeful chase.

So Rex passed the night with the men from Gonzales, who camped where they were, and the next morning started with them on their march back to the Guadalupe. They had not covered more than half the distance, when the three scouts rejoined them, with their sinister mission accomplished; but bringing the sad news that the Mexicans had fired the main house of the Rancho Herrera and burned it to the ground.

With his heavy heart made still more sorrowful by this intelligence, Rex took back the horse he had loaned to Handy, and rode ahead with the other two, reaching Gonzales in the evening of the third day after the fall of the Alamo.

To the townsfolk of Gonzales, most of whom had counted relatives or friends among the defenders of the Alamo, the news of its fall carried the wildest grief and consternation. On all sides were heard the wails of widowed women and orphaned children, mingled with cries of fear. Every one believed that the terrible Santa Anna would now march eastward, and might appear at any moment. So great was the panic that preparations for flight were at once begun in nearly every house.

Amid all this grief and terror there was one bright spot, and in one humble dwelling prayers of gratitude were mingled with tears for the heroic dead. It was a log cabin in which Sebastien Tejada had found shelter for the fugitives from the Rancho

Herrera.   Here Rex was greeted by his mother and the two girls, as one restored to them from the grave.

Late that night, or rather early the following morning, as these four still sat talking of what had happened, and trying to plan for the future, the door of their cabin was flung open, and a man of commanding presence, but so splashed from head to foot with black prairie mud, as to be for a moment unrecognizable, stood before them.

It was General Sam Houston, who had started from Washington for San Antonio on the day of receiving his reappointment from the convention as commander-in-chief of the Texan army. As he now learned, it was the very day on which the Alamo fell. Accompanied only by his military secretary, and riding with all speed to the relief of the beleaguered troops, he had only just reached Gonzales, and came to Rex Harden for confirmation of the terrible news that greeted his arrival.

Again Rex told his sad story, and the General followed its every detail with absorbed attention. Tears of anguish stood in his eyes when it was finished.

"It is a bitter blow," he said, "but I pray God that the sacrifice of those brave souls may not be in vain. Perhaps it was needed to rouse Texans from their apathy in this struggle for freedom. Now we must try and save Fannin from a like fate.

Are you in condition to carry a despatch to Goliad, lieutenant?"

"I am, sir," replied Rex, promptly; "only—" Here the lad cast a perplexed glance at his mother.

"I understand," said Houston, "and, in your absence, will care for these dear ones, as though they were my own, until I can deliver them in safety to your honored father, who still sits with the convention at Washington. Did you know, my boy, that, on the second day of this fateful month, that same convention declared Texas to be a free and independent Republic? This news you will bear to Fannin, as well as the sad tidings of the fall of Alamo. You will also convey to him my order to immediately blow up his fortifications, destroy what public property he cannot carry away, and retreat with all his force to the Colorado, where I will join him; for we dare not make a stand against Santa Anna until we can unite our slender and widely scattered forces. Therefore my policy for the present will be one of retreat. But I will have a despatch prepared for you to deliver. How quickly can you set out?"

"As soon as I can procure a horse, general."

"You can have mine; for, in spite of his recent hard travel, he will be again fit for the road by morning. At daylight, then, I shall expect you to be en route, and may God speed your mission.

After delivering your despatch, you will remain with Fannin and assist in his retreat.

"Ladies, I have the honor to wish you a good night, and I beg that you will not allow any anxieties for the future to disturb your rest."

CHAPTER XXXIV

AGAIN ARE THE TEXANS DEFEATED

So heavy were the roads and so inferior to Tawny
was the horse now ridden by Rex, that he did not
reach Goliad until the 14th of April, or eight days
after the fall of the Alamo. He found Colonel
Fannin in a most perplexing position. No definite
news had been received concerning the Mexican
army known to have left Matamoras about the time
that Santa Anna began his eastward march from the
Rio Grande; but the air was thick with rumors of
its approach. Report located it at San Patricio, only
fifty miles away. A few days previous to the arrival of General Houston's order for the abandonment of Goliad, an urgent appeal had been received
from Refugio, a small mission village thirty miles
away, stating that several loyal families were in
danger of being cut off, and begging for an escort.

In reply, Fannin sent Captain King with thirty-
five men to bring them in. Since then nothing had
been heard from this relief party, nor from the three
scouts, sent out on as many successive days to gain
information of it. Finally, a few hours before Rex

reached Goliad, Major Ward of Georgia had been directed to march to Refugio with his battalion, one hundred and fifty strong ; and now Fannin hesitated to obey even so imperative an order as that brought by our young lieutenant.

"God knows that I realize the danger of my position, Harden, and the necessity for retreat," exclaimed the perplexed soldier. "But how can I go and leave those brave fellows behind to be slaughtered ? No, sir, I can not do it, but must wait for news from them."

Thus four precious days were spent in waiting for news that did not come, days of suspense and sleepless anxiety. In the meantime Goliad was filled with rumors of the near approach of a formidable Mexican army. The native population, some two thousand in number, not only took delight in exaggerating these rumors to increase the alarm of the Americans, but they threw every obstacle in the way of their procuring draught animals, wagons, and provisions, all of which were necessary for the retreat.

Finally, a wounded and blood-stained soldier, nearly dead from starvation and exhaustion, crawled into Goliad with a terrible tale of disaster. The message that had drawn King to Refugio had been a ruse ; and upon his arrival he had been surrounded by an overwhelming force of Mexicans. Throwing themselves into the old mission, the thirty-five Americans had defended it for two days. Then artillery was brought to bear on the walls, and, through the breaches made by it, one thousand Mexicans rushed in assault. The pitiful handful of defenders was wiped out in a minute. Seven of them, including their intrepid commander, captured alive, were immediately taken outside, fastened to trees, and shot.

The Mexicans next advanced to meet Major Ward, of whose coming they had been notified. He, falling into an ambush, still made a desperate resistance, inflicting a heavy loss on the enemy, and finally escaped under cover of darkness with a scanty remnant of his men. For two days these wandered hopelessly amid swamps and drowned timber-lands, dying of wounds and exhaustion, until the few who remained alive surrendered as prisoners of war to a party of Mexican troops near Victoria.

With this information Fannin hesitated no longer ; but gave orders that a retreat to the Colorado should be begun on the following morning. That night was spent in burying the heavier guns, blowing up fortifications, and destroying government property. Scouts, sent out at daylight, reported no signs of an enemy on the eastern road, and, at eight o'clock in the morning, the little army of Texans, only three hundred in number, abandoned Goliad and marched to the river. There two hours were spent in crossing their artillery and wagons. Then the slow march, which must keep pace with laggard oxen, was resumed.

The day was bright and hot, and at noon Colonel Fannin ordered a halt to rest his teams. The point at which this rest was taken was on the open prairie, some eight miles east of Goliad and within five miles of the timber line marking the Coletto, the next watercourse on their route.

After an hour's halt the line of march was again taken up, and the cavalry force of the expedition — only twenty-eight in all — was sent ahead to examine the crossing of the Coletto. Soon after they were lost to view in the timber, Rex, who rode beside Colonel Fannin, called the latter's attention to a couple of horsemen emerging from the same line of trees a mile or so distant.

Focussing his field-glass on these, the commander uttered an exclamation. At the same moment the two horsemen were joined by a strong force of cavalry, that, sweeping from the river bottom, galloped obliquely forward on a line that would intercept the Texans, and cut them off from the timber.

"Mexican lancers!" cried Rex, who knew only too well the gaudy uniform, the waving plumes, and pennoned spears of that corps.

"They are, indeed!" replied his companion; "and there come their supports."

As he spoke, dark masses of infantry were to be seen emerging from the timber at the same point.

"God help us! We must fight them here in the open," exclaimed Fannin. With this he halted his slender column and formed it into a hollow square, with artillery posted at the four corners, and wagons in the centre. As the Mexicans drew near, the guns opened fire at long range, and gave the Texas cavalry their first intimation of trouble. They came hurrying back from the timber, but communication with their friends was already cut off. A few minutes later they were compelled to fly for their lives before a charge of lancers, who pursued them to the river, where they finally made good their escape.

In the meantime, the Mexican infantry charged boldly, in spite of the steady fire of the Texas guns. Advancing from three sides at once, with a furious discharge of musketry, they rushed at the little square as though expecting to overwhelm it by a single effort. Not until the opposing bayonets were actually interlocking, did they realize how deadly were the rifles of those western frontiersmen. Then they recoiled, staggered, and fled, leaving the still unbroken square surrounded by scores of dead and wounded men.

Disheartened by the failure of their first grand charge, the Mexicans attempted but two more, and these were so lacking in spirit as to be easily repulsed by the Texas riflemen. After that their commander contented himself with drawing a close cordon about his intended victims and firing at them from a safe distance until dark. But this was a game at which the riflemen were perfectly at home, and for every American hit by a bullet at least three Mexicans bit the dust.

In this long-range warfare the most serious damage done by the Mexicans was the killing of the American cattle, which precluded the possibility of removing their wounded from that place, even if an opportunity for retreat should be offered.

With the coming of darkness the extended line of Mexican camp-fires indicated their position, and showed how effectively the besieged were cut off from the blessed water, for lack of which they were already suffering acutely. Many of the wounded became delirious from thirst, and their pitiful appeals for water caused their uninjured comrades more distress than even their own parched mouths.

All night long those who were able labored so diligently at throwing up intrenchments, that by morning they could safely defy attack by a force much greater than any that had thus far appeared against them.

Just before dawn Fannin, who was himself wounded, called his men together, and laid before them the desperate nature of their position.

"There is but one hope for you," he said, "and that is to start at once, cut your way through the enemy's line while he is still asleep, and then dis-

perse in small parties. In that way some of you can probably escape."

"But what shall we do with the wounded?"

"We must be left to accept whatever fate the Mexicans may reserve for us."

"It would be the fate of the Alamo," shouted Rex Harden.

Then from all sides rose cries of,—

"We will never abandon our helpless comrades. Whatever fate awaits them shall be ours as well."

So it was settled, and there was no further talk of retreat.

With the coming of daylight, the Mexicans, who had been reënforced by seven hundred cavalry and a battery of artillery, renewed the attack by cannonading the Texan position at long range.

Fannin withheld his fire because of his scanty supply of powder, and because with each minute he expected it would be needed to repel a general assault. Instead of this, to his infinite surprise, the Mexican fire ceased with sunrise, and an officer appeared with a flag of truce. He demanded an unconditional surrender, to which Fannin replied that he would fight so long as he had a man left able to fire a rifle, rather than surrender without terms.

So the flag returned, and the entire Mexican army formed in order of battle. Now every Texan nerved himself for the expected onset, the gunners stood beside their pieces with lighted matches, and the riflemen sighted their long barrels. But it never came. Instead of ordering an attack, General Urrea, accompanied by an officer bearing another white flag, rode out in front of his extended lines.

Colonel Fannin, with Major Wallace and Rex Harden, the latter being asked to act as interpreter, advanced to meet them.

The two commanders greeted each other with grave courtesy, and then General Urrea begged that Colonel Fannin would avoid a further useless shedding of blood by surrendering to the vastly superior Mexican force.

The latter replied that as he was strongly intrenched and well prepared to resist any force that could be brought against him, he should not surrender except on the most advantageous terms.

Rex Harden interpreted for both sides; and it was largely owing to his diplomacy that the following honorable terms were granted:

1st, That the Texans should be treated as prisoners of war, according to the usages of the most civilized nations. 2d, That they must lay down their arms. 3d, That the men should be sent to the coast within eight days, and thence to the United States, as soon as vessels could be procured to transport them. 4th, That the officers should be paroled, and also forwarded to the United States.

Rex wrote out this agreement in both English

and Spanish, the duplicate papers were signed by the respective commanders, and the battle of the Coletto was ended.

Although mortified at being forced to surrender, the Texans rejoiced at receiving such favorable terms, and immediately piled their arms outside their breastworks, where they were taken into possession of the Mexicans. Then the unwounded prisoners, some two hundred in number, were marched back to Goliad, which place the wounded, among whom was Colonel Fannin, did not reach until two days later.

Thus for the fourth time in his short but eventful experience of war did Rex Harden find himself a prisoner in the hands of his Mexican enemies. The present captivity, however, he regarded but lightly; for was he not shortly to be sent to the United States and set free? Certainly he was, if the most solemn pledges that men can exchange were binding upon Mexican honor. At the same time, he would much rather be liberated in Texas, and without giving his parole not to fight against the butchers of the Alamo.

CHAPTER XXXV

" LISTEN ! "

ALTHOUGH the prisoners were so closely crowded into the mission church of Goliad that they had scant room to lie down, and although they were allowed neither bedding nor fuel, while for food they were only given a daily allowance of meat, without bread or salt, and so small as barely to save them from starvation, they were comparatively happy and content ; for were they not to be set free, and sent to their homes within a few days? This was almost the sole burden of their thought and conversation. Most of them were young men from the States, who had been attracted to Texas by the romance with which its name and cause were surrounded. In far-away Ohio and Kentucky, Georgia and Louisiana, it had seemed a gallant thing to fly to the relief of suffering Texas, there to gallop madly over boundless plains in pursuit of flying foes, to feast on unlimited game, perhaps even to invade the strange, foreign land of Mexico itself, and wrest the freedom of Texas from the Tyrant in his palace.

Urged by such anticipations, and by the restless

enthusiasm of youth, these boys — for most of them were little more — had left their homes, enlisted in companies of Blues, or Grays, or Rangers, or Red Rovers, or some other catching designation, and, after undergoing many hardships, had finally landed on the soil they were to defend.

From this point their disenchantment was even more rapid than it had been while buffeted by the billows of the Gulf. They were now drenched by the cold rains of wet northers, forced to make weary marches through mud as black and sticky as tar, or to endure weeks of idleness in dreary and wretchedly equipped camps. Instead of feeding on an abundance of game, they starved on mouldy hardtack and rusty bacon. Instead of dashing on splendid horses across breezy prairies in pursuit of flying foes, they were condemned to weary labor on fortifications with hours of hateful drill thrown in by way of change. They never saw the Tyrant they were to drive across the Rio Grande, nor even one of his soldiers, until he surrounded them with an army to which they must surrender, or die of thirst. Thus their present captivity with its promise of a speedy return to their homes was the very pleasantest episode of their whole experience in Texas. How dear and inviting those far-away homes now seemed ! How the thin-faced boys talked of them, and longed for them ; how they smiled when they thought of what heroes they would be when they reached them, and how firmly they determined never again to leave them!

They had surrendered on the 20th, and, according to General Urrea's pledged word, were to be liberated within eight days. Therefore on the 28th, at the latest, they would be free. How they counted the days, hours, and even minutes as the time dragged slowly by!

One morning Colonel Fannin announced that he was going under guard to Copano, the nearest seaport, to find out what vessels were available for their transportation, and they gave him a hearty cheer as he left them. On that same day eighty more volunteers fresh from the States, who had been captured by the Mexicans the moment they set foot on Texas soil, were marched into Goliad, and huddled with the other prisoners in the old mission church.

But no one minded the extra crowding, since it was done by friends just from home. There would be only four more days of it, anyhow; while, between the veterans who had actually fought for Texas, and the new-comers, who were not likely to have a chance to do so, there was so much to tell and to hear, that the time would pass very quickly. As a hero of the Alamo, Rex Harden was of especial interest to the late arrivals, who regarded him with much the same awe as they would Sam Houston himself.

One thing about these new-comers greatly puzzled

Rex and his companions. It was that each of them wore a white rag tied about his left arm. When questioned concerning these badges, they could give no information, save that a Mexican officer had tied them in place, and charged them not to remove the bits of cloth under penalty of death. All the prisoners discussed this problem at length, but could arrive at no satisfactory conclusion concerning it, though the general opinion was that those wearing the white badges would be held as prisoners much longer than the others, and would probably be sent to Mexico, since they had been obliged to surrender without making terms.

There was a pale-faced, studious-looking youth among the new-comers named Fenno, who was convinced that this was the correct explanation, and was heartbroken in consequence. He was of the same age as our Rex, and the very contrast of their personalities caused an intimacy to spring up between them. Fenno, soft-handed, low-voiced, and of a peculiarly gentle disposition, had never before been away from home, and was, as Rex told one of his comrades, "precociously" ignorant of the world.

"Yes, looks like he would faint dead away at the sight of blood," rejoined the other. "Regular Miss Nancy, and what brought him down here is surely a beater."

Fenno had been brought there through sheer ignorance, and from a romantic desire to become a champion of liberty. Now, with his illusions all vanished, he would gladly give anything that he valued, to be once more back in his Ohio home. So the belief that, as a wearer of a white badge, he would be carried into Mexico for an indefinite imprisonment, made him positively ill. "Oh! If I were only in your place!" he cried, "and sure of being sent to the States within two days."

At this Rex meditated, and then said thoughtfully, "Well, I don't know but what I'd change places with you. I'd a heap rather stay here in Texas than go to the States just now, and I've already thought out a plan for escape. It will take time, though, and I'm afraid they are going to send us off to-morrow. You know Colonel Fannin has just got back from Copano, with the news that several vessels are due there, so they may ship us off any day, perhaps even to-morrow."

As a result of this conversation, Rex assumed Fenno's white badge that night, they exchanged clothing, and each agreed to answer to the other's name at roll-call on the following morning.

That was the night of the 26th of March, and as Major Ward with the survivors of his battalion had just been added to the list of prisoners, the old mission was crowded to overflowing; four hundred and forty-five men being squeezed within its narrow walls. Still they were all in good spirits, for in some way the impression had spread among them that on the next day, which would be Palm Sunday, and also the last of the eight days stipulated for on the Coletto prairie, many, if not all of them, would set out for their far-away homes. So they talked of home, sang "Home Sweet Home," until tears stood in their eyes, and finally fell happily asleep to dream of home.

At daylight soldiers came to waken them, and order them into line. Instantly the report passed from mouth to mouth that the vessels had reached Copano, and that they were to march at once for that port.

" Hurrah for the little old States ! " shouted one.

" Hurrah for good old home ! " cried another.

" And we'll never come back any more ! " yelled a chorus.

All was excitement, bustle, and happy confusion.

Amid the noise the voice of a Mexican sergeant was heard, announcing that the " white rags " should remain where they were.

" That's rough on you Johnnies," called out a sympathetic veteran, who was packing his slender kit for home.

" Four of them," continued the sergeant, " are wanted to assist the doctors. Let any four who can speak Mexican step this way."

The doctors thus mentioned were four American physicians, found among the prisoners, and ordered to duty in the Mexican hospital. To assist them, four of their countrymen were detailed each day.

At the call on this occasion, Rex Harden, who had already congratulated Fenno on his "chance," sprang forward and was accepted. He was given a jacket and cap such as the Mexican hospital stewards wore, and told to put them on. This was in order that he might be recognized as an attaché of the hospital, in case he should happen to be sent outside on errands.

Rex purposely delayed his dressing until his late companions, and Fenno with them, had marched joyously from the church, as he wished to avoid any recognition or inquiries that would attract attention to himself.

The departing Americans had been formed in three separate columns, each guarded by a double file of soldiers. To the surprise of every one who witnessed the manœuvre, Rex among the number, these three columns were marched out of town in as many different directions. One was headed down the river towards Copano, one up stream in the direction of San Antonio, and one due west as though it were bound to Mexico.

While our lad, walking slowly towards the hospital, was wondering at this, and also planning an escape, his preoccupation caused him to come into collision with a young Mexican officer who stood alone on a street corner, gazing after the receding columns of prisoners.

Rex began to apologize, but his words were cut short; for, as the other turned his face he saw that it was his old-time friend Florio Veramendi, whom he had not met since the latter entered the army two years before, and whom he had supposed to be still stationed at the Mexican capital.

At this moment Florio's generally handsome and laughing face was so haggard, and wore an expression of such horror, that the greeting which Rex started to utter died on his lips, and instead of it he asked anxiously :

"My dear Florio! can this be you? When did you come to Goliad? What is the matter? You look as though you were condemned to instant execution. Are you ill?"

" Ill!" cried the young Mexican, fiercely. " I am so sick with shame that my heart is like to break. Condemned! I am condemned forever to wear the brand of infamy because I belong to a race perjured and accursed! When did I come? I reached this place of horror last night, bearing a sealed and urgent despatch from that monster of deceit and prince of human devils, Santa Anna. Of its contents I was ignorant until five minutes ago, else would I have endured tortures rather than deliver it. Having done so, though innocently, as I would swear before the Almighty, I am forever marked with the damnable marks of Cain and Judas."

" You rave, Florio! Something terrible has happened to upset you. I am your friend, even though we fight on opposite sides. Tell me your trouble

that I may help you bear it.   What have you done?
or what has been done to you?"

"I brought the sentence under which those hundreds of defenceless and unprepared men are even
now led out to be slaughtered in cold blood," answered the young Mexican, speaking with deliberate
emphasis.

"But," cried Rex, aghast, "that cannot be.   Those
men are prisoners of war, with lives and liberty
solemnly pledged to them."

"For that very reason no Mexican may ever again
claim to be an honorable man, and I am outcast from
this day."

"Florio, I won't believe it!"

"Listen!"

From far out on the western prairie came a dull
roar of musketry.

"Listen!"

From down the river came another awful crash
of guns.

"Listen!"

But, with a cry as of a wild beast springing on
its prey, Rex was racing madly in the direction
taken by the third column of prisoners, the one with
which Fenno had gone.

CHAPTER XXXVI

A MASSACRE FROM WHICH TWO ESCAPE

TEXAS lay apparently at the mercy of Santa Anna. Her only organized bodies of troops had been wiped from existence, her foes had been everywhere triumphant, and were now marching three strong, well-equipped armies across the state. The government had fled from Washington on the Brazos, to the equally insignificant and defenceless village of Harrisburg on Galveston Bay, near the site of the present city of Houston. The one man upon whom the faint hopes of the Texans rested, and whom they had chosen to lead them in battle, was retreating across the sodden prairies of the Colorado at the head of a few hundred demoralized, barefooted, and wretchedly equipped troops. With these travelled a throng of helpless refugees, mostly women and children, while in hot pursuit marched Santa Anna, leading his strongest army corps.

That he did not overtake and destroy the fugitives was owing to the heavy rains that turned the prairies into quagmires, and made of every stream an unfordable torrent. At each one the Texans, as they crossed, carefully collected and destroyed every boat for miles up and down, or carried them to the eastern bank. Thus at every river the Mexicans were compelled to spend days in constructing rafts for their artillery and baggage. The Texans, moreover, burned all villages as they evacuated them, beginning with Gonzales, besides sweeping the country of provisions, live-stock, and forage.

From all sides Houston was bitterly blamed for retreating ; but, realizing as no other could the folly of attempting a stand under the circumstances, he steadily pursued his own policy, held no councils, and silently bided his time. The news of the fall of Goliad saddened him, but in no way altered his plans, for he had foreseen that it was inevitable.

When, two weeks later, one who had escaped as by a miracle brought tidings of the cold-blooded massacre of prisoners, whose lives and liberties had been solemnly guaranteed, the great heart of the leader seemed like to burst with grief and rage. The effect on his men was to turn them into demons athirst for vengeance, and he promised them that their opportunity should not be long delayed.

Upon the Hardens the blow fell with a crushing weight, for the messenger replied to their anxious queries, that Rex was certainly among the murdered. He knew him by the lone-star badge embroidered on his sombrero. It was the only one in Goliad, and he had seen its wearer fall. Yes, there could be no mistake about it, their Rex — the splendid fearless boy, who was all in all to them — had been sacrificed for Texas, and they felt that they had, indeed, given her their best.

Until now Nelita Veramendi, with her piquant beauty and unfailing cheerfulness, had been the very life of that gloomy retreat; never complaining, always helpful, and full of bright prophecies for the future. From earliest childhood she had regarded Rex Harden as a well-loved brother, but at the news of his death she stared for a moment incredulous, and then sank like one who has received a mortal wound.

That the cruel massacre of helpless prisoners had taken place was true; but he who carried its tidings to Houston's camp was mistaken when he named Rex Harden as among its victims. Santa Anna had received news of the fall of Goliad and the victory of Coletto while at Gonzales, and when he heard of the terms granted to the vanquished, his face grew black as night. Seizing a pen, he dashed off a few words, enclosed them in a sealed envelope, and looked about him for a trusty messenger. Florio Veramendi had that day arrived from Mexico with despatches from the Minister of War, and was in the President's tent awaiting instructions. To him, then, Santa Anna said harshly:

"Carry this order with all speed to General Urrea at Goliad. Tell him to execute it instantly, and to the letter."

So Florio departed; and, taking an escort of twenty mounted men, rode in haste to Goliad, which place he reached during the second night. On the weary journey he wondered much concerning the nature of the urgent message he was bearing, and when General Urrea opened it, he was startled by the expression of horror that flitted across the man's face. The trained soldier was, however, able to suppress his feelings; and, without a word of explanation, merely said:

"Very well, sir. His Excellency's order shall be obeyed, and you may retire."

Thus dismissed, Florio joined certain young officers of his acquaintance, from whom he learned all that had happened since their advance upon Goliad. Then he sought the rest he had so well earned, and slept until morning. So the infamous order he had brought was in the very process of being carried out before he learned of its nature. His informant had just left him horror-stricken at the merciless perfidy of the man whom he owned as master, when his friend Rex Harden, whom he had no idea was in Goliad, appeared upon the scene.

The latter was no sooner convinced of the truth of Florio's words, than he conceived a wild idea of gaining the nearest column of prisoners in time to warn them of their impending fate, and join them in a death grapple for vengeance with their executioners.

Although he ran like one possessed, and was

allowed to pass the sentries on account of his hospital uniform, he only reached the scene of the tragedy in time to see it enacted. As he gained sight of the column, the prisoners were halted in a double line facing the river. Ten paces behind them stood the three hundred Mexican troops who acted as guards, with their muskets aimed at the still unsuspecting prisoners. At that moment one of the latter turned his head, and instantly realized what was about to happen.

" They are going to shoot us, boys ! " he screamed, and had barely uttered the words when a sheet of flame leaped from the long line of muskets. At that fire one hundred men fell dead or dying. The terrified survivors rushed madly toward the river, and after them leaped the Mexicans, yelling like demons, firing as fast as they could reload, and stabbing with their bayonets those whom they overtook. Only a few of the Americans gained the river bank, while not more than one in four of those who leaped into its current, escaped the rain of bullets that beat the clear waters into foam, and reached the other side.

All this happened so quickly that Rex, standing horror-stricken, and temporarily unnoticed, was for a moment incapable of thought or action. Then of a sudden he knew that only by desperate effort could he avert from himself the awful fate that had just overtaken his recent comrades.

Thus thinking, he sprang forward as though to

join the yelling savages who were chasing, shooting, and stabbing the defenceless fugitives. With them he screamed:

"Death to the gringos!   Kill the heretics!"

In the assumed ardor of his chase, he did not pause on reaching the river bank, but, leaping far out into the water, swam after the most laggard of those who had thus far escaped, as though bent on his destruction. The Mexicans on the bank yelled with delight as they saw him gain on the fugitive, and, misled by his uniform into believing him one of themselves, cheered him on to greater exertions.

As the swimmer whom he was following gained the opposite shore only a few feet in advance, and started to climb the steep bank, exhaustion or terror overcame him, and with a despairing cry he slipped back into the water. At this the Mexicans screamed with derisive laughter, but in another moment their tone was changed to one of angry amazement. Instead of forcing his victim beneath the surface and drowning him, as they fully expected the stout swimmer wearing their uniform would do, he was actually assisting the hated Americano to climb the bank.

For a moment they gazed incredulous and then, realizing that they had been tricked, began hastily to reload their empty guns. Two or three shots were fired without effect; and then, to their chagrin, he whom they had supposed to be their friend turned and taunted them with a defiant gesture, while his companion disappeared in the thick timber.

In another instant the young Texan followed, and, gaining the shelter of the trees, found him whom he had saved lying panting on the ground. Until then Rex had not seen his face nor given a thought to his identity. Now, to his joyful amazement, he discovered him to be the very lad whose white badge of safety he had assumed the night before, and whom he had believed to have thus been sent to his death.

"Fenno! Can it be possible?" he cried.

At his words the other opened his eyes and struggled to his feet, gazing at Rex as though he had been a ghost.

"Is it truly you, Harden? Have we both really escaped from that hell of murder, or is it all a dreadful dream from which I am not yet awaked?" he asked. At the same time he shivered and glanced about him fearfully.

"It is no dream, old man, but an awful reality from which, thank God, we have both escaped. But there is no time for talking ; we are still surrounded by deadly perils. So brace up, and come along."

Thus saying, Rex started through the timber, which at that point was but a narrow belt, and Fenno followed him. They were about to emerge from it, when the former halted and sank to the ground, pulling his companion with him.

Not fifty yards away, on the open prairie, was a

troop of Mexican lancers, evidently stationed at that point to cut off the escape of any fugitives. Behind them the lads could hear their merciless pursuers crossing the river. Their position was certainly a desperate one, while, to add to its terrors, several Americans who, like themselves, had swum the river in safety, just then emerged from the wood in blind flight, and were instantly speared to death by the waiting lancers.

After making certain that their victims were dead, and robbing their bodies of whatever was worth taking, the lancers remounted and dashed away as though they had sighted other fugitives. At the same time, the shouts of the pursuing Mexicans who had crossed the river drew ominously near.

" Come," whispered Rex, " we must run for it ! There is no other chance."

So the two broke from their cover, and, nerved by despair, sped like the wind across the open. They had not gone a quarter of a mile, when a backward glance showed the lancers to be returning to their original position. Flinging themselves to the ground, the hunted lads lay trembling, and only partially concealed by the brown prairie grasses.

After a little the lancers again moved away, and the two fugitives resumed their flight, which they maintained until they reached a clump of chaparral in which Rex said they would hide until night.

During that day they repeatedly heard sounds of

firing and saw several parties of Mexican cavalry scouring the country; by which signs they were led to believe that they two were the sole survivors of that awful massacre.

Filled as they were with grief, rage, and apprehension, our lads were spared a knowledge of the further horrors even then taking place in Goliad. There, after murdering their uninjured prisoners, the Mexicans dragged the wounded out into the courtyard of the old mission and butchered them. Colonel Fannin was the last to be put to death, and he met his fate like the brave soldier he was, calmly facing his executioners and baring his own breast to receive their cowardly bullets.

Thus was closed a chapter that, for perfidious treachery and inhuman cruelty, is unsurpassed in all the annals of American history.

CHAPTER XXXVII

THE DARKEST HOUR

With the coming of night Rex and Fenno, somewhat refreshed by their rest, set forth on what they believed to be a northeasterly course. They dared not strike for the Rancho Herrera, or even toward Gonzales, for Rex knew that Santa Anna was marching to the eastward, and that the whole country in that direction would swarm with Mexican soldiers. By going directly east they would become involved in the labyrinth of swamps and bayous bordering the coast; but a course between the two might take them to the Texas army on the Colorado.

The night was intensely dark, and they had not so much as a star to guide their steps. Still they pushed sturdily on until daylight, when they stopped to rest in the timber bordering a small stream. Fenno was so wearied that he begged Rex to let him sleep there all day, but the latter declared they must not think of halting until they had put many more miles between them and their merciless foes. So they forded the stream in icy water that rose above their waists, and pushed on with hardly a pause until night, when they came again to a narrow but deep and rapid stream.

All that day they had been exposed to the drizzle of a wet norther by which they had become thoroughly soaked and chilled to the bone. They were also sick and trembling with the weakness of hunger. They had seen plenty of deer that day, and could now hear numbers of wild turkeys going to roost in the tall timber surrounding them, but as neither of them possessed a weapon of any kind, both deer and turkey were safe so far as they were concerned.

Rex did own one thing fully as valuable as a rifle, and that was a water-tight fire pouch, containing flint, steel, and tinder. He had not dared light a fire up to this moment, and would not have done so now, but that poor Fenno was shaking so violently with the cold, and pleaded so pitifully for one, that he could not refuse him.

"All right, old man," he said at length. "I suppose we might as well run one risk as another, and it does seem as though without a fire we should die before morning. So we'll have one if I can make it. Only let us cross this river first that we may not have it to do in the morning when we are dry."

Fenno shuddered at the idea of entering the black waters; but, urged on by Rex, finally did so with a rush, thinking to have the dreaded task over with as quickly as possible. It was an ill-advised movement, for he stumbled, fell, and was swept away by the strong current. So dark had the night already become, that it was full half an hour before Rex, guided by his faint cries, found him caught in the overhanging branches of a tree, a quarter of a mile below, and dragged him ashore, nearly dead with exhaustion, chill, and fright.

Now a fire was a necessity, and the young Texan made one as quickly as possible. With all his efforts, another half-hour had elapsed before he succeeded in obtaining a blaze from the wet material at hand. While he was thus engaged, Fenno, shivering and moaning, did not speak a word; and when, by the first gleam of fire-light, Rex turned to look at his companion, he was terrified to find him lying with closed eyes and bloodless face, in a sort of a stupor. Dragging the poor lad close to the fire, and pulling off his wet garments, Rex rubbed and slapped the almost lifeless body for an hour before the sluggish blood began again to circulate. A little later Fenno was tossing with fever, and raving of the awful scenes he had so lately witnessed.

All night long he passed in alternate chill and fever, moaning and shaking with one, or tossing and raving with the other. It moved Rex to tears to hear him talk of his far-away home, and call the dear ones left in it, by name. Again he would break into a fury of rage against the wretches who had murdered his comrades. The same train of thought came to his lucid moments, and he begged Rex not to let him die until he had taken vengeance upon at least one Mexican.

The coming of morning found both lads asleep, and the day was well advanced before Rex awoke. Seeing that Fenno still slept heavily, he ventured to leave him, while he went to explore their surroundings as well as to search for food and shelter.

He had not gone fifty yards before he found a well-marked road running parallel to the stream on which they were camped. Although somewhat troubled at the nearness of this highway, as there was no one to be seen on it in either direction, he ventured to follow it in the hope of finding a house.

So anxious was he to make such a discovery that he walked much further than he had intended on setting out ; but was thinking of turning back, when his ear caught a distant rattle of drums and the faint notes of a bugle call. He wanted to run, but, determined to know whence the ominous sounds came, he forced himself to proceed to a bit of rising ground, from which he hoped for a wider survey. To his amazement, he saw, not more than two miles away, a town. He could not believe the evidence of his eyes, and rubbing them he looked again. Then his heart sank like lead, and he groaned aloud, for not only did he see a town, but he recognized it to be Goliad. He tried to think himself mistaken ; but could not, for the whole storm-blurred landscape was too terribly familiar. So in all their sorrowful tramping he and Fenno had only moved in a circle, and were again almost at the awful starting-point of their despairing journey.

So disheartening was this discovery that for a moment Rex was ready to give up the struggle and resign himself to the fate that appeared inevitable. Only a thought of the helpless lad awaiting him caused him to think better of such a cowardly resolve, and begin to retrace his steps. He had not gone more than half-way back when he caught a distant glimpse of approaching figures. Leaping to one side, he threw himself down in the tall grass, through which he crawled until the sound of approaching voices warned him to lie low.

The new-comers were half a dozen Mexican foot-soldiers straggling along the road toward Goliad, and Rex, peering through the grasses, saw that while two of them supported a comrade who was covered with blood and evidently severely wounded, the other three carried *seven* muskets between them. Thus one soldier was missing and unaccounted for.

When the squad had passed out of sight, Rex rose and hastened forward, apprehensive that they might have seen the fire he had left burning, and so discovered his helpless comrade. So fearful did he become of this, that he ran the last mile of the way as though in a race with death. When he at length reached the place from which he had set forth, he found that he had indeed been racing with death, and that the latter had won the victory.

Close beside the fire lay Fenno, pierced with a dozen wounds and dead. His rigid fingers were clutched about a bloody bayonet, and near him lay a Mexican soldier of similar uniform to those who had just passed, also dead. On all sides were evidences of the struggle in which the lad from Ohio had taken that vengeance for which he had prayed, before yielding up his own life.

The whole story of the tragedy was so plainly written that Rex could see its every detail, and for a while he could only sit and stare at the outspread page. Birds sang above him, squirrels raced and chattered on all sides, and the river flowed placidly close at hand, but he heeded none of these things and saw only his dead comrade. His first feelings were of horror, loneliness, and utter despair. Then came a bitter rage and a longing for revenge.

"I will live!" he cried, springing to his feet. "I will live, if only to fight those wretches once more, even if I shall die fighting as this poor, brave fellow has done. Yes, I will! and I will make my way to Houston's army. First, though, I must bury this poor body beyond reach of buzzards and wolves."

With the bayonet that, in his final struggle, Fenno had wrested from his murderer, and with which he had avenged his own fate, Rex now laboriously dug a grave beside the peaceful river. The task occupied him for several hours, and as the body of him who had given up his life for Texas was laid to rest in her soil, the sun was near his setting. It had broken from the clouds in time for a last look at the dead, and to direct the living on his course.

When his sad duty was finally completed, Rex again crossed the river, carrying with him the bayonet that killed, avenged, and buried poor Fenno. Then, guided by the lone star of evening that shone low in the west, our young Texan again set forth to traverse the wide wilderness lying between him and safety.

Two days later, gaunt, famished, footsore, and in the last stages of exhaustion, he stood beside the swollen Guadalupe and gazed despairingly at its swiftly rolling flood. With his ordinary strength he could easily swim it, but in his present state of weakness he knew the attempt would be suicidal. In four days he had not tasted food save a few grass seeds and leaf buds.

As he sat gloomily on the bank, concealed by an undergrowth, and wondering if the end of all things had indeed come for him, a slight sound attracted his attention. Glancing in that direction, he saw three deer walk daintily down to the water's edge, not two hundred feet from him. Oh, for a rifle, or a gun of any kind! And then — venison steaks for supper!

"But I might as well wish for the moon," thought the starving lad bitterly.

The sight of those deer was so tantalizing, that he was about to hurl a chunk of wood at them, and so dispel it, when his arm was arrested by a slight movement on the limb of a tree overreaching the place where they stood. He had just made out that it was caused by the tip of a waving tail, when, with a mighty spring, a great tawny body launched itself through the air and lighted on the back of one of the unsuspecting deer. Like a flash the others were gone, and a puma or Mexican lion was beginning to make his supper off the one he had stricken.

Rex watched him enviously and anxiously. " Will he eat it all? " he asked himself. " Oh, if he would only go away, leaving just a little of that venison! " And the puma did just as the famished lad wished he would. In half an hour his appetite appeared to be satisfied, and a goodly portion of the deer still remained. This he dragged a short distance and carefully concealed beneath a pile of branches, sticks, and leaves, as a dog would hide a bone. Then, taking a drink from the river, and making a long, slow survey of his surroundings, the powerful animal walked leisurely up the bank and disappeared.

Two minutes later, regardless of whether the great cat were watching him or not, Rex was robbing his larder. That night he ate venison steaks hacked off with a bayonet, and broiled over coals, until it did not seem as though he should ever care to eat another mouthful of meat so long as he lived.

Y

CHAPTER XXXVIII

DESPAIR AND HAPPINESS

AFTER that Heaven-sent supper, Rex slept dream-
lessly beside his smouldering fire until daylight, when
he awoke feeling happier and stronger than at any
time since leaving Goliad. Now he wondered if the
puma had come back to renew his feast during the
night, and trembled to think how easily the great
brute might have punished him for his theft if it
had been discovered. So uneasy was he at this
thought, that he decided not to remain within reach
of punishment any longer; but to place the Guadalupe between him and danger as quickly as possible.
Lashing his meat, together with his clothing, to a
floating log, and pushing this before him, he swam
the river in safety; but at the expense of a serious
loss. This was his bayonet, which he had sharpened
to a knife-like edge, and with which he would not
have parted for many times its weight in gold. But
in some way it slipped from the clothing in which
he had wrapped it, and now only the Guadalupe
knew where it lay.

While greatly cast down by this loss, and in spite
of his enormous supper of the evening before, Rex

realized that his appetite was as ravenous as ever; and so, as soon as he gained the opposite bank, he set about preparing another meal. While thus engaged he had the satisfaction of hearing a succession of angry roarings from the timber he had so recently left, that caused him to smile at his own cleverness.

After this Rex made two more good meals from the puma's venison, and then the remainder was stolen from close beside him as he slept, so skilfully that he never knew what animal took it. However, what he had eaten gave him strength to reach the Lavaca River, which lay mid-way between the Guadalupe and the Colorado where he hoped to find his friends. But now he was again very hungry, and so nearly barefooted that his feet were bleeding from innumerable cuts and bruises; unless he could soon find a pair of boots or something to take their place, it was evident that his journey was nearly ended.

As he hobbled painfully along the edge of the dense timber of the river bottom, which at this place was miles in width, seeking for some road or trail that should penetrate it, he caught sight of a house, the very first he had seen in all his wanderings. It was a small structure of logs, standing in a little prairie bay that made into the timber, and was enclosed by it on three sides. After cautiously watching this house for a while from the concealment of the timber, and seeing no evidence of human presence, Rex finally hobbled up to its door and entered. Not only was it deserted, but everything movable in it had been so wantonly destroyed that the floor was littered with broken furniture, smashed crockery, and ripped bedding. There was no sign of food, nor could our lad find a scrap of leather with which to resole his worn-out boots.

Still the outlook was not wholly gloomy, for in a crib outside he found half a dozen ears of corn, which he speedily converted into meal by means of a steel mill that was nailed to a tree in the yard. Returning to the house with his precious meal and building a fire in one of the chimneys, he soon had prepared that simplest of all bread forms, an "ash cake," which, unsalted and unleavened as it was, yet tasted a little better than anything he had ever eaten except the venison of the Guadalupe.

After disposing of this extremely frugal supper, the tired lad collected a heap of tattered bedding, and lying down on it, only kept awake long enough to reflect how thoroughly comfortable he was and how he wished he might look forward to as good a bed every night. Then he fell asleep.

When next he wakened it was with a start and at sound of gruff voices. Daylight was streaming in at the open door and windows, and standing beside him, looking at him curiously, were two strapping Mexicans in the dress of rancheros.

"Ho! Gringo!" said one.

"Probably escaped from Goliad," remarked the other.

" And therefore worth money if we shall take him back, for a reward is offered."

" As it is also the place to which we are going, there can be no harm in letting him live till we get there."

"Certainly no harm, unless he should escape."

"We will attend to that. Stand up, gringo! Quickly! So!"

With this, the speaker gave our lad a kick that assured him he was not dreaming, and brought him stiffly to his feet. There was not the slightest chance for resistance, and filled with despair he was led outside, where two other Mexicans were guarding a small herd of horses. One of these was caught and held until the prisoner, with arms pinioned behind him, could be securely lashed to its bare back. Then it was turned loose with the others, and the whole cavallard was started on a swinging lope to the westward, or back over the very way Rex had just come.

Never in all his manifold experiences had our lad suffered such tortures both physical and mental as fell to his lot that day. The pains that shot through every joint of his body were those of one stretched upon the rack, while his mind was filled with humiliation, rage, and despair. When night came, he was loosed from his horse on the bank of the Guadalupe. He slipped to the ground like a log, while his brutal captors jeered at his sufferings, and told him they were nothing to the torments he would endure after he had been shot. They still did not wish him to die just yet, so they loosed his bonds, gave him food and drink, and then tied him securely to a tree for the night.

The following morning he was again bound to a barebacked horse, and the terrible journey was resumed. Rex thought he should be drowned when the horses were made to swim the river, and hoped he would be ; but to his disappointment he was not, though it very nearly happened. By the time he found himself on the western bank and being rapidly borne through the timber, his body had become partially numbed by long-continued torture, and at intervals he lost consciousness. From one of these unconscious spells he was aroused by a confusion of shots, yells, and the furious galloping of horses. Then all was once more a blank.

When he next awoke he was lying on the ground, and being bathed with hot water. He did not ache, and it was so pleasant to lie still that for some time he did not open his eyes. When he did, he knew that he was in a dream and not really awake after all; for he saw his own dear Tawny standing only a short distance away; while bending anxiously over him was Cochito, the young Comanche with whom at some remote period he had contracted a friendship.

Of course all this was absurd, for Tawny had died

long ago, and so had Cochito; at least he believed he had, though he was not quite sure. But thinking was too hard work, especially when one could only think foolish thoughts not to be distinguished from dreams; and he was very tired. So the poor lad, who was too weak and weary to care for anything except rest, again closed his eyes and fell asleep.

For weariness and pain, and unhappiness and despair, there is no restorer and comforter to equal sleep. Thus when Rex had slept for a day and a night, he awoke strengthened and refreshed in body and mind.

Immediately he sat up and looked about him. He was under a spreading tree, on a soft bed made of Spanish moss overlaid with robes. Not far away was a fire, about which were gathered a number of Indians. Beyond them a herd of horses was feeding. At his first movement one of the Indians rose and came toward him.

It was Cochito, who said in Mexican, "It is good to meet my white brother once more, and to see that he is well."

"Indeed, it is very good to see you, Cochito, though I can't quite make out how it has come about. You see, I thought I was dreaming, and in my dreams you came to me together with my horse Tawny, — the one, you know, that brought you to me once before. But, of course, that couldn't be really, for he is dead."

For answer Cochito only smiled and breathed a shrill whistle, the very one that Rex had formerly used to call Tawny. At sound of it a horse in the distant herd threw up his head; and, when it was repeated, he came swiftly to where they were.

It was Tawny, not only alive, but as strong and well as ever. No other horse in Texas had so free a stride, could show a coat of such satiny gloss, or mane and tail of such admirable texture. Besides, no other would have answered that whistle, or thrust his velvet muzzle into Rex Harden's very bosom to be petted.

Flinging his arms about the proud neck, and burying his face in the silken mane, Rex almost sobbed for joy ; and when he found words he cried:

"Oh Tawny ! Tawny ! I never expected to see you again, and now I am the very happiest fellow in all Texas. But, Cochito, how does it happen that you and he are here? Where did you find him? I can't seem to understand it at all."

"It is very simple," replied the young Indian, smiling. "I found him more than a moon ago, wounded on a prairie, and knew him for the horse of my white brother. So I cared for him and made him well, and he followed me because of the whistle with which I had heard my brother call him. When I came again I would have restored him; but the lodge of my brother was burned, and he was not there. Then with my comrades I gathered many horses and much else of value. With these we were riding once more to the lodges of our own people, when, at this place, we met my brother and four of his enemies. They will not trouble him more, but their scalps will make glad the hearts of the Comanches who dwell by the Nueces."

" And Tawny! Am I to have him back again?" cried Rex.

" Why not? Is he not the horse of my brother?"

" Am I also free to go where I please?"

" Could one be the brother of a Comanche warrior and not be free?"

" Cochito, old man, you are one of the very finest fellows I ever met. I am proud to be called your brother, and to call you brother. For this day's work I shall love you as long as I live."

CHAPTER XXXIX

CAPTURED BY A FRIEND.

ALL that day Rex rested and regained strength, happy in gazing at his beloved horse, whose every movement filled him with joy, and in talking with Cochito, whom he found to be so intelligent that a decided respect for the young Indian was added to his feeling of friendship. From him he learned that General Houston had already retreated beyond the Colorado, and would probably be found on the Brazos, while Santa Anna was sweeping the country with his armies.

" Why is it so ? " asked Cochito. " Are the white men cowards, that they dare not stand before Los Mexicanos ? "

" Does not a small band of Comanche warriors sometimes run from a strong war-party of Lipans, until they have led them into an ambush where they may be destroyed ? " asked Rex.

" It has so happened."

" In this case it is the same. The Texans are few, and their enemies many. So, for a time, the white men retreat; but at the proper place they will turn and fight. Then let my brother open his eyes, and he will see Mexicans flying over the prairie like antelope before the lobo wolf."

" If my brother says so, then will it come to pass, and Cochito will remember his words."

Bright and early the following morning was the camp of rest astir; and though Rex parted with regret from the young Indian who had proved so true a friend, he was impatient to be off, the more so that he was to ride his own incomparable Tawny. Besides the horse saddled and bridled, all that the Indians could give him were provisions, guns being with them too scarce and too precious to be spared. But Rex was more than content; for, with Tawny, he felt that he could travel to the world's end and defy pursuit.

Cochito watched them swim the Guadalupe, and the two lads waved a farewell to each other as the dripping stallion scrambled up the eastern bank.

Oh! how glorious was the ride across the broad prairies that Rex had already traversed twice in sadness and pain. So swiftly were the miles spurned by Tawny's flying feet, that the Lavaca River was reached before noon, the Navidad was crossed a few hours later, and that same night found our young Texan camped in the heavy timber bordering the Colorado.

He had just finished cooking his evening meal, and was about to eat it, when two big, black, and very ugly-looking negroes walked into the circle of firelight and informed him that they had waited quite long enough for him to prepare their supper. They also ordered him to cook some more at once.

As one of them carried a gun which he kept constantly pointed at Rex, the latter thought best to comply with their demand. So, inwardly fuming with rage, but outwardly calm, he again set to work, while they took turns at eating and threatening him with the gun, until his whole slender stock of food had disappeared down their black throats.

While his unwelcome guests ate, they informed him that General Houston had been driven across the Brazos, that Santa Anna was "gwine run him clar outen de state," and that no white man would ever again be allowed to dwell west of the Sabine. This news Rex received in contemptuous silence, though with a fear that part of it, at least, might be true.

After the negroes had eaten all they could, or rather, all that there was to eat, they argued as to whether they should kill their prisoner or not, and finally decided, that as the Mexicans would do that very soon anyhow, they would not waste good powder on him. "Same time, boy," said one of them, "we'se gwine take dat 'ar hoss of yourn."

"Very well," replied Rex, quietly, "if you insist upon taking him, I suppose I can't help myself. Please don't abuse him, though, for he is very gentle, and not over strong."

"Yah, yah!" guffawed the negroes. "Oh no, sah, we won't 'buse de hoss, certainly not, only jes' ride him to def, an' den leav' him go: dat's all."

With this, one of them approached Tawny, who was quietly feeding near by, caught up the trailing picket rope, and gave it a yank.

The stallion uttered a scream of rage, sprang at the man, knocked him down, and struck furiously at him with his fore feet. The attention of the other negro being thus attracted from Rex, the young Texan leaped forward, snatched away his gun, ran back a few paces, and pointing it at his head cried:

"Down on your knees, you black scoundrel, or I will kill you!"

Instead of obeying, the negro advanced so threateningly toward the lad, that the latter pulled the trigger. There was no report, and with a fiendish laugh the black bounded forward holding a knife in his uplifted hand.

At that moment Tawny was ready for another victim; and, instead of meeting a defenceless boy, the negro was confronted by a raging demon, before whose onset he was as helpless as a child. His uplifted arm was seized and crushed between the animal's powerful teeth; and, in another instant, he too was flung aside to lie as motionless as his companion.

Then Tawny, still quivering from excitement, with head and tail uplifted, stepped proudly over to his young master, with an inquiring air as though to ask "Are there any more?"

"You are a noble fighter, old fellow," cried Rex, passing an arm across the horse's neck and petting him, "and I am mighty glad that you are my friend instead of an enemy."

An examination of the gun that had first intimidated, and then failed him, disclosed the fact that it was not only unloaded, but broken and worthless. So Rex threw it into the river. Then satisfying himself that neither of the negroes was dead, and having no desire for further dealings with them, he mounted Tawny, and taking advantage of the light of the newly risen moon, started to cross the Colorado.

Although the western bank and the broad surface of the river were flooded with light almost as bright as day, the eastern bank was still in blackest shadow. Thus while Rex was plainly visible to several pairs of eyes that watched him from the shore he was approaching, he was unsuspicious of a human presence, until as Tawny was in the act of leaving the water, his bridle was seized from both sides, and at the same time a harsh voice, accompanied by the ominous click of a pistol, ordered the young rider to dismount and surrender.

"Out of the frying-pan into the fire," groaned Rex, as he reluctantly obeyed, for the command had been given in Mexican, and he realized that he was again occupying the now familiar position of a prisoner in the hands of a pitiless enemy.

He was conducted up the river far enough to overcome the distance he and Tawny had drifted downstream in crossing, and then into a gully through which a red clay road, ankle deep with mud, led to the top of the bluffs. Just back of these was a cluster of houses, to one of which our lad was taken. Without formality he was ushered into a lighted room containing a Mexican officer, who was seated at a table, with his back to the door, eating supper.

" A prisoner, Señor Teniente," announced one of the two men who held Rex by the arms.

At this the officer partially turned his head, and revealed the familiar features of Florio Veramendi.

In the water-soaked, mud-bespattered, tattered, and long-haired youth of whom he caught only a glimpse, Florio did not recognize the friend of his boyhood, and asked carelessly:

" What sort of a prisoner ? "

" An Americano, señor."

" A soldier ? "

" It is doubtful."

" What is his name? "

" Your name, gringo, announce it," said the soldier in a low tone to Rex, and the latter answered in a clear voice:

" Lieutenant Rector Harden, of the Texas army."

" Holy Mother ! " cried Florio, springing from his

chair. Then recalling his position, he added in a
calmer tone: "This is a most important capture,
sergeant, for which you deserve and shall receive
great credit. Now, however, you may retire and
leave the prisoner with me, for I must question him
in private. You have taken the precaution to see
that he is unarmed?"

"I have, Teniente."

"Very well, then, I can take care of him," —
here Florio laid a hand significantly on his sword, —
"though you will, of course, station a sentry within
call."

"I understand, Teniente," replied the sergeant,
saluting and marching stiffly from the room, followed
by the other soldier.

The moment the door closed, and it was certain
that the room was not exposed to observation from
the outside, Florio's manner changed as by magic.
With a beaming face he sprang forward, and seized
his prisoner's hand.

"My dear, dear Rex! How can I ever say how
glad I am to see you? How can I express my
thankfulness that you should come this night of all
nights, the only one on which I happen to be in command of the river guard? This, too, when I
believed you to have been killed at Goliad, through
an infamous order delivered by my hand. Imagine
what I have suffered! Imagine my position! With
your blood on my head, I could never again face

your family or my own. With my hatred of Santa Anna for that act of devilish perfidy, I could no longer serve him. I handed my resignation to General Urrea on the day that I last saw you. He would not accept it, but ordered me to report in person to the President. This I determined never to do, but rather to desert, since I was not allowed to resign. For that purpose I strove to get as close to the Texan army as possible, and came to this point, where Filisola ordered me to remain with Captain Gregorio, who commands the river guard.

" Unable to form any plan, I obeyed ; and now, see how kindly the saints have directed my steps. Gregorio was summoned to the Brazos, where the army is crossing, but will return on the morrow. In the meantime we will plan together a flight, for now that I can again look your father and mother and sweet sister in the face, I am no longer a Mexican, but one devoted soul and body to the cause of Texas. So, while we have time, let us consult. But, dear boy, you look famished. Have you supped ? No ? Sit down, and as you eat, tell me of the miracle by which you escaped on that dreadful day. Oh ! the horror of that time ! the happiness of this ! "

An hour later the sergeant was summoned and told that, on account of important disclosures made by the prisoner, the lieutenant had determined to escort him in person to the Brazos, leaving him — the sergeant — in command of the river guard for

z

that night.   " You will therefore have my horse and the horse of the prisoner at the door in five minutes, besides detailing one man to accompany me," ordered Florio.

Within five minutes everything was in readiness, and when Rex was mounted on Tawny, Florio bade the soldiers pinion his arms securely behind him. Then they set forth, the lieutenant and the soldier riding on either side of the prisoner and holding straps attached to Tawny's bridle.

They had thus gone a mile when the lieutenant suddenly discovered that he had left his pistols behind, and ordered the soldier to ride back for them. " We will proceed slowly until you again overtake us; and you will leave your carbine with which I may shoot the prisoner if he attempts to escape," added the young officer.

The soldier saluted, obeyed, and disappeared, whereupon Florio loosed his prisoner's bonds, handed him the carbine just acquired, and with lighter hearts than either of them had known in many days, the two lieutenants dashed away in a direction very different from the one they were supposed to have taken.

CHAPTER XL

TEXAS FREE AT LAST

FOR a whole week Rex and Florio, leaving all travelled trails to avoid the Mexican armies, struggled through tangled canebrakes, swamp, and drowned timber lands, swam swollen rivers, or rode heavily over endless prairies sodden with rain. They were generally bewildered and often lost, they had scanty food, and less of rest, but always they pushed steadily forward. After crossing the Brazos they rode toward Harrisburg, the seat of government, where, if anywhere, they believed the Texans would make a stand.

Now they met many stragglers, Mexican soldiers wandered from their commands, and refugee settlers. Whenever our two lieutenants encountered the former, Rex was a prisoner in the hands of Florio, but when they met with Americans, their position was reversed. Every one whom they questioned told them a different story; but by piecing these together they gained a fair idea of the situation.

Santa Anna, leaving the main body of his army still crossing the Brazos, with an utter contempt for the little force of farmers under Houston, had pushed ahead with but eight hundred men and a single piece of artillery, so rapidly as to leave the Texan army in his rear.   His objective point was Galveston, and he only delayed his march to that place long enough to burn Harrisburg, which had been deserted by its terrified inhabitants but an hour before.   Then he continued down Buffalo Bayou amid a network of creeks and salt-water inlets toward Galveston Bay.

Until he reached the San Jacinto River he had no idea that he was being hotly pursued by the enemy whom he had passed and left in his rear with such contemptuous indifference.   On the San Jacinto prairie they caught up with him, drove in his rear guard and shelled his camp.   With this he moved to a timbered ridge slightly elevated above the surrounding level, and began to fortify his position, at the same time sending back for reënforcements.

Thus matters stood on the morning of the 21st of April, 1836.   General Martin Cos had just joined his illustrious brother-in-law with seven hundred fresh troops, several pieces of artillery, and a report that Filisola would arrive the next day with one thousand more.

"I shall not need them," remarked Santa Anna, scornfully.   "We are strong enough now to sweep Mr. Houston and his horde of ragged rebels from the face of the earth, and this very day I mean to do so.   But there is no haste, my dear Martin.   Take your time to rest, and after siesta will we set about our task of teaching the dogs their lesson."

The noon hour was long past when two young horsemen dashed up to the only bridge across a bayou, bordering the San Jacinto prairie. To their amazement, men were cutting away its supports, and they had hardly clattered across when it fell. One of the axemen, clad in buckskin, sprang forth to bar their passage. He was Deaf Smith the scout.

"It's all right!" shouted the foremost rider. "I am Rex Harden. Where is the Texas army?"

"Hurrah, lad! You're just in time for the fight. Ride one mile further, and you'll be with them!"

So the two hastened on, and five minutes later Rex, reining Tawny to a stand beside General Houston, saluted and reported:

"Just arrived, general, but ready for duty."

"Why, lad, they told me you were dead! Never mind. Thank God you are alive. Now get a sword and help us strike the blow that shall make Texas forever free. Come on!"

"Take my sword," said Florio, hurriedly, at the same time thrusting the weapon into his comrade's hand. "I cannot draw it against men of my own race, and so will await you here. God bless you, my friend, and send you the victory."

Thus far Rex had seen no enemy, and was wondering where the battle was to be fought, when, from a clump of timber in front of the thin Texas line, there came a roar of artillery. A moment later the thrilling order:

"Forward *march!* Double-quick, *charge!*" rang out, and was repeated from mouth to mouth along the line.

As they burst through the fringe of timber, and emerged from it, Rex saw a long, low breastwork and beyond it the tents of a camp. A narrow strip of prairie lay between him and it. Already the Texans were running across this, yelling like madmen their battle-cries :

"Remember the Alamo! — Remember Goliad!"

The startled Mexicans fired one wild volley into the on-rushing line; but they might as well have tried to stop it with pea-shooters. This was the moment for which the men of Texas had waited for months, — the terrible moment of vengeance. Not a shot did they fire until the breastwork was reached. Then a withering sheet of flame leaped from the brown rifles, and swept with the shriek of death through the devoted camp that was barely wakened from its siesta.

Over the breastworks the Texans sprang like famished tigers. They had no bayonets, but they had pistols and bowie knives, while, with sinewy arms, they swung their clubbed rifles like flails of Heaven's wrath.

For five minutes the struggle was fierce, and to the death. Then the Mexicans gave way at every point and fled in utter panic. Within fifteen minutes from the first cannon shot, the decisive battle of

San Jacinto had been fought and won. Santa Anna, " the Napoleon of the West," who had never before been defeated in battle, had been whipped at last by " Mr." Houston and his seven hundred ragged rebels. The Alamo and Goliad were avenged. Texas was free!

That evening a report was handed to General Houston. " Eight Texans killed and twenty-five wounded; 630 Mexicans killed, 208 wounded, 730 prisoners, and not more than a dozen escaped."

Horses and mules with gorgeous trappings, camp equipage, arms of every description, ammunition in quantity, and a military chest, containing $12,000 in gold, all had fallen into the hands of the victorious Texans.

But one thing was wanting to crown their victory, and it was the capture of Santa Anna. Houston had issued strict orders that he was to be taken alive if possible, and now he was not to be found. Could he have escaped? It must not be ; for only the Mexican President could command the four thousand Mexican troops still in Texas to face about and march beyond the Rio Grande. Until dark the adjacent country was scoured for him, and with earliest dawn the search was renewed.

Rex Harden knew not what he had done in the wild excitement of those terrible fifteen minutes of battle, or how he had borne himself. When they were over, he found both himself and Tawny covered with blood that was not their own, and that he was tightly clutching the hilt of a broken sword. As soon as he found that Santa Anna was missing, he entered eagerly into the search for him, and by his side rode Florio Veramendi, the only man in camp who knew the Mexican President by sight.

The morning after the battle, as these two and three others were riding at some distance from camp, Rex spied a Mexican in the uniform of a private soldier, skulking beside a bayou, and they rode up to him. At their approach, he drew a blanket over his head; but Florio had already recognized the man who, in all the world, he most despised. "It is he! It is Santa Anna himself!" he shouted.

In another minute, Lieutenant Rector Harden of the Texas regulars, riding Tawny the superb, was leading the horse of Florio, on which was seated his prisoner, General Antonio Lopez de Santa Anna, tyrant by trade, and President of the Republic of Mexico by profession.

Three hours later, Florio Veramendi, Texan, who had begged for the mission and been backed in his pleading by Lieutenant Harden, to whom nothing could now be refused, was galloping westward accompanied by Deaf Smith, the scout. The former bore to General Filisola, now commanding the Mexican forces in Texas, an order written and signed by Santa Anna for the immediate retirement of all his troops beyond the Rio Grande. With the signing

of that paper was the freedom of Texas forever assured.

Miles away from the battle-ground of San Jacinto, on which myriads of red mallows, snow-white Texas lilies, and the blue bells of buffalo clover were stained with blood to an all-pervading crimson, was a camp of refugees. In it were the sick and wounded, men too old to fight, and boys too young, women and children, cattle driven from many an abandoned ranch, and a few wagons containing the scanty savings from hundreds of deserted homes. It was a camp of distress and suffering, of mingled hopes and fears. Its occupants were at the end of their strength, which had been exhausted by weeks of terror and ceaseless flight, and now they must await their fate, for they could go no further.

They knew that a battle was about to be fought. If it should result in defeat, the end of all things would have come, so far as they were concerned. If a victory should be theirs, — and oh ! how they prayed for one, — the joy would be inconceivable.

So, on that 21st of April, they waited with such intent listening, that they hardly dared speak above a whisper, for fear of losing one of the dreaded, but longed-for sounds. They had heard a boom of heavy guns the day before, and were fevered with anxiety, until they learned that it indicated but a preliminary skirmish, and that the battle would be fought on the morrow. Now the fateful morrow had come.

Squire Harden, suffering such pain from his old-time wound as to be nearly helpless, was in command of the pitiful camp, and on that morning he visited every part of it, with words of hopeful cheer and kindly wisdom. But its inmates hardly heard him, and made scant reply to his courtesy, for they fretted at being interrupted in their listening.

From daylight they listened until long past noon, and the strain became almost too intense to be borne; but no sound had come to them. The afternoon was half spent ere they heard the far-away, but unmistakable note of a heavy gun. At the dread sound, their pent feelings found relief in shouts and shrill screamings. But only for a moment, and again they listened in breathless silence.

For ten minutes the distant cannonading was continued; then came a heavier volume of firing, a confused murmur, and all was as quiet as before. The sun set, and they still knew not what had happened. All that night they waited in dread anticipation, but in the morning the messengers came. There were so many of them, that, when first seen they were believed to be the earliest fugitives of a defeated army, and the refugees watched their approach with despairing eyes. Especially was their intent gaze fixed on one who so far outstripped the others, that he seemed to have left them at a standstill, and to be coming on the wings of the wind.

Squire Harden would have ridden to meet him,

but his wife begged him not to leave them, while Mabel and 'Lita Veramendi clung to his arms. So they waited together until Mabel, staring intently at the approaching figures, exclaimed:

"Father, that horse is Tawny, for there cannot be another like him in all Texas."

"Nonsense, daughter! It can't be."

"But father, it is!"

"And Rex, our Rex, is riding him," almost screamed Nelita.

"Child, hush! Rex is dead."

"He is not dead! He is alive, and is coming!" cried the girl, leaping forward, with outstretched arms, as though to greet the brave young rider. Then, realizing what she was doing, she turned and fled to the shelter of the wagon, there to hide her confusion and her unspeakable joy.

Now the speeding horseman waves his hat madly, and utters the ringing Texas yell, — a fierce cry of jubilation and victory. With that one sound the whole story was told, and in an instant the breathless camp was shouting, cheering, laughing, sobbing, and praising God.

A few seconds later, Rex Harden had leaped from Tawny's back, and, with the hot tears, that alone can give adequate expression to overwhelming joy, streaming down his sun-tanned cheeks, had clasped his trembling mother in his strong young arms.

Charles Scribner's Sons'

New and Standard Books for Young Readers for 1897=98...

MRS. BURNETT'S FAMOUS JUVENILES

An entirely new edition of Mrs. Burnett's famous juveniles from new plates, with all the original illustrations. Bound in a beautiful new cloth binding designed by R. B. Birch, and sold at very much reduced prices.

LITTLE LORD FAUNTLEROY
TWO LITTLE PILGRIMS' PROGRESS
SARA CREWE and LITTLE SAINT ELIZABETH AND
    OTHER STORIES (in one vol.)
PICCINO AND OTHER CHILD STORIES
GIOVANNI AND THE OTHER

Five Volumes, 12mo, each, $1.25

The original editions can still be supplied at the former prices:

LITTLE LORD FAUNTLEROY. Beautifully illustrated by REGINALD B. BIRCH. Square 8vo, $2.00.

TWO LITTLE PILGRIMS' PROGRESS. A STORY OF THE CITY BEAUTIFUL. By Mrs. FRANCES HODGSON BURNETT. Illustrated by REGINALD B. BIRCH. Uniform with "Fauntleroy," etc. Square 8vo, $1.50.

SARA CREWE; OR, WHAT HAPPENED AT MISS MINCHIN'S. Richly and fully illustrated by REGINALD B. BIRCH. Square 8vo, $1.00.

LITTLE SAINT ELIZABETH, AND OTHER STORIES. With 12 full-page drawings by REGINALD B. BIRCH. Square 8vo, $1.50.

GIOVANNI AND THE OTHER: CHILDREN WHO HAVE MADE STORIES. With 9 full-page illustrations by REGINALD B. BIRCH. Square 8vo, $1.50.

PICCINO, AND OTHER CHILD STORIES. Fully illustrated by REGINALD B. BIRCH. Square 8vo, $1.50.

G. A. HENTY'S POPULAR STORIES FOR BOYS

New Volumes for 1897-98.   Each, crown 8vo, handsomely illustrated, $1.50.

Mr. Henty, the most popular writer of Books of Adventure in England, adds three new volumes to his list this fall—books that will delight thousands of boys on this side who have become his ardent admirers

WITH FREDERICK THE GREAT. A Tale of the Seven Years' War. With 12 full-page illustrations. 12mo, $1.50.

This story, more than any other of Mr. Henty's, follows closely the historic lines, and no better description of the memorable battles of Rossbach, Leuthen, Prague, Zorndorf, Hochkirch, and Torgau can be found anywhere than is given in this volume. Through the historic part there runs the record of the daring and hazardous adventures of the hero, so that the charm of romance is given to the whole narrative. It is one of the most important volumes Mr. Henty has written.

A MARCH ON LONDON. A Story of Wat Tyler's Rising. With 8 full-page illustrations by W. H. Margetson. 12mo, $1.50.

This book weaves together, in a most interesting way, the story of Wat Tyler's rebellion under King Richard, the civil war in Flanders which occurred soon after, and the ill-planned attack upon the French led by the Bishop of Norfolk. The whole story is singularly interesting, covering as it does a period of history which is but little known and which is well worth narrating.

WITH MOORE AT CORUNNA. A Story of the Peninsular War. With 12 full-page illustrations by Wal. Paget. 12mo, $1.50.

A bright Irish lad, Terence O'Connor, is living with his widowed father, Captain O'Connor of the Mayo Fusiliers, with the regiment, at the time when the Peninsular War against Napoleon began. Under the command of Sir John Moore, he shared in the same marching and sharp fighting which that expedition experienced up to the battle of Corunna. By his bravery and great usefulness, in spite of his youth, he received a commission as colonel in the Portuguese army, and during the remainder of the war rendered great services, being mentioned twice in the general orders of the Duke of Wellington. The whole story is full of exciting military experiences and gives a most careful and accurate account of the conduct of the campaigns.

SOME OF THE NEWEST BOOKS

WILL SHAKESPEARE'S LITTLE LAD. By IMOGEN CLARK. With illustrations and cover design by R. B. Birch. 12mo, $1.50.

A story, full of warm color and brisk movement, of Stratford life in Shakespeare's day, the local atmosphere being reflected with rare fidelity, and the hero, the poet's son, being drawn with sympathy and charm.

CHILD POEMS. By EUGENE FIELD. With an introduction by KENNETH GRAHAME and profusely illustrated by CHARLES ROBINSON. Uniform with Robert Louis Stevenson's "Child's Garden of Verses," also illustrated by Charles Robinson. 12mo, $1.50.

THE STEVENSON SONG BOOK. VERSES FROM "A CHILD'S GARDEN," by ROBERT LOUIS STEVENSON. With music by various composers. A companion volume to the Field-DeKoven song book printed last year. Large 8vo, $2.00.

AN OLD-FIELD SCHOOL GIRL. By MARION HARLAND. With 8 full-page Illustrations. 12mo, $1.25.

LORDS OF THE WORLD. By ALFRED J. CHURCH. A STORY OF THE FALL OF CARTHAGE AND CORINTH. With 12 full-page illustrations by RALPH PEACOCK. 12mo, $1.50.

The scene of this story centres in the overthrow and destruction of Carthage by the Romans. The story is full of valuable historical details and the interest never flags.

HEROES OF OUR NAVY. By MOLLY ELLIOT SEAWELL. Illustrated. 12mo. *In press.*

Never has this entertaining writer been more felicitous than in the present volume.

THE LAST CRUISE OF THE MOHAWK. By W. J. HENDERSON. Illustrated by HARRY EDWARDS. 12mo, $1.25.

The book is crowded with dramatic incident—mutiny, shipwreck, Farragut's great fight in Mobile Bay—and the narrative is as simple as the events and characters are entertaining.

KIRK MUNROE'S STIRRING TALES

THE WHITE CONQUEROR SERIES

WITH CROCKETT AND BOWIE   AT WAR WITH PONTIAC

THE WHITE CONQUERORS   THROUGH SWAMP AND GLAI

Each, illustrated, 12mo, $1.25. The complete set, 4 vols., in a box, $5.00.

JUST PUBLISHED

WITH CROCKETT AND BOWIE; OR, FIGHTING FOR THE LONE STAR FLA A TALE OF TEXAS. With 8 full-page illustrations by VICTOR PÉRARD.

The story is of the Texas revolution in 1835, when American Texans under Sa Houston, Bowie, Crockett, and Travis, fought for relief from the intolerat tyranny of the Mexican Santa Aña. The hero, Rex Hardin, son of a Texas ranc man, and graduate of an American military school, takes a prominent part in t heroic defense of the Alamo, the terrible scenes at Golead, and the final triump at San Jacinto. The historical side of the story has been carefully studied and i localities rendered familiar by a special trip to Texas undertaken by the auth for that purpose within a year.

PREVIOUS VOLUMES

THROUGH SWAMP AND GLADE. A TALE OF THE SEMINOLE WAR. Witl full-page illustrations by VICTOR PÉRARD. 12mo, $1.25.

In this new story Mr. Munroe opens to view an exceedingly interesting period American history—the period of the Seminole War in Florida. Coacoochee, tl hero of the story, is a young Indian of noble birth, the son of Philip, the chiefta of the Seminoles. He is a boy at the time of the beginning of the Semino troubles and grows up to lead his tribe in the long struggle which resulted in tl Indians being driven from the north of Florida down to the distant southel wilderness. It is full of strange adventure, of stirring incident and rapid actio and it is a true and faithful picture of a period of history little known to youl readers.

AT WAR WITH PONTIAC; OR, THE TOTEM OF THE BEAR. A TALE OF RE COAT AND REDSKIN. With 8 full-page illustrations by J. FINNEMORE. 12mo, $1.2

A story of old days in America when Detroit was a frontier town and tl shores of Lake Erie were held by hostile Indians under Pontiac. The her Donald Hester, goes in search of his sister Edith, who has been captured by tl Indians. Strange and terrible are his experiences; for he is wounded, take prisoner, condemned to be burned, and contrives to escape. In the end there peace between Pontiac and the English, and all things terminate happily for tl hero. One dares not skip a page of this enthralling story.

THE WHITE CONQUERORS. A TALE OF TOLTEC AND AZTEC. With 8 ful page illustrations by W. S. STACEY. 12mo, $1.25.

This story deals with the Conquest of Mexico by Cortes and his Spaniards, tl " White Conquerors," who, after many deeds of valor, pushed their way into tl great Aztec kingdom and established their power in the wondrous city whei Montezuma reigned in barbaric splendor.

BOOKS BY WILLIAM HENRY FROST

JUST PUBLISHED

THE KNIGHTS OF THE ROUND TABLE. Illustrated and cover designed by S. R. BURLEIGH. 12mo, $1.50.

Mr. Frost's volumes of folk-lore stories have achieved a deserved popularity, and his last one, dealing with the ever-fascinating theme of the Round Table and its knights, is equal to either of his earlier books.

MR. FROST'S FORMER BOOKS

THE COURT OF KING ARTHUR. STORIES FROM THE LAND OF THE ROUND TABLE. Illustrated by S. R. BURLEIGH. 12mo, $1.50.

Mr. Frost has had the happy idea of making a journey to the different places connected with the Arthurian romances by history or legend, and of relating the ever new Round Table Tales on their sites, to the same little girl, now somewhat older, to whom he told his charming Wagner stories.

THE WAGNER STORY BOOK. FIRELIGHT TALES OF THE GREAT MUSIC DRAMAS. Illustrated by SIDNEY R. BURLEIGH. 12mo, $1.50.

'A successful attempt to make the romantic themes of the music drama intelligible to young readers. The author has full command of his subject, and the style is easy, graceful, and simple."—*Boston Beacon.*

ROBERT GRANT'S TWO BOOKS FOR BOYS

JACK HALL; OR, THE SCHOOL DAYS OF AN AMERICAN BOY. Illustrated by F. G. ATTWOOD. 12mo, $1.25.

'A better book for boys has never been written. It is pure, clean, and healthy, and has throughout a vigorous action that holds the reader breathlessly."
—*Boston Herald.*

JACK IN THE BUSH; OR, A SUMMER ON A SALMON RIVER. Illustrated by F. T. MERRILL. 12mo, $1.25.

'A clever book for boys. It is the story of the camp life of a lot of boys, and is destined to please every boy reader. It is attractively illustrated."
—*Detroit Free Press.*

THE KANTER GIRLS

By MARY L. B. BRANCH. Illustrated by HELEN M. ARMSTRONG. Square 12mo, $1.50.

The adventures of Jane and Prue, two small sisters, among different peoples of the imaginative world—dryads, snow-children, Kobolds, etc.—aided by their invisible rings, their magic boat, and their wonderful birds, are described by the author with great naturalness and a true gift for story-telling. The numerous illustrations are very attractive, and in thorough sympathy with the text.

SAMUEL ADAMS DRAKE'S HISTORICAL BOO

JUST ISSUED

THE BORDER WARS OF NEW ENGLAND

COMMONLY CALLED KING WILLIAM'S AND QUEEN ANNE'S WARS. By SAM
ADAMS DRAKE. With 58 illustrations and maps. 12mo, $1.50.

Mr. Drake has made a consecutive, entertaining narrative of the border v
which the French and Indians waged against the English settlers in New I
land during the reigns of King William and Queen Anne. The story is fu'
adventurous interest and is told with that minute attention to suggestive anc
structive details which have been the distinguishing feature of Mr. Drake's o
books. The illustrations, many of them from photographs of historic spots ar
buildings still standing, are of exceptional interest.

FORMER VOLUMES

THE MAKING OF THE OHIO VALLEY STATES. 1660-1837. Illustra
12mo, $1.50.

THE MAKING OF VIRGINIA AND THE MIDDLE COLONIES. 1578-1701.
lustrated. 12mo, $1.50.

THE MAKING OF NEW ENGLAND. 1580-1643. With 148 illustrations
with maps. 12mo, $1.50.

THE MAKING OF THE GREAT WEST. 1812-1853. With 145 illustrations
with maps. 12mo, $1.50.

STORIES OF LITERATURE, SCIENCE, AND HI
TORY BY HENRIETTA CHRISTIAN WRIGHT

A NEW VOLUME JUST ISSUED

CHILDREN'S STORIES IN AMERICAN LITERATURE.—1860-1896. 1:
$1.25.
Miss Wright here continues the attractive presentation of literary history be
in her " Children's Stories in English Literature," taking up the literary fig
that have appeared since the time of the civil war, and treating their works
personalities in a simple manner, interesting to young readers.

CHILDREN'S STORIES IN AMERICAN LITERATURE.—1660-1860. 1:
$1.25.

CHILDREN'S STORIES IN ENGLISH LITERATURE. Two volumes: TA
SIN TO SHAKESPEARE—SHAKESPEARE TO TENNYSON. 12mo, each, $1.25.

CHILDREN'S STORIES OF THE GREAT SCIENTISTS. With portr
12mo, $1.25.

CHILDREN'S STORIES IN AMERICAN HISTORY. Illustrated. 12mo, $1

CHILDREN'S STORIES OF AMERICAN PROGRESS. Illustrated. 1:
$1.25.

THREE BOOKS OF SPORTS AND GAMES

THE AMERICAN BOY'S BOOK OF SPORT. OUT-DOOR GAMES FOR ALL SEA-SONS. By DANIEL C. BEARD. With over 300 illustrations by the author. 8vo, $2.50.

This is an entirely new book by Mr. Beard, containing altogether new matter of great interest to all young lovers of sport. It is a companion volume to the author's well-known "American Boy's Handy Book," of which over twenty-five thousand copies have been sold, and will undoubtedly rival that famous work in popularity as it does in interest.

THE AMERICAN BOY'S HANDY BOOK; OR, WHAT TO DO AND HOW TO DO IT. By DANIEL C. BEARD. With 360 illustrations by the author. Square 8vo, $2.00.

" The book has this great advantage over its predecessors, that most of the games, tricks, and other amusements described in it are new. It treats of sports adapted to all seasons of the year ; it is practical, and it is well illustrated."
—New York Tribune.

THE AMERICAN GIRL'S HANDY BOOK. By LENA and ADELIA B. BEARD. With over 500 illustrations by the authors. Square 8vo, $2.00.

"I have put it in my list of good and useful books for young people, as I have many requests for advice from my little friends and their anxious mothers. I am most happy to commend your very ingenious and entertaining book."
*—*LOUISA M. ALCOTT.

THOMAS NELSON PAGE'S TWO BOOKS

AMONG THE CAMPS; OR, YOUNG PEOPLE'S STORIES OF THE WAR. With 8 full-page illustrations. Square 8vo, $1.50.

"They are five in number, each having reference to some incident of the Civil War. A vein of mingled pathos and humor runs through them all, and greatly heightens the charm of them. It is the early experience of the author himself, doubtless, which makes his pictures of life in a Southern home during the great struggle so vivid and truthful."*—The Nation.*

TWO LITTLE CONFEDERATES. With 8 full-page illustrations by KEMBLE and REDWOOD. Square 8vo, $1.50.

"Mr. Page was 'raised' in Virginia, and he knows the 'darkey' of the South better than any one who writes about them. And he knows ' white folks,' too, and his stories, whether for old or young people, have the charm of sincerity and beauty and reality."*—Harper's Young People.*

EDWARD EGGLESTON'S TWO POPULAR BOOKS

THE HOOSIER SCHOOL-BOY. Illustrated. 12mo, $1.00.

"' The Hoosier School-Boy ' depicts some of the characteristics of boy-life years ago on the Ohio ; characteristics, however, that were not peculiar to that section. The story presents a vivid and interesting picture of the difficulties which in those days beset the path of the youth aspiring for an education."
—Chicago Inter-Ocean.

QUEER STORIES FOR BOYS AND GIRLS. 12mo, $1.00.

" A very bright and attractive little volume for young readers. The stories are fresh, breezy, and healthy, with a good point to them and a good, sound American view of life and the road to success. The book abounds in good feeling and good sense, and is written in a style of homely art."*—Independent.*

BOOKS BY HOWARD PYLE

BEHIND THE GARDEN OF THE MOON. A Real Story of the Moon Angel. Written and illustrated by Howard Pyle. Square 12mo, $2.00.

Out of the truth that great deeds are achieved and high character moulded by entire spiritual consecration, rather than by direct and interested effort, the author has evolved a winning and delightful piece of fanciful fiction, and has illustrated it copiously in his happiest and most characteristically poetical vein.

THE MERRY ADVENTURES OF ROBIN HOOD of Great Renown in Nottinghamshire. With many illustrations. Royal 8vo, $3.00.

" This superb book is unquestionably the most original and elaborate ever produced by any American artist. Mr. Pyle has told, with pencil and pen, the complete and consecutive story of Robin Hood and his merry men in their haunts in Sherwood Forest, gathered from the old ballads and legends. Mr. Pyle's admirable illustrations are strewn profusely through the book."—*Boston Transcript.*

OTTO OF THE SILVER HAND. With many illustrations. Royal 8vo, half leather, $2.00.

" The scene of the story is mediæval Germany in the time of the feuds and robber barons and romance. The kidnapping of Otto, his adventures among rough soldiers, and his daring rescue, make up a spirited and thrilling story."—*Christian Union.*

THE BUTTERFLY HUNTERS IN THE CARIBBEES

By Dr. Eugene Murray-Aaron. With 8 full-page illustrations. Square 12mo, $2.00.

"Our author only reproduces the incidents and scenes of his own life, as an exploring naturalist, in a way to capture the attention of younger readers."
Chicago Inter-Ocean.

JUST PUBLISHED

THE KING OF THE BRONCOS

And Other Tales of New Mexico. By Charles F. Lummis. Illustrated by Victor Pérard. 12mo, $1.25.

A charming collection of stories of life and adventure in the Southwest. The last story, " My Friend Will," is a masterpiece, with a brainy moral for adult as well as juvenile readers.

A NEW MEXICO DAVID

And Other Stories and Sketches of the South-west. By Charles F. Lummis. Illustrated. 12mo, $1.25.

" Mr. Lummis has lived for years in the land of the Pueblos; has traversed it in every direction, both on foot and on horseback ; and it is an enthralling treat set before youthful readers by him in this series of lively chronicles."—*Boston Beacon.*

STORIES FOR BOYS

By Richard Harding Davis. With 6 full-page illustrations. 12mo, $1.00.

" It will be astonishing indeed if youths of all ages are not fascinated with these ' Stories for Boys.' Mr. Davis knows infallibly what will interest his young readers."—*Boston Beacon.*

HEROES OF THE OLDEN TIME

By JAMES BALDWIN. Three volumes, 12mo, each beautifully illustrated. Singly, $1.50; the set, $4.00.

A STORY OF THE GOLDEN AGE. Illustrated by HOWARD PYLE.

"Mr. Baldwin's book is redolent with the spirit of the Odyssey, that glorious primitive epic, fresh with the dew of the morning of time. It is an unalloyed pleasure to read his recital of the adventures of the wiley Odysseus. Howard Pyle's illustrations render the spirit of the Homeric age with admirable felicity."
—Prof. H. H. BOYESEN.

THE STORY OF SIEGFRIED. Illustrated by HOWARD PYLE.

THE STORY OF ROLAND. Illustrated by R. B. BIRCH.

THE BOY'S LIBRARY OF LEGEND AND CHIVALRY

Edited by SIDNEY LANIER, and richly illustrated by FREDERICKS, BENSELL, and KAPPES. Four volumes, cloth, uniform binding, price per set, $7.00. Sold separately, price per volume, $2.00.

Mr. Lanier's books present to boy readers the old English classics of history and legend in attractive form. While they are stories of action and stirring incident, they teach those lessons which manly, honest boys ought to learn.

THE BOY'S KING ARTHUR   **THE BOY'S PERCY**

THE BOY'S FROISSART   **THE KNIGHTLY LEGENDS OF WALES**

FRANK R. STOCKTON'S BOOKS FOR THE YOUNG

"His books for boys and girls are classics."—*Newark Advertiser*.

THE CLOCKS OF RONDAINE, AND OTHER STORIES. With 24 illustrations by BLASHFIELD, ROGERS, BEARD, and others. Square 8vo, $1.50.

PERSONALLY CONDUCTED. Illustrated by PENNELL, PARSONS, and others. Square 8vo, $2.00.

THE STORY OF VITEAU. Illustrated by R. B. BIRCH. 12mo, $1.50.

A JOLLY FELLOWSHIP. With 20 illustrations. 12mo, $1.50.

THE FLOATING PRINCE AND OTHER FAIRY TALES. Illustrated. Square 8vo, $1.50.

THE TING-A-LING TALES. Illustrated. 12mo, $1.00.

ROUNDABOUT RAMBLES IN LANDS OF FACT AND FICTION. Illustrated. Square 8vo, $1 50.

TALES OUT OF SCHOOL. With nearly 200 illustrations. Square 8vo, $1.50.
"The volumes are profusely illustrated and contain the most entertaining sketches in Mr. Stockton's most entertaining manner."—*Christian Union*.

THINGS WILL TAKE A TURN

By BEATRICE HARRADEN, author of "Ships That Pass in the Night." Illustrated. 12mo, $1.00.

One cannot help being fascinated by the sweet little heroine of this tale, she is so engaging, so natural; and to love Rosebud is to love all her friends and enter sympathetically into the good fortune she brought them.